MW01152944

Last Days

A NOVEL

ROBERT POLLOCK

Copyright © 2015 Robert W. Pollock.

All rights reserved. No part of this book may be reproduced, stored, or
transmitted by any means—whether auditory, graphic, mechanical, or
electronic—without written permission of both publisher and author, except
in the case of brief excerpts used in critical articles and reviews. Unauthorized
reproduction of any part of this work is illegal and is punishable by law.

ISBN: 978-1-4834-3549-7 (sc)
ISBN: 978-1-4834-3548-0 (e)

Library of Congress Control Number: 2015912005

Because of the dynamic nature of the Internet, any web addresses or links contained in
this book may have changed since publication and may no longer be valid. The views
expressed in this work are solely those of the author and do not necessarily reflect the
views of the publisher, and the publisher hereby disclaims any responsibility for them.

Any people depicted in stock imagery provided by Thinkstock are models,
and such images are being used for illustrative purposes only.
Certain stock imagery © Thinkstock.

Lulu Publishing Services rev. date: 08/26/2015

Contents

Dedication

This book is dedicated to all of those suffering from the ravages of Alzheimer's, and their families who must love, support, and fight this battle with them every day.

Acknowledgements

In writing this novel, I based my characters and story lines on various real experiences in the lives of people who lived through caring for parents or relatives with Alzheimer's. In particular, I must posthumously recognize the influence of both my grandmother and grandfather, Helen and Thomas MacArthur of Tampa, Florida. Witnessing the family tragedy created during the last years of their lives was a significant factor leading me to write this book. Their son, Don MacArthur, of Brandon, Florida was their main means of family support in those final years, and I must extend to him a special, long overdue thank you for everything he selflessly did in support of his parents and this family.

There are others whose stories likewise contributed to the development of this novel. In particular, I must thank Kathy, Paul, and Lori Taylor for their role in supplying input for some of the story's main character, Stan Beecher. Their descriptions of events surrounding the last years of their father, George Diamond helped me understand both the level of pain family members suffer, and the kinds of behavior a late-onset Alzheimer's patient might exhibit. Finally, I must acknowledge my aunt, Emily Pollock, who I have watched decline, and who today still suffers in the final stages of advanced Alzheimer's.

I must also extend a personal thank you to L. J. Robinson, Executive Director of Manorhouse Assisted Living in Knoxville, Tennessee. Through her willingness to open the doors of her facility, and describe how Assisted Care and Memory Care units function, I was able to create a backdrop for our main character's final years.

I was once told that all good writing is the final product of good editing. I have found those words to be true. To that end, I must thank my primary editor, Kate Neary. Her work and advice was invaluable in bringing this book to life. In addition, I must thank one of my primary readers, Ms. Joan Smith for her insight and assistance. In writing this novel, it was critically important to hear and consider the comments and suggestions from Kate and Joan. Their perspectives and thoughts helped give context and color to the characters and story.

In everyone's life they have a few people who have inspired them. For me, the motivation to actually write came later in life, but the inspiration came many years ago from a truly gifted professor at Tusculum College. Dr. Francis Overall was an extraordinary teacher who continuously urged me to write and use my creative side. She was so passionate in her teaching of literature, poetry, and writing that it was impossible for someone to experience her class without leaving a better person. Even though she has now passed away, it is to her I offer my profound and deepest thank you for the gift of writing she provided.

My only intention in writing this novel was to provide a brief insight as to how Alzheimer's can not only affect its victims, but also their families. I doubt anyone can adequately describe the level of pain and sense of helplessness someone battling Alzheimer's must endure each day. In some way, however, I hope this book can serve as a small comfort to those now living with this illness.

Importantly, a great deal of credit must also go to Eben Alexander, famous neurosurgeon and author of the blockbuster book, *Proof of Heaven: A Scientist's Case for the Afterlife*, published in 2012. It was the descriptions of his personal journey and near death accounts in *Proof of Heaven* that provided the foundation to portray Stan's late life experiences. In constructing those final days, I researched a great many near death experience (NDE) stories to make what I wrote as credible as possible. Dr. Alexander's account was among the most vivid and well articulated of those descriptions.

In sum, I must recognize and dedicate this book to all the families and people wrestling with this tragic disease. Their stories are each an individual journey filled with small victories and heartbreaking moments. To them I wish God's peace and grace to fill their lives, and hope this book might represent just a small insight into what they must face every day.

Beecher Family Tree

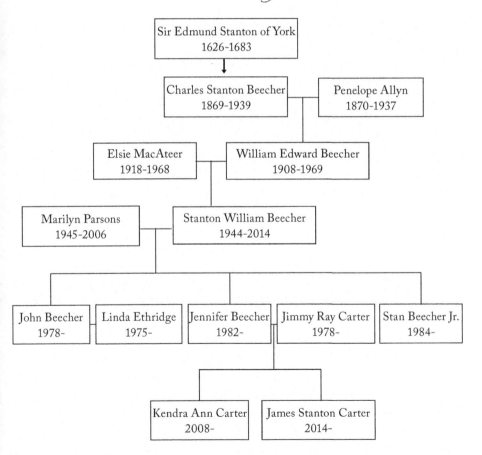

Sir Edmund Stanton of York
1626-1683

Charles Stanton Beecher
1869-1939

Penelope Allyn
1870-1937

Elsie MacAteer
1918-1968

William Edward Beecher
1908-1969

Marilyn Parsons
1945-2006

Stanton William Beecher
1944-2014

John Beecher
1978-

Linda Ethridge
1975-

Jennifer Beecher
1982-

Jimmy Ray Carter
1978-

Stan Beecher Jr.
1984-

Kendra Ann Carter
2008-

James Stanton Carter
2014-

1

The Last Day

I t is said that one of the blessings in life is one never knows exactly what day will be his last. That was not to be true for Stanton Beecher. He knew precisely what was to be his last day; it was today. Today, at approximately 3 PM, his life as he had known it would come to an end. Oh, he wasn't going to die, at least not today, but everything that had made up his life to this point was about to end. He was about to lose the freedom to simply go outside and walk the streets, to drive to his friend's house to watch a sports event, to take a trip downtown for breakfast on a whim, or to plaster his car with orange T's, and travel to Knoxville's, Neyland Stadium for a tailgate party. At three o'clock today, two men would arrive in a small van to load up what few belongings he would keep. His son would then drive him to Willow Grove Assisted Care where he would spend whatever days of his life remained. In that moment, everything was to change; as far as Stan was concerned, not for the better.

Stanton William Beecher, age 68, had been the rock of his family. It was he to whom everyone looked for strength, for advice, for support.

The family he loved was now in turmoil, on the brink of permanent separation, and he was its only hope of salvation. The tables of life were about to turn in a most unfortunate way, and Stan could not have been less happy than he was this day.

*****

Stanton Beecher was the only child of Elsie and William Beecher, who had married in 1940. His grandfather, Charles Stanton Beecher, had immigrated to America back in 1887 at the tender age of 18 with only forty five dollars and a suitcase of second hand clothes. He was one of many children in the Beecher lineage that traced all the way back to William the Conqueror, the first Norman king of England in 1087. Sir Edmund Stanton of York, a man of significant stature in the court of King Charles I in 1655 was also somewhere back in the family tree, and his grandfather, Charles had been very proud of this heritage.

As was common in his grandfather's time, craftsmen and tradesmen made up a large portion of the population. Charles had learned his trade as a stone mason, and ultimately came to live in the northern English town of Durham. Stone masons tended to go where there was work. Charles had heard America was a place where there was "good work to be had." He was certain prosperity would follow, and set off from Durham to seek his fortune in a new and exciting land: America.

Soon after arriving and settling in a small neighborhood of New York, he married Penelope Allyn, and began life in the New World. Unfortunately, the promise of good work did not materialize in New York. Instead, he found that many craftsmen had left the city to relocate in North Carolina and the eastern counties of Tennessee.

In 1888 he set off for the city of Asheville, North Carolina. It was not an easy life for Charles and Penelope; they trembled on the cusp of poverty much of the time. His previous employment had been church construction, but in Asheville all that was about to change. Having found work on the new Vanderbilt mansion, the Beechers finally found themselves ready to raise a family. Their son William was born in 1908. Times were good.

Once Biltmore, as it was named by the Vanderbilt family, was completed, Charles was again looking for work. For years he bounced from one project to the next until he heard of a large building to be erected on the campus of the University of Tennessee in Knoxville. So it was that in 1918 Charles, Penelope, and ten year old William moved to Knoxville, Tennessee. The work provided a steady income, and life improved again.

Charles and Penelope were very proud of what they had accomplished in life. He had made a good life for his family, and wanted to transfer all he had learned to his son, William. He was a hard father. He expected a great deal of William. There was little tolerance for laziness, mischievous behavior, or poor performance in school. The expectation was, "every Beecher would work hard, make something of himself, and forge his own way in the world."

As a result of his membership in the Masonic Lodge and an acquaintanceship with Mr. Simon Whitcomb, Charles found young William an apprenticeship as a typesetter in a small local publishing business. At age fourteen, William was set off to work with his father's admonishment: "You best make good of this opportunity, boy, or you will be answering to me! Be sure of it." As it turned out, William did make good of his opportunity. Due to the sound work habits his father had instilled and his ability to acquire skills quickly, William soon became a valued employee. Still, his father's stern warning often rang loudly in his ears whenever he feared he was not living up to Mr. Whitcomb's expectations.

As William matured, he became much like his father – authoritarian, stubborn, and determined to "be somebody." Although he never went to college, he gradually worked his way up the ladder in Mr. Whitcomb's publishing company.

At 32 he married the much younger Elsie MacAteer. Their only son, Stanton William Beecher was born shortly thereafter. Stanton was raised with as much love as one could have wanted. World War II was just ending, and an ethic of hard work was the order of day. Wages were fair and provided a secure living, but not much more. Much of his father's work ethic and love of country was passed on to Stanton. William hoped his son would follow him into the publishing trade where he knew chances of success were high.

Stanton, however, had different ideas. Much to his father's disappointment, Stanton did not follow him into the publishing business. Instead, he and his friend Ted Newsome joined the police force. Stan was bright, hard working, and intuitive. Those skills ultimately led him to the rank of detective. He was decorated numerous times, and proud of his service. He was even more pleased by the fact that people respected him as an example of what a good citizen should be.

The center of Stan's life was his family. He met Marilyn Parsons at the annual church picnic. At age 32, he had already been through two courtships that ended badly. But with Marilyn, there was something different. He knew from the first day he had seen her that she was special.

Marilyn paid little attention to Stan, and seemed quite disinterested in his advances. Stan was not disheartened by Marilyn's seeming disinterest. Ultimately, he convinced her to allow him to court her. From that time on, Stan and Marilyn were inseparable. He proposed after only three months, and they were married that same summer. By their eleventh anniversary they had been blessed with three children: John, Jenny, and Stan Junior.

Marilyn was totally in charge of the house, schooling, church attendance, and manners. Stan dealt with larger discipline issues and finances. They partnered to share responsibilities, and relied totally on one another.

One of the Beecher family's great achievements was the purchase of their own home. It was a modest, craftsman style home in a quiet neighborhood. The white frame, brick two-story home sat on a small plot of land with a low white fence framing its boundaries. Small shrubs and a low hedge lined the concrete walk that led to the full-length porch. For Stan and Marilyn, it was a dream come true.

On the day they went to the lawyer's office to finalize the purchase of their home, Stan was full of pride. He was careful to make things look routine, as if this were just an everyday occurrence. Marilyn knew better, and was proud of her Stan. She knew how long and hard he had worked to be able to afford his own home; *their* own home.

The first home of Stanton William Beecher, he thought. His father would have been proud of him, although he would have done his best to conceal his emotion in the same way Stanton had.

As their family grew, the Beecher children became the center of focus for Marilyn and Stan. The first to be born was John. Stan could not have been more proud, a son. He was a fine looking boy who quite honestly looked much more like his mother than Stan. That was fine with Stan. He was a bright child, full of mischief, with a streak of independence that always seemed to give him the lead with other children.

John was an excellent athlete, and excelled as a student. It was rare that he came home with any grades under an A, although Language Arts was never a strong suit.

"I frankly don't understand why any school would make someone labor through something as mind deadening as Milton's, *Paradise Lost*," he would lament.

"Have you ever read that, Dad? I mean, your IQ goes down nearly 2 points with every stanza! Doctor Overall just gushes about it, and thinks it's really great stuff; but everyone in the class I talk to thinks its complete crap."

Stan looked sternly up from his newspaper and replied, "John, the assignment is the assignment, so just stop complaining, and do what's asked."

John looked over towards his mother to enlist her help and said, "Mom. Help me a little here. Dad is not getting the point I'm trying to make."

Marilyn looked at her son, and shook her head, "No, John. Your father is right here. You just have to do what you have to do."

"Never mind," John added. "There's no talking to you about such things because you two *always* take the side of the school. You're both the same on these things."

John went on to graduate magna cum laude in Business and Finance from the University of Tennessee, the first in the Beecher family to graduate from college. He distinguished himself in his studies and as a campus leader. His mother was brimming with pride as she hugged her son on graduation day. The picture of John in his cap and gown with his parents hung proudly in the house on Gill Avenue.

John ultimately used his sound finance education wisely when he joined an investment firm in Knoxville. Again, it was John's grandfather's contacts in the Masonic Lodge that had come to pay dividends. Henry Wright was managing partner of Wright, Johnson, and Willoughby Investments. He "had known his grandfather William," as he put it, "a half century ago, at least." Mr. Wright spent hours reminiscing about old times, and what a great man his grandfather had been. John had the good sense to politely listen, with the occasional addition of, "Really? I never knew that." In actuality, John knew quite a bit about his grandfather William because his father constantly referred to the man as if he were a saint.

From time to time Stan offered advice he had gotten from his father, but the most valuable was that if you want to live a prosperous life, then you have to live *below* your means, not *at* your means. His father also strongly suggested he find himself a good woman to be his partner in life.

For years, John was married to his job – climbing the corporate ladder. Then, he met Linda Ethridge at a charity event. She was a beautiful woman who was cultured, intelligent, well-traveled, and independent. Best of all, she adored John. He was just the kind of man for whom she had been waiting, and so it was the two of them seemed destined to meet and fall in love.

Professionally, John had begun to rise through the ranks of Wright, Johnson, and Willoughby, where he found his forte as a specialist in retirement securities, annuities, and estate planning. John became a respected member of the community; all his father dreamed he might be, in fact, he exceeded his father's expectations. Yet, he was to learn that success had a downside and a price.

Jenny was very different. She was the sensitive one. As a child, she was the girl who formed the *Save the Whales Club*. She was the one who brought the cupcakes to school for Valentine's Day. If there was someone in the cafeteria sitting alone, Jenny sat with her or invited her to sit with the larger group. Jenny was constantly involved in some cause, and was a champion of the "little guy."

As a student, Jenny always managed to pass, but perhaps not excel. Jenny meticulously organized everything, took copious notes, and kept painstaking records. She was a talented reader and writer, but mathematics was an altogether different story. Without her brother's help, it was unlikely she would have ever passed Algebra. She found math to be as frustrating as her brother had found Milton.

"Dad, I am about ready to throw this textbook, the notebook, AND the teacher right into the nearest dumpster!! I mean really! Just tell me one time, just one time when anyone will *ever* use the quadratic equation for any-thing," she said.

Stan looked up at Jenny, and seeing her sad face, stepped in to rescue his daughter.

"How about we get John down here to help with this situation, honey?"

John always came to lend assistance, but not always happily. It was useless to complain, however, because when he had done so in the past, Dad had gotten angry, and lectured him on being a good brother.

"Now we are not having that attitude in this house, young man," his father would explode. "In this family we help one another, and we do it happily! And I don't want to hear anything about what is simple to you, and why others can't just work things through. Just because things came easy for you doesn't mean everyone else can see things so clearly. Now, go help your sister, and I better see a smile on your face as you do it!"

John knew better than to debate the topic. He loved his sister, and didn't totally begrudge spending the time, but like all smart people to whom things come easily, he found it frustrating when the same wasn't true for others.

Ultimately Jenny graduated from high school, and went on to community college. She studied nursing for a time, but after struggling with the clinical classes, changed her major to Health Care Administration. Once graduated, Jenny found a position in the admissions department of Parkwest Hospital.

It was at Parkwest that Jenny met Jimmy Ray Carter, a nurse practitioner. The courtship was short and passionate. The two of them were a perfect pair. They were soon married in Saint John's Episcopal Cathedral in downtown Knoxville.

In the years ahead, Jenny and Jimmy had two children, Kendra Ann, and then much later James Junior. While Kendra was too young for school, Jenny stayed home so as to raise her "the right way." Her brother, John, was a dutiful helper during this time. He bought groceries, invited them to his home for dinner, helped pay for small projects around the house, and occasionally baby sat so Jenny and Jimmy could have a night out. Even though John had his own life to lead, he always tried to make time for his sister; although Jenny was never certain of Linda's opinion of his help. John was their mentor in other ways as well. He helped Jimmy organize a good family budget, provided advice on big decisions, and helped steer them through numerous financial hardships.

Once Kendra was old enough for pre-school, Jenny was able to return to work part time. Just that little extra money made a big difference in their life. Finally, they were able to get a larger rental home, and Jimmy was able to afford the used truck he wanted. Jenny believed life was good, and the hardships were behind her.

Stan Junior was the third of Stan and Marilyn's children. Marilyn wanted to name him Stanton to honor his father, but Stan Senior objected to the idea.

"I've always disliked my name, Marilyn. You know that. Why would we want to saddle this poor boy with that same cross to bear? He'll grow up disliking it just like me." He had that stern look in his eye that Marilyn had come to know so well, and it was always best to just go along once he had that look. But, she could not allow that, "cross to bear" comment to go unaddressed.

"Good grief Stanton William!" she jumped in. "Cross to bear? Really? Your name was such a horror that it's been a 'cross to bear?' Isn't it a shame that mean ole William of Beecher was so insensitive as to give you the family name he cherished and revered?" she added for good measure.

If there was anything that could get under Stan's skin, it was mention of his father in an unfavorable light, even humorously.

"Fine, whatever; but please, Marilyn. Can we just not name him Stanton? Please." Marilyn yielded, and the boy became just plain Stan.

Unfortunately, the name was not the worst of Stan Junior's difficulty in life. Stan Junior was born with a serious cognitive processing problem.

Stan Junior spoke clearly enough, although if he got nervous, or tried to put his thoughts together too quickly, one might notice a slight stutter. From a physical standpoint, he looked much the same as other boys. He was lean, and by middle school was already a heady 5'9" tall. He fit in with most boys, though it was clear Stan didn't always grasp what was going on around him in quite the same way as everyone else.

The school placed him in special education by second grade, and he was often not included with his peers in such things as class plays, trips, dances, or other activities. Stan Junior could never understand this exclusion, but he tried to live with it.

"Why can't I go with the class on the trip to Asheville, mommy?" he would ask. "I'd like to go see the big house and have lunch there," he said with such a plaintiff voice that his mother's eyes welled with tears.

His father, on the other hand, would just become enraged, and it was all Marilyn could do to keep him from driving down to the school, and accosting everyone in sight, beginning with the principal who he held personally responsible for these decisions.

This particular trip had special meaning for the Beecher's because Stan Junior's great grandfather had worked on many of the stone staircases and buildings at the Biltmore Estate. Ultimately, Stan Junior was allowed to go on the condition one parent would also attend to "insure the safety and well being of the boy on the trip."

As Stan Junior got older, he developed a strong sense of love for animals. He was particularly passionate about birds. He could tell you the name of every bird in Tennessee along with numerous other birds from all over the country. He knew them by sight or song. Whenever the family went out, Stan shared his knowledge about any birds he saw or heard in the area.

"You hear him, Dad? That's a red winged blackbird. He probably lives over near that marshy area...they like water, you know. Oh wait. There's a cardinal. Boy, they have a pretty song."

Talking about birds was one of Stan Junior's true pleasures in life, and the family was careful not to squash his enthusiasm. They purchased every book or object dealing with birds they could find. Stan Junior spent hours in his room pouring over these materials, learning facts about each bird. Later, he regaled the family with the litany of new things he had learned on owls, eagles, or hawks. These talks went on until someone was able to deftly change the subject.

A boy like Stan Junior was invisible to almost everyone in school. Very few ever paid him much attention. He was, however, often bullied. One group had even given Stan the unkind nickname; "Short-cheese Stan." Students often referred to yellow school buses as, "the cheese." There were also smaller school buses used to transport the more severely handicapped students. These buses were known as, "the short cheese." Students would say things like, "Oh his father took away his car, so now he has to ride the cheese." With special needs students, they would say, "Yeah, he comes in on the short cheese." This was how Stan Junior came to be known by this group as, "Short-cheese Stan."

One afternoon, the group came, and plopped down at Stan's lunch table to have some fun at Stan Junior's expense. Stan looked up and smiled, pleased that the boys had chosen to sit with him.

The group's leader, Kyle, began, "So, Short-cheese, you see any birds shitting on a fence or some other interesting bird-thing today?" Everyone laughed, and repeated the same humiliating question.

Stan, mistaking the question to be legitimate, answered back, "No, n n-nooo. Actually, birds are more active later in the ye-year. I don't see that many now. Besides, I take the b-bus to school, so I don't get much chance to to see any."

The group howled with laughter. "Yep…you take the bus. That, by the way is why *you* are, SHORT CHEESE STAN," Kyle said loudly enough for the entire cafeteria to hear. Now there were lots of people laughing at Stan Junior.

Unfortunately for Kyle, he never saw Stan Junior's sister, Jenny, coming up from behind. Before he knew what was happening, she hit him across the front of his face with one of her books. He fell back, then forward, his nose and forehead gushing blood. But, Jenny was not done. She pushed him into the table while hitting him with a food tray, called him names, and swore at him until two teachers arrived to pull her away. As they pulled her away, she continued kicking at Kyle and issuing threats to everyone in earshot.

"Go ahead, assholes. Keep calling my brother 'the cheese.' I promise you the next person I hear say that will be super sorry!"

Stan Junior sat there in total shock and amazement. He had never heard his sister this angry or swear before. This was a total meltdown. He had no idea exactly what Jenny meant by, "seeing to it they would be sorry," but he did know she meant it, and those boys should pretty much take her at her word. Nor did Stan Junior know exactly what it was about "cheese" that Jenny had found so offensive.

Stan Junior later heard that his brother John had come, and picked Jenny up from school. She had received a three day suspension, and couldn't return without a parent. That was bad. Dad was a terror about any trouble at school, and he felt really sorry for his sister.

By the time Stan Junior arrived home, Jenny had already gone to her room. As he walked into the living room, he could hear his Dad on the phone with the school. Of course, he could only hear his Dad's half of the conversation, but could pretty much guess what the other half was saying.

"Yes...yes I heard the boy was hurt. He got just what was coming to him. No, you listen! This kid's been bullying my son all year. How many times have I brought it to your attention, and you have done nothing. Well; his sister took care of it for you, didn't she. What?...of course I know I have to come in. But I can tell you this right now; if you are expecting some kind of apology, you will be on your pensions in nursing homes before you hear one. By the way, what about the other boys? Yes, them; what's happening to them? What do you mean you have no grounds to take action? What are you going to do? Wait for them to hurt someone else?"

Stan Junior looked at John, who was just sitting in the chair listening to his father do battle with the school principal.

"Dad's really mad, isn't he, John."

"Yeah, Stan. Don't worry. He'll take care of it."

Stan Junior wasn't worried that his Dad would take care of things. His Dad *always* took care of *everything*. That was one of the great things about being in this family, and having this father.

"Yes, yes, yes. I know. Jenny's suspended for three days. And now I suppose you expect me to take disciplinary action here at the house, but you people take no action at all with the people who caused this in the first place. Is that it? Well, I'll deal with this, but you need to know I'm proud of the way my daughter stood up for her brother. So,

I'll see you at the meeting, but you people better come up with some better ideas than the ones you had today as to how you're going to deal with these bullies!"

Down went the phone so hard that the cradle in which it sat flew off the table.

"Dad?" Stan Junior said.

"What, son," Stan answered, not really looking in his son's direction but just continuing with his angry train of thought.

"Am I in trouble like Jenny?"

"What? No. No, of course not. You're not in trouble, son...and Jenny isn't...I mean you guys did nothing ...," and he stopped mid sentence to get his temper under control.

"Well," Stan Junior continued, "am I suspended from school for three days like Jenny?"

"No. Why would you even think that, Stan?"

"Well. I was just thinking that if I *was* suspended, maybe I could just stay here, and keep Jenny company so she won't be here all by herself."

With that, Stan Senior stopped dead in his tracks and looked at his son. Then he looked over at John, and the two of them smiled.

Stan Senior approached his totally bewildered son, and hugged and kissed him on the forehead.

"You, my friend are absolutely the best brother ever! The best."

John then came and put Stan Junior in a fake head lock, and proceeded to give him some make-believe punches to the head.

"You are my kind of guy, pal...my kind of guy."

Stan and Marilyn realized early on that Stan Junior would probably never live independently. It would be best if he could live with them or some family member, and continue to feel that family love and support. Ultimately, John decided to have Stan Junior come live with him and his family. He and Linda lived in a large house, and had plenty of room for Stan Junior. In addition they had a good sized yard, and a yellow lab named, Bonkers that Stan Junior absolutely adored. Somehow, Bonkers and he made a perfect pair. For Stan Junior, life could not have been better. But that did not mean some unhappy times were not to come. They were.

Today, Stan Senior saw all that history, and all that family unity about to disappear. In fact, nearly his entire previous life was over. He was to be put by the wayside for his remaining days. At least that was how he saw it.

Yes, he had signed the power of attorney papers John said were absolutely essential. Yes, he had somewhere agreed that he needed "some assistance" in his daily living, and perhaps an assisted living arrangement made sense. Yes, he had even signed those dumb papers over at Willow Grove, dammit! He had been, as he saw it now, "skillfully walked down the garden path to his own demise." He hated the thought of it.

"It was a bloody act of betrayal is what it was," he thought. And the more he thought about it, the angrier he became. "Those two just piss me the hell off! I really can't stand it. And to think of all the crap I went through on their behalf, and now where are we? Now, how are things working out?" he thought.

Stan had noticed over the last year that his temper had become increasingly more explosive. Perhaps it was circumstances, he thought. "Yes, that must be it. I'm just angry at the way things are turning out, and the way I allowed myself to be manipulated." In reality, however, Stan knew it was more than that. He had feared there was something wrong for a long time. He passed it off to his family as "old-timers disease," but he knew it was more than that. Stan had become a near expert at creating plausible denial for all the things he saw going wrong in his life. He had been willing to blame nearly every ailment known to man for the symptoms he so obviously displayed. Ultimately, however, the doctors cleared all those other excuses he had used from the table, and called the demon by its name…Alzheimer's.

He was now often given to fits of anger over the smallest incidents. Inanimate objects trembled at his mere approach. On one occasion his bathrobe got caught on a newly poured cup of coffee, inconveniently spilling it onto his leg, all over the counter, and onto the floor. Outraged, he cried, "You son of a bitch!! You bastard!" With those epithets, the coffee cup flew against the wall making an even bigger mess, while the coffee maker was swept off the counter and into the sink, crashing and breaking the carafe.

"Oh great," Stan exclaimed. "Just great!" He felt so stupid, and was almost immediately sorry for what he had done. "What a dummy you are."

There was another thing that angered him. If he was going out, his children preferred he have a companion. "Who the hell do they think they are," he raged. "I'm the parent here. I'm the boss, not them." The more he thought about it, the angrier he became. Just because he had gotten a little disoriented a time or two, these kids wanted to make a federal case of it.

Worse than his fits of anger, were his bouts of forgetfulness. He knew things were getting worse, but he was still confident that with a little more help, perhaps a little more patience, he could remain right where he lived now. He wasn't that bad! Hell, he saw people forget crap all the time. He just needed a little help. He forgot the many occasions when his safety and sudden outbursts of anger had become significant issues.

Once John got that power of attorney, wheels were set in motion that made it nearly impossible for Stan to remain where he was. As he saw it, the forces of evil had taken over, and he was helpless to stop them. First, the house was placed on the market for sale. Furniture and other possessions had been given to charitable organizations. Visits to assisted living establishments had been organized until finally Stan resigned, and said, "Fine. Yes, this will do." Oh how skillful those little bastards had been, Stan now thought. As far as the facility he accepted was concerned, it was not much different than any of the others they had visited. One look around at the residents, Stan concluded this place was about the same as everywhere else they had looked.

Today, Stan had finally reached the last day he would spend in his family house on Gill. He was sad. He was angry. He was depressed. He didn't really know which emotion occupied him most. He just knew it was a tangle of irreversible gloom. He had long stretches of time where he was perfectly lucid, like his old self. Then, however, he would seem to drift off; be forgetful, lose his temper, ignore everything around him. He now sat by his front window, and waited for his son to arrive. It was almost that time. Just then, John pulled up in his new car.

"God; look at that," thought Stan. "Another new car for this kid! Does he do this just to aggravate me and show off, or does he really enjoy spending 800 unnecessary dollars every month? How many times did I tell this boy to 'live below his means?' How many? Three thousand if it was one. Did he listen? Did he follow direction? Of course not. It's John, and John always sees himself as the smartest person in the room." Already, Stan's temper was about to run away from him.

With that, the door opened, and in walked John with his cheery, "Hi Dad. How are we feeling today? Having a good day?"

"*WEEEE*, are *NOT* having a good day! Jesus but I didn't get much for my money out of that asshole University of Tennessee if you can come waltzing in here with that kind of dumb ass question!! I'm about to be hauled off by the Bonzo Brothers to some foreign place of lifetime incarceration and you ask me, 'are we having a good day,'" Stan exploded.

"Dad. Really. First of all, it isn't 'The Bonzo Brothers.' It's Art and Sal from Willow Grove who you met and liked because they told good jokes. They are simply coming with the van so they can make sure you are bringing the things you want to have in your new apartment." John knew his father was unhappy, but he was going to do his very best to avoid confrontations, and make this transition go as smoothly as possible. But things would not be so easy.

"Oh yes, yes, yes. I forgot. My '*neeeeew* apartment,'" Stan answered. "You make it sound like I am going to the damn Ritz! Well it's not. It's an assisted living deal where the average age of the '*residents*' is about 152, and their IQ's are in the single digits. And that's the ones still able to communicate with something more than a grunt or burp."

"Dad, really. This is really a nice place, one of the best in all of Tennessee. And by the way, Dad, what's with all the swearing recently? All the time we were growing up, you hardly used a word worse than 'damn.' Now, you are like a sailor on leave. In fact, even worse, I now sometimes hear you even taking the Lord's name in vain. I mean, to me that's nearly unbelievable. When we were kids, you heard me say GD just once, and I was put on punishment for forty five minutes. As far as you were concerned, that one was even *worse* than the F word. Lately, I've heard you use it several times. What is with that? Why? It isn't a very appealing characteristic, I can assure you."

Stan responded almost before John could even complete the last syllable. "Ooooh, you can assure *me* can you? Well, that's great. I feel so much better with all that reassurance. And as for where did all that swearing come from, there are certain occasions that call for stronger language. Let me '*assure you*,' THIS is one of them! And as for God, he apparently asked for and received a divorce from his ole servant Stan."

John felt an overwhelming sadness at hearing his father speak this way. He knew it was the disease talking, but the knowledge that his father was going through these emotions and fears was almost too much to bear. He was so glad Jenny was not here listening because she would want to cancel the entire arrangement on the spot.

"I'm sorry to hear you talk this way, Dad. I don't think God abandoned you, and I don't think you really believe that either. But you're mad, and you're just venting a little bit," John said trying to relieve some of his father's feeling of abandonment.

"Oh, you don't think so, John? Let me tell you some of the other bad news that may have escaped your most observant notice. Not only does God give you the heave-ho at some point? Ohhhhhh no no, no. That's not good enough. No sir. First he robs you."

"Dad, what in the world are you talking about?" John asked, wondering just what crazy direction this conversation was going now.

"Well. First, God takes away your wife; a woman who never did a single thing to hurt another human being; someone who never spoke an ill word about anyone. But oh no, that's not good enough. Not for God. No sir. He wants her there for himself, so He just barges in and takes her, leaving you to figure out how to reinvent life."

Losing Marilyn was a family tragedy that had left a scar on his father that would never heal. Stan had always harbored the idea that he was supposed to go first, and somehow God had cheated him by taking Marilyn before him.

"Then, just to make things interesting, He chips away at shit like your eyesight, your hearing, your sense of balance. Once you're totally on the ropes, He swoops in with the coup de grace. Yes sir. The coup de-damn grace. Know what that is, John-boy?"

John didn't even want to ask or further encourage his father's tirade.

"Well, listen up there, Johnny, 'cause this good news is allllll coming your way, and coming a lot sooner than you think."

Stan was on a roll now, whatever thoughts were jumping into his mind, there was no filter; they were flowing off his lips like a snowball careening downhill.

John tried to help his father regain some control. "You're mad at everything, and right now you just don't want to hear any discussion from me. Let's just leave it there for now, OK?"

With that, Stan somehow began to regain his temper, but with it came an almost overwhelming feeling of remorse. He was feeling so alone, so totally helpless to do anything to make his situation better. He didn't feel good about having just yelled at his son. He sat there looking straight ahead. It sounded as if people in the room were speaking, but he wasn't paying attention, and probably they weren't speaking to him anyway. Was there a way out of this he wondered?

"Tell me, John," he said calmly. "Why do I have to go to this place? Why are we going there? Isn't there something we can do so I can stay? How about another home helper?"

Stan was near desperate at this point, even though he knew his situation was beyond hope. Could there be *any* last minute reprieve?

"Dad, you *know* why this is the best arrangement. You know you've had so many issues, and why there's a concern..." John hadn't even finished the sentence before Stan erupted again.

"Best arrangement! Best arrangement for who?!! Not best arrangement for me, that's for damn sure. Maybe the best arrangement for you...not for me! I want the one that suits *ME*!"

"And don't think I'm too far out of it to know what's going on here, John. Oh ho ho no, I get it entirely. You guys all want to get on with your lives, and I'm in the way. I wasn't getting *out* of the way fast enough was I? So you two just figured you might hurry things along under the banner of, 'let's do the right thing for Dad.' Right, but it's not really about what's right for Dad, is it! It's about what's convenient for you. We've had this discussion before; BIG TIME, haven't we. That's what we're dealing with here, isn't it John. You forget that nice little family pow-wow we had a few months back; but I don't. No sir; I don't"

The doctors had warned that Stan's temper and paranoia were likely to get worse and erupt. Yet, now, today, it caught John off guard. It was killing him to see and hear his father feeling this way; worse yet, to know he was a part of it. Although he had been assured a large element of what was taking place was a common component of the disease, somehow at this point, that assurance was not comforting.

"Dad, this is not about convenience for Jenny and me at all. You know as well as I that you have had any number of episodes that were outright dangerous. There are lots of good reasons that more professional support is the best option for you. We've been over them many times. You've even agreed yourself it was a good idea."

"Yes. I know. But I'm rethinking things. This may be some sort of 'try and convince Dad' game you and your sister are playing here, but it's damn well not a game to me. To me its life and death, and *I'm* the one here losing his life. I can see what's happened, the die is cast; but don't expect me to be happy about it!"

Before John could even answer, his Dad fell silent, walked over to the front window, and looked out onto Gill Avenue. Standing there, Stan's mind began to wander. It was as if he was staring at a deep, dark, and foreboding tunnel directly in his path; a dark abyss full of unknowns; full of darkness. In another time and day Stan might have been afraid; but here, at this moment? Now, he just felt this overwhelming sadness and emptiness. He had a sense that he would simply cease to exist; not so much in physical way, but rather he would just stop mattering to anyone or to the world in general. Worse, there was not a single thing he could do to change his fate. There was, he thought, nothing worse than dying of old age too early.

At that exact moment, Stan saw his fate arrive. The white panel van with the words, "Willow Grove" written in large green script on the side pulled up. Underneath the title, in smaller print, were the words, "living with dignity."

"Living with morons," Stan said sotto voce.

"What Dad?" John asked.

"Nothing, John, absolutely nothing. The Bonzo Brothers are here, that's all."

John immediately went over to the window, and saw that the truck was here with Art and Sal who would help move the heavy pieces out of the house.

"I better go out and help Art and Sal get organized. I'll be right back. You gonna be OK for a minute?"

"No. Actually, I was going out to the backyard, and play on the dangerous damned swings for a while. Maybe you better come back there, and watch so I don't fall off and skin my damn knee," he answered sarcastically. "No, no, go on...I'll just watch the two Bonzo's do their thing."

Then he yelled as an afterthought, "Better tell them to organize all their fucking nets and straight-jackets before they come in. You never know what kind of asshole, lunatic jackass might be inside. Could be their worst damn nightmare.....*me*! Sons-of-bitches," he added in an inaudible voice.

With that, John went outside to head off Art and Sal to let them know what they were walking into.

"Hey guys. Thanks for coming. I just wanted to let you know, this has been a bad day for Dad. He might say some really mean or aggravating things in there, so I just wanted to apologize in advance. I think the best thing is to just try to ignore everything as best we can."

Art answered, "Don't worry, Mr. Beecher. We both know this is a tough day for everyone. We've done this lots of times before, and we understand how people feel. It's a big emotional break. We'll be as quick and gentle as we can be. He's going to ride with you, though, right Mr. Beecher?"

"Oh yeah...he comes with me," John answered, relieving their concern that Stan might be riding in the cab with them. They had had that situation once before when a new resident decided he didn't want to go, and then tried to get out of the truck to make a run for it when they arrived.

John quickly added, "Jenny and Stan Junior are going to meet us at the place with Sandy, his dog. We thought it best to keep things here simple and moving. I hope that's OK."

As they re-entered the house, John said, "Anything with a red ribbon on it is what's going with us. If you have any questions, you can just let me know."

"Thaaaaaat's right boys...you can just ask my son here. Don't bother to ask me. I only own the place, but I don't know shit from shinola about anything around here. Hey, make sure you take that big dining room table. I plan to do a lot of entertaining in these new digs. You two are invited. Just bring some hot women and good whiskey."

Art just smiled and said, "OK, Mr. Beecher, we'll be sure to get it for you. Sal and I hate to miss good parties."

As Sal and Art worked to load the van, Stan sat on a dining room chair looking out at nothing in particular. John was speaking to him, but no response was coming back.

In a little less than an hour, everything was loaded, and the Willow Grove van pulled out.

"OK, Dad. I guess we're ready. You want to get in the car? Dad? Dad…we need to get in the car."

Stan said nothing, and did not move. After several tries and no response John was getting nervous that his father might just become adamant and refuse to leave the house. He was hesitant to try and physically move his father because such actions in the past had sometimes caused violent responses. He tried again.

"Dad, Dad…we're ready to ride in the car. We're going out, OK?" This time, he breathed a sigh of relief; he at least got a response.

"Yeah. Well, you're ready at any rate. Fine. Let's get in that fancy new car, whatever it is. I hate to see all that dough you don't need to spend go to waste."

John ignored the car comment. He was just happy to get his father moving in the right direction. As they moved toward the car, his father never looked back; never even acknowledged he was leaving his house for the last time. John wondered just how much of this had been simply blocked from his father's mind.

On the ride to Willow Grove, Stan was amazingly silent. He just looked out the window, and occasionally said something under his breath like, "last time I'll see that." Stan was afraid. He was certain this had all been one big conspiracy of which he had somehow become the victim. What was going to happen to him? He was almost sure as soon as he got wherever they were going, that warden lady was going to put him in some sort of lock down from which he'd never escape.

Would they let him have a TV? No...he doubted their prisoners would be allowed that kind of thing. How had he gotten here? He couldn't really remember. But yes. It was a ruse; he knew it! He remembered signing a bunch of stuff, but hell, he didn't know what any of it said. He just knew John had pushed things in front of him, so he just signed whatever it was. No, there were people trying to get him, he was sure of it. Maybe it was that nursing home place...maybe they saw a way to get him over there and get hold of his money. He was trapped by them. Now, there was no place to run.

As they were going through town, John suddenly thought of a way to make the ride happier for his father.

"Hey, Dad! I just thought of something. Since we're already going that way, why don't we drive by Neyland Stadium one more time. That would be fun for both of us."

His Dad had always loved going to Tennessee football games at Neyland Stadium. For years he had held season tickets, although recently, John had taken him to only a few games each year. Every game day, Stan wore his orange UT shirt and dilapidated old hat with Phil Fulmer's autograph.

With that suggestion, Stan's face suddenly lit up with a big smile. "That's a good idea, John. Let's go by the stadium."

John thought it funny in an ironic way that of all the things his Dad had forgotten, one of things he hadn't forgotten was Tennessee football and Neyland Stadium. He had always said, "Once Tennessee Orange gets in your blood, it never leaves."

As he passed World's Fair Park, John said, "Do you remember how we used to walk this way to the game, and see all the people going up this hill? I think my favorite part was always when you bought me those big hot dogs as we went to our seats. And the band; you loved the Pride of the Southland Band. Do you remember that, Dad? Those days were really special."

Stan just looked at his son with a slight grin. He felt better to see his son smiling.

As they rode down Northshore, they came onto a small grove of trees with a long circular drive. The drive was ringed with dogwood trees, weeping willows, and flowering azaleas. The two-story building had an elegant antebellum entry, and a bold green portico to greet visitors. They rolled up towards the graceful Willow Grove entrance; outside waiting were Jenny, Stan Junior, and Sandy. Of everything his Dad might have seen, the only thing that caught his eye was his dog, Sandy.

"Hey look, John...its Sandy!! They found her. Awww...look how excited she is." Sandy saw Stan getting out of the car, and immediately started barking and pulling at the chain to get free. She could hardly contain herself with Stan so nearby. Finally, Jenny let her go, and she ran to Stan, jumping and barking in what could only be described as sheer dog delight. She was wagging her tail so hard her entire body quivered.

"Yes, yes. That's my girl. You still love me, dontcha." As Stan bent down to greet her, Sandy put her paws up over his shoulder, and began licking his face. Stan just laughed and said, "Yeah, you're my good girl."

Stan stood up while Sandy continued to jump and run around him, tangling her leash in his feet. Then, he looked ahead at the doors in front of him. Jenny came over, took his hand in hers, and with tears running down her cheeks the two of them walked toward the front door. Stan Junior took Sandy, and it was the four of them walking together, walking toward the end of one chapter in their father's life and into another.

2

The Early Years

The Beecher family of Gill Avenue was a typical southern family. Their children attended public school, they were members in good standing at Saint James Church, and they were well regarded in the community. Stan had always been of the belief that good children were raised in two primary places; the church and the dinner table. Marilyn made a home cooked meal every evening, and the family sat to enjoy one another's company, and talk about their day. Family values were transmitted and reinforced at mealtimes.

"Whose turn is it to say the mealtime prayer tonight?" Stan asked.

Marilyn looked around the table for one of the children to speak; all but Stan Junior's heads were down. Marilyn let everyone off the hook, "I think it's mine. Stan Junior went last night."

With no further discussion, Marilyn continued, "We thank you Lord for our many blessings and this food. Please bless all around this table, and the food to our bodies that we can continue in a Christian way with love and thanksgiving. Amen."

"Amen," everyone echoed with knives and forks at the ready.

"So then," Stan began, "What's happening in your worlds that is new and exciting?"

Looking around the table, there were few takers on Dad's opening question.

"Jenny? How about you? What's going on there," Stan asked.

Jenny thought a moment as to what would be something even worth introducing and said, "Well, Teddy McKnight got his as… uhh…got suspended from school for starting a fight in gym class. The word was he got pissed at someone in the basketball game and punched him."

Marilyn winced at her use of the word, "pissed" in her statement, but let it roll by, hoping her husband would not zero in on it. At least she pulled up short from using the a-s-s word, so small blessings were to be counted.

Jenny continued, "It doesn't surprise anybody he got suspended. Teddy is a real jerk. He is always trying to bully somebody, and today he got called on it. 'Good' is what I thought. Nobody likes him."

Marilyn looked at Jenny as she put down her fork, "Well, Jenny, maybe that's why he has such a hostile attitude; he thinks no one likes him."

Jenny looked back at her mother, and rebutted the argument. "Mom, they don't like him because he's a jerk. If he wants people to like him, maybe he's the one who needs to change."

"I know, dear, I was just thinking that if others were nicer, maybe he would be too. Of course, I don't know this boy, so maybe I'm missing something," Marilyn added, making somewhat a retreat.

"Well, you know Jenny, in a way, your mom here has a point," Stan added, coming to the aid of his wife. "It costs us nothing to be nice to someone. If they don't return the kindness, at least our conscience is clear that we reached out first, right?"

Stan Junior, feeling he knew a little on this subject of kindness to others joined the fray, "Yeah, Jenny, people can be mean all the time, but I just try to be nice."

Marilyn looked at her son with one of her loving smiles and said, "Absolutely right, Stan Junior; absolutely right."

Character and values were a common theme of discussion at the Beecher dinner table, this was another prime example. Of course, there had been many times where Stan tried to steer the subject onto some "lesson to be learned" topic when Jenny and John would just roll their eyes and groan. Even Marilyn sometimes had to leave the table when Stan would climb into his pulpit for a short sermonette. But that was their father, and as corny as he sometimes sounded, the Beecher family had become accustomed to his little lectures.

As a recently promoted detective on the Knoxville Police Force, Stan Senior's hours were long, and not defined by a regular forty hour workweek. It was not uncommon for their father's best friend and partner, Ted Newsome to show up late at night, when he and their Dad would talk in hushed voices in the kitchen. Sometimes Stan Senior would even leave at that late hour calling to Marilyn on the way out the door,

"Don't wait up, Sweetheart. I'll probably be late."

The absence of their father was not unusual. On the other hand, their father seemed to always be present for significant family events at the school or church. He had attended almost every sporting event for John, been to all Jenny's flute recitals (although she readily admitted to being painfully horrible at that instrument), and appeared at Stan Junior's "class parent days."

As the children grew up, family traditions and values grew stronger. That was a good thing, because in adulthood, those values would be put to the test.

*****

Oddly enough, the family's first test came from Jenny, just after she had decided to date Jimmy. As everyone sat down for dinner, conversation proceeded at the usual pace until Stan asked Jenny how things were going at the hospital.

"So Jenny, how's the new job? You getting along OK over there?"

Jenny, looked up, smiled, took a deep breath and said, "It's pretty great, Dad, pretty great. Actually, I met someone, and he asked me out for Saturday. I'm looking forward to finally getting out."

Stan stopped eating; everyone stopped eating.

John was the first to speak out. "Wow. That's super, Jenny. Are you going anywhere special?"

Stan could wait no further, "Sooooooo, you going to tell us about this young man, or do I need to read it in the Society Section of the *Sentinel*," he laughed.

Jenny looked up at her father and said, "Well, his name is Jimmy Ray, he's just a little older than me, and just joined our staff as a nurse practitioner. He's very nice; we have lunch at the same time, so one of the other staff introduced us. Anyway, he wants to go to dinner and a movie, so I said yes."

"That's great," Stan Junior said enthusiastically. "I love going to the movies. That should be a lot of fun."

Marilyn finally asked her own question. "So, Jenny, will we get to meet your new friend at some point here; will we see him Saturday?"

Jenny felt this was as good a time as any. "Yeah, he's coming by to pick me up, so I'll have him come in for a minute." Then she looked at her father admonishingly, "A minute Dad, not a half hour for interrogation about his entire life history."

Stan objected with vigor. "Oh for goodness sakes, Jenny, of course. Why would you suggest I would do that? No, no, no, just introductions will be fine. *'Interrogations'* indeed. You must think I'm some kind of ogre!"

Stan Junior wanted to know, "Can I be here to meet him, too?"

"I'll introduce him to you first, Stan Junior," Jenny laughed. Stan Junior smiled, and looked about the table in his moment of victory.

"Oh…there *is* one other thing you should know now, just so you won't be surprised Saturday…he's an African American."

All forks stopped moving except for Stan Junior's. All conversation came to a halt. All breathing was temporarily suspended. Stan Senior looked straight up at Marilyn. Marilyn was looking back at him with that, "say nothing" look.

It was Marilyn who broke the silence. "Oh. Well, that's fine. I'm sure he's very nice, and we all look forward to meeting him."

"Uhhhhh. Yes. Yes, of course. Yes, bring him round…we all want to meet who this is taking our daughter out on the town," Stan said trying to sound nonchalant, but falling well short.

John added, "So, Jenny, how long have you known this guy?"

Jenny knew what he was asking, and shot back, "About a hot five minutes, just long enough to say yes and suspend my membership in the Knoxville Wallflower's Association. Any problem with that, John?"

"Jeez, Jenny, it was just a question. You don't have to bite my head off." John decided he wouldn't say another word. This is what Jenny wanted to do, fine with him, time to leave the party.

"Right…well, I've got some work to do, so if everyone will excuse me, I think I'll go upstairs and get started."

"John, you've hardly eaten a thing, why don't you finish up a little more," his mother pleaded.

"No, I wasn't all that hungry, Mom. Maybe I'll come down for dessert later." Retreat was what was on John's mind. He'd seen Jenny's temper, and he didn't need it directed at him.

"No dessert for children who don't finish their dinner," Stan Senior shot back, trying to add humor, and break the tension hanging in the room.

Jenny knew her parents were taken by surprise, but she was also pretty confident they'd be fine once they met Jimmy; how could they not? He was one of the sweetest guys she'd ever met. Things would work out; she knew it.

After everyone had left the table for their rooms, Marilyn looked over at Stan who had a somewhat pained look as he was wiping the last crumbs of his dinner from his lips. She knew he was less than comfortable with Jenny's announcement, but this was a topic best addressed in advance, and with honesty.

"So, Mr. Beecher, I'm looking at you, and wondering if there's a problem with all this? You seem awfully quiet over there, and I know the wheels are turning in your head," Marilyn said with her own head cupped in her hands.

"Noooo, nooo...no problem; just a little surprised I guess," Stan answered but with the word "lie" written all over his face.

"Uh huh," Marilyn answered. "Now let's hear the real story. What's biting you about this? Is it that he's black? You're thinking she should stay in her own race or something?"

"Oh, my goodness, Marilyn," Stan shot back, looking up with a hurt expression. "Try not to make me a racist. No, but you know, relationships have problems in the best of circumstances, and mixed race relationships, well, they present even more problems. I don't know...I guess I'm just being a little overprotective, and don't want to see her get hurt."

Marilyn's gaze never left Stan's face. "Mmmmmm hmmmmmm...'overprotective'.....is that the word we're using tonight?" she asked. "Maybe you and I should just let *her* worry about whatever problems others might have, and we just be there for her if and when something does go wrong...and I think it's a little premature to think *anything* will go wrong, don't you?"

Marilyn was not yet done. She knew her husband well enough to know when he was wrestling with something. His face showed no signs of resolution.

"And one more little thing, Stanton William," she added in a bit more sharpened tone of voice. "If you don't want to alienate your own daughter, I would suggest you just get by whatever reservations you have up there in your head. She's a grown woman, not 14, and I think she knows what she's doing. Besides, this is a date, not a marriage proposal. So how about we meet this young man, and just cross bridges when they arrive. Who knows, you might even like this fellow. I'm pretty sure if Jenny likes him, he must be a pretty good guy."

Stan knew his wife was right. He wasn't certain it made him any more comfortable with the situation, but he did know he better just paint a smile on his face, and go along with things for now. Besides, his wife was definitely right about the possibility of his liking the young man. Jenny had always been a good judge of character.

Jimmy pulled in front of Jenny's house at 5:55, while Jenny waited near the front window. She was thinking; "my God, I feel like a teenager waiting for her first date, then again, that's about what this is."

As soon as Jenny saw the car pull up, she went and opened the door so Jimmy would know he had the right house. She waved him in.

If Jenny thought she had some misgivings as to how her family might react to hearing Jimmy was African American, they were small potatoes compared to the apprehension Jimmy was feeling. He had never dated outside his own race before, so he had no idea what kind of reception awaited inside. "It's just dinner and a movie," he told himself, but he was hoping this would turn out to be much more in the future.

Jimmy came to the door, and Jenny grabbed his hand as she led him inside with a big smile.

"Mom, Dad; this is Jimmy Ray who I told you about from the hospital."

Marilyn smiled, and was the first to shake his hand.

"Well, my, my. Jenny, you didn't tell us he was this tall," her mother joked.

Stan was right next to his wife, "Jimmy...very nice to meet you. Jenny told us a little about you, but I'm sure we'll hear a lot more as time goes on. By the way, this over here," he said motioning Stan Junior's direction, "is Jenny's younger brother, Stan Junior."

Jimmy shook everyone's hand and said, "Well, I'm very pleased to meet everyone. Jenny and I haven't had a lot of time to get to know one another yet, but from what little she's said, I knew she had a real nice family. I'm a family guy too; that's important."

Music to Stan's ears...of course, everything you hear on first meeting someone needed further verification as far as Stan Senior was concerned. But, first impressions are important, and Jimmy had made a good one.

Jenny, wanting to limit the time for further interviewing, moved Jimmy toward the door.

"OK, everyone; we'll be back later. I don't want to be late for our reservations."

Marilyn went over and opened the door, "Alllll right, dear. You kids have a good time. It was nice meeting you, Jimmy."

With that Jenny briskly moved down the sidewalk, pushing Jimmy out in front of her. They got in the car, and looked at one another a minute, then the two of them burst out laughing.

"Oh my God," Jenny said. "Poor Dad didn't know which leg to stand on or what to say next. Don't worry, you made a great impression, I can tell. This is going to be just fine. But really, it was so funny."

Jimmy said, "Here is my word to sum up the entire meeting... *awkward.*" Then he laughed again. "Thanks for getting us on our way, and not letting me twist in the wind. You have no idea how nervous I was. I thought I was fourteen again."

Jenny laughed out loud, "That's exactly what I was thinking as you came up the steps. Isn't that funny?"

They decided on the Downtown Grill for dinner. It was a casual place which always attracted good sized crowds, especially on the weekend. It was a good location to talk and get better acquainted. Once their orders were placed, the conversation shifted.

"Well, you've met my parents; tell me about yours. Do they live in Knoxville?" Jenny asked.

Jimmy thought a minute about just how much he wanted to tell about his family, but then decided, "Hell, let's get all this out on the table now."

"Right…well, my Dad is actually a Professor of Urban Studies over at UT, and my mom is a full professor in the music department. Once upon a time my mother was quite a singer. Her biggest claim to fame was performing with the Birmingham Civic Opera in the early days when she and Dad were first dating. Actually, my father met my mother when she was singing at the Baptist church he attended. At the time he was just starting out in the teaching field, so initially he was a little intimidated by Mom's near celebrity status."

Jenny listened to Jimmy's description of how his parents met with great interest. It was not so different from that of her parents.

"Oh my God," Jenny smiled. "Isn't this a riot; my parents met in church too. Their first date was actually to a church supper. My Dad had to chase my mother for some time before she agreed to even go out with him. Isn't it ironic?"

Jenny had another big question on her mind about Jimmy's parents, but hesitated to ask. She was somewhat afraid of what she might hear.

"I'm almost afraid to ask, but I'm going to anyway. How did your parents take the news that I'm white? Of course, I'm just assuming you already told them, right?"

Jimmy smiled across the table. He too was a little hesitant to tell the entire story.

"Let's just say, my mother seems OK, but my father has some reservations."

"About me?" Jenny added with her heart slowly sinking.

"No, no," Jimmy quickly added. "No. You see, my father is one of those people who is just a bit slow on anything new or a surprise. Telling him about you was both. He had always imagined that I would just do what everyone else in the family has done, meet a nice girl at the Baptist church, get married, and have children. Of course, he also thought I would go to college, get a doctoral degree, and take my place in some high profile profession; nurse practitioner didn't fit that design either. So, I guess this was just one more instance where I did something he didn't plan. But don't you worry. Between mother and me, we will get him on board."

Jenny felt much better, and was now breathing easier. She hoped that this was the beginning of something big in her life. And it was.

At the house, the two of them stood outside talking a bit longer. Jenny knew Jimmy would never have the guts to kiss her, so she pulled him down and kissed him, a nice long, tender kiss.

Jimmy was a bit shocked...pleasantly shocked, but shocked nonetheless. And to think this entire thing took place under two watchful eyes peering out from a top floor window.

Marilyn went to bed smiling. "This is going to be some ride, she thought...some ride."

By the end of the year, Jenny and Jimmy had announced their engagement. During that time, Jimmy had become a welcome guest in the Beecher home. He could frequently be found playing catch with Stan Junior; the two had become good friends. The Beecher and Carter families had reluctantly come to terms with the union.

*****

John came down the stairs wearing a new suit which cost what would have been a week's pay for his Dad. His hair was perfectly trimmed, along with the hint of a small goatee on his chin. Stan took one look and said,

"I got some new blades up there for my razor if you've run short."

"No Dad. I just thought it might make me look a little older. I have an interview today."

"Hope it's not with the Gillette Company," Stan sarcastically answered without looking up from the morning paper.

"No, Dad...not the Gillette Company," John answered with a long sigh. "It's with the accounting firm of Widbey and Strong over in the First Tennessee Building. I think I've pretty much got this. One of the UT guys I went to school with put me onto it. He started there two months ago; great salary, good benefits, real up and coming organization according to him. It's only the first round, so my guess is there will a second, more intensive interview down the road. Whatever; I've been up there preparing, I'm ready to go," John said with a confident smile.

"Do yourself a very big favor, son," his Dad cautioned. "Don't get your heart settled on any one position until the ink is dry on the contract. Construction projects can often fall in on the unwary workman if you know what I mean."

John knew what he meant, and the metaphor sucked as far as he was concerned. Why argue, he would just let his Dad be surprised when the offer came in.

The interview was in the offices of Widbey and Strong, on the 24th floor of the First Tennessee Building, a modern glass and steel structure commanding the south end of Gay Street, overlooking the Tennessee River and mountains. As John sat waiting, the neatly dressed woman managing the office busily shuffled papers, made entries on her keyboard, and paid him no attention whatever. She was a fiftyish woman, very well dressed, and official looking. Her phone rang,

"Yes sir. Now? OK."

As she hung up, another man exited the inner office. He was in his early 30's, also sharply dressed, and carried a brown, high end, leather briefcase. He nodded to John,

"Good luck...it wasn't too bad," he smiled as he walked toward the exit.

"You can go in now. Mr. Highsmith is ready," said the woman.

As John went in, the HR director, Jacob Highsmith came over, shook his hand, and led him to a seat. The surroundings included a long conference table, a buffet table with coffee, Danish, and assorted drinks, and an expansive window with a view of the west city and Great Smokey Mountains in the background.

Mr. Highsmith led off, "Would you care for anything to drink, or a pastry?"

John politely refused, preferring to just move ahead with the interview. It was a fairly standard beginning, about what John had expected, including the customary background questions followed by more specific accounting questions. John was confident in his answer to each question.

"OK, John. Well, I've very much enjoyed meeting you. We are on a somewhat short timeline, so I will personally call everyone to let them know if they will be moving forward. I should be making those calls early next week at the latest. Do you have any questions or last minute things for us to know?"

"No," John answered. "I'm very happy to have had the opportunity to come in today. I look forward to seeing everyone at the next step. This is a great company, and I'm eager to be part of the team."

Mr. Highsmith rose from his chair, walking John toward the door. "You're an impressive young man; it was nice speaking with you. Have a great week."

As the door shut, John felt good. He said goodbye to the secretary, and made his way to the elevators.

The call came four days later.

Stan Senior answered the phone, and called up to John's room.

"It's for you, John; a Mr. Highsmith. I think you were expecting this call."

John had deliberately given the secretary, who he was later informed was an executive assistant, not a secretary, a landline because he was afraid his cell phone might drop the call.

"Yes, this is John Beecher, nice to speak with you again Mr. Highsmith."

"Nice to speak with you also, John. Let me come directly to the reason for my call. We are going ahead with three final candidates, but I'm afraid you were not one of those we selected. You are a good prospect, and had some very fine answers indeed; but at the end of the day, it was simply a matter of which candidates we thought might fit our organization best as far as hitting the ground running. I want to thank you for your interest, perhaps at a later time, our paths may cross again."

John was stunned. No, he was crushed. He thought he had nailed the interview, made a great impression; done everything right. "Now I don't even make the second round? Really? Unbelievable. What went wrong?"

"Oh; I see. Well, I'm disappointed, this was a position I had really hoped to get. Can I ask where I fell short?"

"Of course, John; you have every right to know the difference. By the way, the term 'falling short' isn't quite accurate. As I said, you presented yourself well, and had some very fine answers. No, the biggest thing that separated you from your competition was their level of understanding about our company, what our major initiatives were as we move forward, and our overall service mission. As a result, their answers were perhaps a little more tailored to our immediate needs. I'm sure you understand; it was an extremely competitive field."

"I see, and yes, I understand how that could make a difference."

Mr. Highsmith then brought the call to an end,

"Good; well again, thank you for your interest. I wish you nothing but the best for your future. Regardless of this outcome, you have a lot to offer. We all wish you well."

Mr. Highsmith hung up. John could not have felt lower. He had never before been unsuccessful in something he attempted; he was totally deflated. He went to his room without telling his father the results, although he didn't need to. Listening from the kitchen to half the conversation provided Stan all the information needed.

Stan looked over at Marilyn, who was cutting vegetables for dinner.

"Looks like our boy got hit with his first big punch," Stan said, looking grimly at Marilyn. He knew this was going to be tough on his son. Lack of success had always been one of his son's great fears from as early as he could remember. John had never been able to settle for anything less than top of the ladder.

"You think you should go up there?" Marilyn asked.

"Nope...not right away. I think I want this feeling to sink in on him a bit. I want this bitter taste to last a while. His ego's bruised right now, but I want to see if he has the will to get up from the canvas and do something; or is he going to wallow in self pity and stay down? Whenever he gets up, that's when I'll get in the fight with him," Stan said.

Marilyn didn't like the idea. She wanted to run up there herself and give him a hug, but she knew her husband was right. Her son needed to learn to get up for himself.

Except for Stan Junior's excited talk about what he thought was an eagle's nest on the highway towards Gatlinburg, dinner was fairly silent. Jenny was out with her new boyfriend, Marilyn was waiting for Stan to say something, and Stan was waiting to hear what John was going to say.

"So, I guess you know I didn't get that job, Dad," John began in a subdued, sad voice.

"Yep," Stan said, not even looking up from the stew Marilyn had prepared.

"They said I didn't know enough about their 'corporate goals,' and my answers were kind of general," he continued in his beaten voice.

"Well," said Stan. "What was the lesson learned," he asked as he laid down his soup spoon, wiped his mouth with a napkin, and looked over at his son.

"What?" John asked.

"You heard me, boy; what was the lesson learned? When you get your butt kicked, there is always a good lesson to be learned; otherwise, what was the sense in allowing your butt to get kicked?" Stan was delivering these messages in sharp terms, not understanding ones.

Marilyn was already uncomfortable. Why did Stan have to be so harsh? That seemed like just kicking her son when he was down. She bit her tongue and stayed quiet, continuing to eat, but not enjoy, her stew.

"Lesson?" John responded, not certain what lesson it was to which his father referred, or where this conversation was going. "Well, I guess I need some inside help to know what's going on within the company... although I don't know how the heck I'll do *that* for every interview."

"Nope," said Stan. "Not quite."

"Ever hear of the internet? Ever hear of corporate annual reports? Ever hear of brochures and public advertising? *That's* where you get that kind of information. So...if you decide you're not beaten yet, then maybe next time you do a little homework and advance planning. I bet you'll do a hell of a lot better than you did this time."

Dad had a good point, John thought. He hadn't really considered there was a lesson in this. He'd have to think about how to make this a learning opportunity instead of defeat. When he finished his stew, he excused himself and returned to his room.

As soon as he left, Marilyn looked directly at Stan, "That was a little rough for a first day, don't you think?"

"Maybe," Stan said. "But the message is always a bit more memorable if you pour salt directly in the wound; learned that from Grandpa William," he added waving his fork at his wife.

"Great," thought Marilyn, "another lesson from Stan's father." She wasn't sure Grandpa William's brand of tough love was what the situation called for, but it was certainly one John would be unlikely to forget.

Stan looked up, and saw his wife's sad face, "Awwww, Marilyn; don't worry. He'll survive; it's just a little black eye. He's a fighter. You wait and see how he comes out of the corner swinging. I'll be there for him every step of the way. Now give me a smooch, and perhaps I can be persuaded to help with the dishes."

Marilyn smiled. This brief moment of tenderness reminded her of why she loved this man.

It took a few days, but eventually John emerged from his self-imposed exile and announced, "OK, I'm done worrying about old Widbey and Strong. The more I think about it, the more certain I am that it was a bad fit anyway. I'm going down to UT today, and look in the Business Placement Office to see what they have for openings. If that doesn't work, I am going to scour the internet. Something will turn up."

Life has its way of bringing surprises in the most unlikely ways. For John, his break was to unexpectedly come at the next meeting of the Rotary Club. John had joined Rotary right out of college, and periodically attended meetings. Many of the business leaders in Knoxville were members, and it was a good place to meet men and women on the rise. At the luncheon, John was seated at a table across from an older man who looked over at his nametag, and made an immediate connection. The man's name was Henry Wright, managing partner of a major investment firm in town.

"John Beecher," Henry said, "you any relation to a William Beecher?"

John looked over at the gentleman's nametag and answered, "Actually yes, Mr. Wright. He was my grandfather; did you know him?"

"Know him," Mr. Wright blurted out with a laugh. "You should have seen the stuff we got up to down at that Masonic Lodge. No, we were great friends back then. I actually attended his funeral. Sad to see him pass...he was a damn good man. So, what are you doing with yourself, John?"

Just that simply, a door opened. It is strange how somewhat simple choices in life can have such far reaching consequences. John's last minute decision to attend the Rotary luncheon was about to change his entire future.

"Well, since you ask, Mr. Wright, I have to be honest. I am now doing mostly temp work, but I've got my resume out there, and I'm fairly confident this is just for the short term."

"Really," Mr. Wright added. "What kind of work do you want?"

"I'm a little flexible on that, Mr. Wright. I'm applying for things in accounting, banking, marketing...something in the business field where there is good upside potential would be the best way to describe it."

"Ever think of investments," Mr. Wright asked with a grin.

"I haven't, but that would be another avenue I would certainly consider," John said, wondering if this Mr. Wright might have something in mind.

"Tell you what...we might have an opening or two down at Wright, Johnson, and Willoughby come the end of the month. Why don't you drop by the office, and give us your resume. I can't promise anything, but we'll get you on the interview list; from there, you're on your own. Isn't that wild; old Will Beecher's grandson shows up at the Rotary," Mr. Wright added with a chuckle.

Henry Wright was an older man, standing a modest four inches short of six feet tall, always dressed in a dark grey, vested suit with a handmade silk bowtie. He was a bit portly, but that only added to his conservative appearance. He was a lifelong bachelor, and on any given evening could be found dining at the Downtown Club, a gentleman's only facility that catered to many of Knoxville's leaders and businessmen. Henry was a no-nonsense man who was more comfortable talking business than sports. He had a somewhat stand-offish, almost grumpy demeanor at times, but inside was a man who greatly valued friendships. That was why he had been so anxious to offer one of his best friend's grandsons an opportunity to interview at his firm. He hoped the young man would do well, but he had to get past that first round of interviews before Henry would ever see him.

John went to his interview that morning with a new sense of purpose. He had researched the firm of Wright, Johnson, and Willoughby. His research had suggested the firm was primarily interested in annuities and long term income. Not wanting to make the same mistake twice, John had looked at everything he could find on retirement strategies from a variety of investment firms, and felt he had a strong understanding of what was needed. In short, for a second time, John felt ready.

Two weeks after the second interview, John was notified he was being given a six month contract to "see how things would go." As far as John was concerned, that was a great first step. His father had told him time and again, "get your foot in the door and take it; it's a job!" John was sure this was good advice.

On John's first day, he was invited into Henry Wright's office. The Henry Wright he found sitting behind the large desk today was quite different from the affable man he had met at the Rotary Club, and the one who had silently sat in at the second interview. The man today was of an entirely different stripe.

"Good, good, John; come right in," Henry said as motioned John to a chair. "Congratulations on the job. First days are important, so I wanted to get a few points across to you right away. That way everything is above board, and we can get off with a clear set of expectations."

John was anxious to hear Mr. Wright's thoughts on his role in the company. Investments were a new field for John; he wanted to hit the ground running.

"First thing to understand is this; we pay a very high salary for a reason. Wright, Johnson, and Willoughby now own you...24/7 we own your time. If we need you on a weekend, you are here. If we need you to work nights, you are here. If we need a financial plan by Friday, you hand it in on Thursday. Are you getting the drift of what I'm saying here?"

"Crystal clear, sir, crystal clear," John answered and thought to himself, "That damn well better be my answer if I don't want to be on the outside looking in from the lobby."

"Good. Now another thing - we are a results oriented firm. We don't care about your hard work, what kinds of steps you took, or any of that kind of business. Did you get financial returns for our clients; that's what we are interested in. We want to know what new business and clients you've added, and how much additional investment has been bought to the firm. What value have you added to our bottom line? If you have to stay up all night getting the results from the Nikkei over in Japan, we don't care. Do it! Results and financial returns will be reviewed monthly, not quarterly, and they damn well need to be up to snuff. You do that, and you'll succeed and prosper here. In the process you'll be well rewarded financially. You don't - well, you know that answer."

John took a breath. Wow. "This," he said to himself, "is going to be a high stress job, but what a fantastic opportunity! The sky is the limit here."

John threw himself into his work with abandon. He *had to* succeed. He saw now why Wright, Johnson, and Willoughby had an opening at the very moment he and Mr. Wright had their initial conversation; they were constantly looking for high energy talent, but they went through people at a staggering rate to find that talent. They ground up new associates on a regular basis; if you couldn't keep pace, you became a "former employee" rather quickly. John was determined that would not be him. His initial work schedule was brutal, often piling up to 60 or 70 hours a week. He was eating and sleeping his position, and he loved it.

As John was making breakfast one Saturday morning, his mother came into the kitchen and said, "It's Saturday, John. Don't you ever get a day off over at that place?"

Not lifting his head from a financial report, John laughed and reminded his mother, "I vividly remember what Dad once said when I told him I was taking a day off. He said, 'days off don't pay the bills,'" as he mimicked in his father's stern voice. "So, Mom, no, I don't get any days off." He then mimicked father's companion quote, "People who are always looking for time off are the first ones fired, and rightfully so! They bring nothing to the table." John smiled to himself, realizing he could now recite nearly all of his father's advice on work ethic. With that, he got up, kissed his mother on the forehead, and went out the door.

John's work ethic and dedication were paying off. He was becoming a rising star in the firm. Mr. Wright had even once said, "We're glad to have you on our team, young John. It's been an impressive start; but don't slack off," then laughed as he briskly made his way through the outer office toward the partners' meeting.

Although seemingly a passing remark, Mr. Wright's comment was no small thing. Mr. Wright rarely handed out compliments to employees, especially those on the bottom rungs of the firm's ladder. More than that, this acknowledgement came with a bonus when he was called into Mr. Wright's office.

"Just going over your reports here, John...nicely done. But you know; most of the new business I see you bringing in includes accounts of a half-million or less. Now that's good, so don't get me wrong. Those smaller accounts add up, and we value them. But Tom Willoughby thinks that with the right kind of exposure, you are the kind of young man who could bring in much bigger accounts. So, we all talked it over, here's what we're going to propose - let's see what you think. We are going to get you a membership over at the Cherokee Country Club where you will come in contact with more high power people. Do you play golf? If you don't, you should learn; some really good business gets done out there on those links. Get involved with organizations, too. You cannot undervalue that networking. Now don't worry about the money, we will pay for the membership, and your monthly payments can be put on your expense account, with receipts of course. How's that sound to you? Oh, and one more thing. If you begin bringing in the kind of business of which Tom thinks you're capable, we might even spring for a car allowance - get you out of that clunker you park in our lot every day," Mr. Wright added as a rare joke.

The expectation bar had just been raised. Yes, it came in the form of some very nice perks, but they were not without their price. The hidden message was he now had to go after bigger accounts. John was happy, but this seeming good fortune had just added another layer to the high expectations of his firm. Little did he know, however, this benefit package was to also change his life in another very major way.

*****

It was just one more black tie charity event to attend for the Knoxville Opera at the country club.

Linda Ethridge was what one might call a "local blue blood." She was a tall, slender woman with mid-length, brunette hair framing the high cheek bones of her face. She was wearing a long black dress with a low-cut back, along with a diamond pendant necklace and matching bracelet. She carried herself with grace and a slight air of sophistication just as her mother had taught her.

The Ethridge family had made a very good living in the tobacco industry. Her grandfather started a small tobacco farm up near Greeneville, Tennessee, and over the years built that enterprise into one of the largest suppliers of tobacco to Phillip Morris. Her father, Jed Ethridge, had continued in the family business, and expanded it through ten counties. The Ethridge family was considered very well off.

The round tables had been prearranged with seating cards, and Linda was seated with her escort directly adjacent to John Beecher. Perhaps it was just good fortune that had placed her in that particular chair; or perhaps it was the fifty dollar bill she had slipped the club manager to switch the nametags. Whatever the case, Linda had been waiting for this opportunity ever since her father mentioned that John was expected to attend. Her family had used Wright, Johnson, and Willoughby to handle their investments for years. Henry Wright had been talking about this young, human dynamo they had hired, and how he had such a brilliant future. Linda had seen John several times on her visits to their offices, but John had never paid her much attention. Tonight would be different.

Linda smiled in John's direction as soon as his gaze came her way. "So, John, you enjoy opera, or is this just another tedious business meeting for Old Henry," Linda asked.

John wondered, "Who is this woman, and how does she know me? Have we met? I doubt that; I can be a little spaced out, but this woman I would remember."

"I'm sorry. Have we met before?" John asked.

Linda just tapped her spoon on his place card. She laughed, and then further explained, "My family is a client of Mr. Wright's. I should learn not to play jokes on people."

"Oh, right…of course; the name card. Duh." Taking his cue, he looked at the name card in front of this mystery woman and said, "Ahhh, Linda; Linda Ethridge. I wish I could say I knew the name, but 'ole Henry,' as you call him, rarely confides much inside information to us underlings," John laughed.

"Oh, I think you are selling yourself a little short there, John, don't you? I don't think the term 'underling' applies to you; not from what my father tells me."

"Really? Well, I shall have to hear what *your father* is telling you, then. Tonight might be very eye opening," John laughed.

"Oh, you have no idea how 'eye opening' it will be," Linda slyly added.

As the night proceeded, John and Linda spent the majority of the evening in one another's company, much to the chagrin of her escort. John had even ventured onto the dance floor for more than his share of the usual dances. It took a little coaxing from Linda, or perhaps the three Basil Hayden bourbons had had their impact, but soon John was out there just where Linda wanted him, in her arms.

In the months that followed, John and Linda spent as much time together as their schedules allowed. In John's case, that was not always as much as he would have liked. Fortunately, Linda was also occupied with her various organizations, and role as chair of two major Knoxville festivals to be held the following spring. The time they were together, however, was more than simply casual. Linda found John to be everything for which she had hoped and more. He was caring, romantic, and attentive. Often, flowers would show up at her house with a card that simply read, "Thinking of you today." Little presents such as books in which she had expressed an interest, or a jacket she had admired in a store window would unexpectedly arrive by courier. The moments they were able to find together were filled with laughter, happy conversations, and countless caring embraces. John, it seemed, had captured her heart, and their engagement was welcomed by both families.

For Stan, John's growing love for Linda had been just the thing for which he had been hoping. He had been urging John for over a year to slow down a little, find a good woman, marry, and settle down. John laughed to himself about the irony of events because this was the same father who had forever preached "hard work and nose to the grindstone as the secret to a prosperous life." Now he's interested in grandchildren, and having his son marry "a fine woman."

John had now found someone of substance, a woman who understood the corporate world, someone who could be his true partner in life. Instead of begrudging his time at the office, Linda lauded him for his initiative and rewarded him with her devotion. For all of his life, John had felt he had lived in Jenny's and Stan Junior's shadows vying for affection in his family. Of course his father and mother loved him, he knew that. But it seemed it was always Jenny who had received his father's attention and warmth. It was always Jenny who received understanding when she made a mistake. It was always Stan Junior whose every word or action inspired their love and approval. The love he received, at least as he perceived things, was more a "tough love."

This time, with Linda, it was different. Having never genuinely felt such a singular love directed toward him, he became consumed with his newfound partner in life. Marriage and a European honeymoon were but steps away.

*****

The next test of Beecher family unity was to come in the most horrible way imaginable. Stan Senior had retired to bed early that evening as Marilyn had attended a church meeting, only to be awakened by a loud knocking at the door. At first he wasn't sure what he heard. The knocking then became pounding. As he threw on his bathrobe and slippers, he was thinking what the heck can this be? He was hoping it wasn't some urgent case needing his immediate attention down at police headquarters. In retrospect, he would have far preferred that to have been the case.

Stan Junior came down the stairs right behind his father as the door was opened. Standing before them was his friend and partner, Ted Newsome and a uniformed officer. A car with its bright lights idled in the driveway.

"Jesus, Ted. I'm going to have to go to Home Depot and buy a new door. What's up?" Stan quipped. Ted's somber expression did not change.

"Stan...let's go sit down a second. I have something really bad to tell you." They went into the living room; now Stan's heart began racing as Ted continued, "Its Marilyn. I'm afraid there's been a terrible accident and..." Ted paused not wanting to tell his best friend this news. His eyes filled with tears. "I'm afraid it was fatal. Marilyn couldn't be saved. Trust me, the EMT's were right there and did everything possible, it just wasn't enough."

John and Linda arrived less than ten minutes after the police, with Jenny and Jimmy not far behind. Ted had asked the officer to phone them to come over as soon as the police car arrived at the house.

Now, everyone joined Stan in the living room. Jenny was holding her Dad, crying bitterly while John had gone over to Stan Junior, and placed his arm around him. Stan Junior asked only one question.

"Does this mean mom's dead, John?"

John simply held his brother and nodded. Stan Junior wept too.

"Wait, Ted. Are you sure it was Marilyn? I mean there could be a mistake or something. I mean, this can't be…there's *got to be a mistake*," Stan almost shouted, tears rolling down his face.

"No, Stan. I'm afraid not. I've already seen her. It's definitely Marilyn."

"OK, I've got to go to her right now. You take me. I have to see her. Whoever is going, get your things, we're going right now."

"Sure, Dad; sure…I'm ready right now," John hurriedly answered. "Linda, could you and Jimmy stay behind just in case anyone calls or comes over?"

"Just let me throw something on and get my shoes," Stan said as he virtually walked in circles. "Oh my God, oh my God; this can't be. This isn't happening. Ted, I just saw her two hours ago. It can't be, please… there's a mistake somewhere."

The ride to the coroner's office was quiet. No one talked to one another, although Stan could occasionally be heard muttering to himself, "it can't be." As they arrived for the identification, the entire Beecher family went inside.

Ted said, "Stan…perhaps John could do this identification part, and you could wait until the folks from the funeral home have had a chance to fix her back up. I need to warn you, she's not in good shape right at the moment. It was a head-on and …well, you know those are bad."

Stan took a deep breath. There was no way he wasn't going to see his Marilyn, and exactly what had happened to her. There was no way he wasn't going to be absolutely certain it was her, and some idiot hadn't screwed up the identification.

"No, Ted. Thanks, I know what you're saying, but I have to see for myself. It's my Marilyn. Just, let's go."

As they wheeled the table out, John and Stan stood waiting. Jenny had Stan Junior in the outer room. They didn't want Stan Junior to see his mother like this. Once you see such a thing, you can never un-see it. No, it would be better if he just remembered her as she was.

The attendant pulled back the sheet from Marilyn, and John literally gasped. The violence of the accident had changed the beautiful mother he knew into something he could no longer recognize.

Stan's tears had stopped at this point. He was in shock, and the only thing keeping him going was adrenalin. He looked over at Ted, and had but one comment: "Please tell me, Ted; she didn't suffer. She wasn't lying somewhere in pain with no one to help. Tell me that didn't happen."

"No," said Ted. "The EMT's said she had died pretty much on impact. There were no signs of any struggle."

Stan nodded as he and John went out to get Jenny and Stan Junior. Ted Newsome drove the family home. By the time they arrived, it was almost three in the morning.

Ted asked, "Would you like me to stay with you guys a while, Stan? Maybe I could make a few calls for you, take care of people who might phone you?"

"No thanks, Ted. Kind of you to offer, but I think we have plenty of people to handle things. I'll arrange for Click to come down and get her. Larry will know what to do. He's a good man...good man," Stan softly repeated, almost in a trance. "I guess I'll have to work with him later in getting her funeral arranged. John will help me."

"Absolutely...We'll all do that together, Dad. You won't have to do that by yourself," John offered.

News like this travels fast. By nine the next morning the house was full of people. Family members, co-workers, neighbors, it seemed everyone was coming and going. For Stan it was a big blur.

Linda was a champion through all of this. She had arranged a variety of food plates, extra chairs, folding tables, additional china, and several caterers to help keep dishes replenished and do cleanup. John had already phoned Larry Click to have his mother's body removed from downtown to the funeral home. Jimmy and Jenny were welcoming people, thanking them for coming, and generally hosting everyone who passed through the door. At this point, none of the family had had any time to personally grieve. Everyone was just doing what they had to in order to survive to the next event. It was hell.

Once the funeral and initial weeks had passed, everyone returned to the chore of living their lives. Jenny went back to the hospital, John went back to his investment duties, and Stan returned to the police department with a vengeance. Probably as a defense mechanism to keep from being in a house without Marilyn, Stan was keeping longer and longer hours at work. Stan Junior, on the other hand, was spending longer and longer hours at home by himself. Jenny didn't like it.

After several meetings, John and Linda agreed it would be better for everyone if Stan Junior came to live with them. Stan Senior agreed perhaps that was a better arrangement. Stan Junior liked the idea as well. Jenny volunteered, but their little rental unit had so little space an added person would have been difficult. Once Stan Junior had moved in with John and Linda, things began to settle down, and return to a more normal routine in the Beecher family.

In his grief and loneliness, Stan bought a one year old golden retriever from the rescue center. Her name was Sandy. She ran around the house carrying an ugly voodoo doll in her mouth at all times. Her "toy" was never far away, and it was one of the few things that seemed to make Stan smile these days.

Over the weeks and months following Marilyn's death, Stan was not himself. He was not the man the Beecher children had known. Only rarely did that dry sense of humor emerge, and he was bitter over the loss of his wife. He was especially angry with God. A man who had gone to church all his life, met his wife there, and been a stalwart of the Sunday service had suddenly stopped attending. The priest from Saint James had reached out to Stan a number of times to offer comfort and support, but Stan never took advantage. He was polite in his refusals, but steadfast.

The scar of Marilyn's death was deep, and would never heal. Gradually, however, Stan did reinvent his life, and begin to re-emerge as the father the Beecher children had known. Unfortunately, down the road lay another test; this time, the family was not to be so united.

3

The Beginning

Who knows when such things really begin? The fact is all of us forget things, and think nothing of it. Often we even make jokes about it. Stan certainly did.

"Can you believe it, Ted," he said to his partner Ted Newsome. "I was damn near late for work this morning because I lost my car keys again!" Stan offered with a chuckle. "I looked for a half hour for those suckers. Where do you think I found them?" he continued.

"No idea Stan, but I do know you are about the most 'key-losin' guy on the force," he laughed. In truth, Ted knew he shouldn't be talking because that very same morning he had misplaced his wallet.

"You're going to die when you hear where I put them," Stan laughed on. "I put them *inside* the cabinet where I keep all the glasses! I mean, I have no clue as to why I would do that. You know, this case has been on my mind so much, sometimes I just lose track, then later say, 'hey, what the heck have I been doing this last half hour?'"

Ted looked over at his friend, smiling, "Really? Geez, Stan, that's bizarre. How the hell did you even think to look there?"

"Yeah, well...had I not wanted orange juice, you would have had your sorry butt coming over to pick me up, that's for sure," Stan concluded.

Currently, he and Ted were working on a very serious case of homicide that had taken place at the Riverwood Apartments, a complex just off the Henley Street Bridge going out toward the airport. As the two rolled up in their unmarked car, they were met by the large steel and glass building rising up among ill kept grounds and graffiti. As Stan and Ted made their way toward the door, a crowd of people milled outside the doors hoping to catch a glimpse of what was taking place inside.

When Ted and Stan entered the scene, the apartment was mobbed with police and the KPD forensics unit. They found a completely trashed living room; lights knocked onto the floor, broken mirrors, an overturned table, and blood stains everywhere. Whoever this victim was, he or she put up one hell of a fight.

"Victim's in here," said one of the county coroner's men on his way by.

The bedroom was not in much better shape. Next to the window, near the nightstand, was the slumped body of a middle aged male in his trousers and a blood soaked undershirt.

Ted said, "I want a total inventory of everything visible in this room. Make sure we get plenty of photos; I mean everything in this room, and not just the body. Check the drawers, see if they've been rifled, and let's get an ID on this guy."

"Already in process, sir," said one of the too many uniformed police officers in the room.

"And I want this place depopulated right now except for the forensics guys, Stan, and me. NOW! We could sell out Neyland Stadium with everyone standing around in here. How do we sort this out with this kind of menagerie," barked Ted.

Stan was just standing next to Ted, staying quiet. Once Ted took charge of a scene, there could not be two people giving orders. Stan walked out to the living room, found the uniformed officer in command, Sergeant Krujkhold, and offered some additional direction.

"Sergeant, before you go out there and send these people home, be sure to find out if any of them saw anything, heard anything, knew anything about the guy who lived here, whatever. I want interviews from as many people as we can find who might help us," directed Stan in a quiet voice. He knew if he were to say this loud enough for everyone to hear, many of the people who might know something would start disappearing.

This case had something else unique. It was the first time Stan noticed his memory problems were affecting his work. The memory lapses had been happening more often. At first he thought, "Am I getting sick?" Then he wondered if he was under too much stress. He had even gone to the internet to find possible causes of "forgetfulness." Memory lapses had become too frequent and too inexplicable.

The body of Frank Calabrese was found on Friday evening, and Stan intended to work through the weekend to gather as much information as possible. He and Ted met Saturday morning for breakfast at Pete's, a local café on Union Avenue, so they could compare notes and discuss where this case was going.

"So, Stan...what do you think about our good Mr. Calabrese?" Ted began; "an interesting situation, no? He's like the invisible man. Nobody seems to know much about him. He kept to himself and no one has seen him. He is like a cipher. Shows up in town from somewhere in New York a few weeks ago, rents an apartment and just hibernates. He's Claude Rains." Claude Rains was the actor who played the *Invisible Man* in the original movie, and Ted loved to throw around trivia from old movies just to see if he could stump people.

"You do know who Claude Rains is, right Stan," Ted asked with a big smile on his face.

"Yeeeees, Ted. I know who Claude Rains is, but only because you've stumped me on that same question a thousand and six times before," answered Stan. Stan also had a habit of making up astronomical numbers to drive his point home. With Stan's response, the two of them laughed out loud.

Joyce, one of Pete's long time waitresses appeared. "Hate to break up the comedy club guys. Morning Ted…Stan. You fellows of the Big Blue Line having your usual today?"

Joyce and the other waitresses knew all the regulars, especially the police, and what they generally ate. It was without question *the* friendliest restaurant you'll ever be in; hence the waiting line to get a table almost every day. More than that, Pete made the best blueberry pancakes in town, *and* he had the best southern breakfast in Tennessee. Just ask him.

"Yep, Joyce, same ole same ole. Scrambled eggs and a special pancake with sausage for me…and of course, keep this coffee cup filled," Ted said.

"Now Sweetie…do I *ever* let your coffee cup get empty? Really, Ted. You must be confusing me with that ex-wife of yours," she laughed. "And eggs over with bacon, home fries, and a biscuit for you there Stan, right?"

Stan replied, "Yes indeed. Hey, Joyce…did you hear about the horse that came in here last week for lunch? And Pete said "Hey pal, this is Pete's, why the long face?" With that Stan just howled with laughter at his own joke. Ted and Joyce just looked at one another, then back at Stan. Neither cracked so much as a smile; they just shook their heads as they looked back at one another.

Joyce said, "Stan, you have told I don't know how many bad jokes in here…but that one? That one? That one goes into the Hall of Fame of sad jokes! Where *do* you get them?" she said.

However, there was a more serious concern in Stan's mind this morning. He had forgotten his notebook at home, now was completely helpless to talk about the case they were there to discuss. He thought he would just let Ted do the talking, and hope Ted wouldn't notice his unpreparedness.

"This guy, he's down here in Knoxville for what reason, Ted? Hiding out? Dealing? Escaping his ex-wife?" Stan said, trying to cover up the fact that he had just offered absolutely nothing to the analysis.

Ted chuckled. "Yeah…well, I would certainly know all about that ex-wife revenge thing; I've got the alimony papers to prove it. Kidding aside, we have to find out more about what this guy was doing here, and just who he might have been associating with. What did that friend of yours turn up in the interviews? What was his name, the officer you told to survey the area?"

Stan swallowed. He now had to confess he didn't have his notes. He knew Ted wouldn't be happy, but there was no use trying to fake it. Ted would see through any cover up in a second.

"You know what Ted…I need my notes, and the fact is I ran off in such a hurry this morning I left that notebook in my other jacket." Stan knew even that wasn't true. Actually, he didn't know where he had left that notebook. He just knew he didn't have it with him.

Ted looked at him with surprise. "What, Stan? First you put your keys in a juice glass, now you forget your notebook at the house? Really?" he added with a little tone of frustration. "Well, do you remember his name at least? Maybe he's over at the station, and we can see if he left a report on your desk."

"Nooooo. But he had an odd name; I do recall that….."

"Wait a second. Odd name," Ted pondered. "I know. Wasn't it Krujkhold? Sure, we know him. He's been with force twenty years. You know him better than I do. You used to work with him when you were in the Special Crimes Unit. Come on, Stan. Snap out of it," Ted laughed.

Inside Ted wasn't laughing; he was worried about his friend. This was unlike him. Stan had always been one of the most detailed, dependable men in the division. Almost nothing escaped his notice. Something was wrong.

*****

Stan was awakened in the usual way... a cold nose and slurp across his face with a long wet tongue.

"Yes, yes, girl. I know. You want to go out for a walk."

With that sign of life from Stan, Sandy jumped on the bed, off the bed, ran to the door, ran back, and barked at Stan, then ran out of the room only to return a moment later dragging her leash.

"OK, OK, I'm up, calm down, calm down." But "calm down" had never been part of Sandy's vocabulary, especially when it was morning walk time! She just continued to stand up on her hind legs and hop alongside Stan on his way to the bathroom.

"Do you mind if I get dressed first, Sandy? Gee, you're a Looney Lucy today."

Stan always enjoyed his morning walk with Sandy. This morning had a particular air to it. There was the sweet smell of magnolias coming into bloom along with the brilliant colors of white and pink dogwoods filling his senses. Spring mornings in Knoxville always made him feel good to be outside breathing the fresh air, walking, and saying hi to neighbors.

"Morning, Mrs. Standridge. Everything getting a good drink today?" Stan shouted over to her.

"Oh yes, Mr. Beecher. In this heat, you have to keep water on things. But I'm Mrs. Wilson," she laughed. "Mrs. Standridge lives on your side, next to you. Are you drinking again?" Mrs. Wilson joked as she continued dousing her plants.

Stan immediately tried to cover his blunder with a quick quip, "Of course, of course...I know that. I think I left my glasses inside."

Stan turned to go home. As he did so, he thought to himself, "I wonder if there really is something wrong with me?"

*****

John arrived at his father's house with the usual lack of notice. He pulled into the driveway, bounded up the front steps, and entered through the unlocked front door. Not seeing his father, he shouted out.

"You forgot to lock the front door again, Dad. You want the North Knoxville Mugger to come in here, and steal all your prized possessions; like that dopey looking Tennessee hat with Phil Fulmer's signature? I don't know what's going to wind up in a museum first, you or that dumb hat you insist on wearing. And by the way, if you think this fearsome watchdog you have is going to somehow ward off the mugger, you can forget that, unless of course there is some possibility a person could be licked to death."

Still, there was no answer.

"Dad?" John cried in a little louder voice. He began looking through the house, thinking, "Gee, I hope he's ok. Where the hell is he?" Once John looked through the inside of the house, he went through to the backyard. "Nope," he thought. "Not here either. This is ridiculous; let me try his cell phone."

The cell phone rang followed by the familiar voice of his father. Stan saw the caller ID, and said to himself, "Damn. I hope I wasn't supposed to be meeting him somewhere."

"County Lockup and Soup Kitchen, Jed Clampet speaking," answered Stan in his best Beverly Hillbilly voice.

"Dad. What the heck? You left without locking the front door, Sandy on the loose running all over, and the place is a mess."

John was relieved that he found his Dad, but the situation at the house was bizarre. For all his life, John had been admonished, "Clean your room. Put things where they belong. Don't leave me a mess to fix." Dad wasn't a neatness fanatic, but he wouldn't tolerate disorganization.

"Oh, that. Ted needed me down here at the station for a little emergency meeting, so I guess I ran out kind of half-cocked. I'll get it when I get home. Did you need something?" Stan's answer was anything but the truth. The only real truth was that Ted had picked him up, and they had gone back to the crime scene to see if there had been something they missed the first time through. As for the mess, that had been mounting for days.

"No. No. I don't need anything. I was just stopping by to see if you wanted to go with me to Tangers. I hoped to have lunch with you at the Applewood, and just poke around the outlets."

"Oh, yeah. I would have liked that, but I'm kind of stuck down here. Why don't you take Stan Junior, he likes to go out there."

"Yeah," said John, "already tried that; it was a no go. He had some bird lecture at the park he wanted to go to. Jenny took him over."

"OK, Dad. Well, glad you're OK. I'll straighten up out here, and go have lunch…Another time." John hung up.

"Wait, no. Don't bother cleaning up. I'll get to it as soon …" but John had already rung off. "Hell!"

Recently, Stan had become very fearful of others being around any of his affairs, or even in his house for that matter. He was worried they would find something they shouldn't, or see something out of place, or come across something important left undone. He didn't know what he feared most, he just knew he was increasingly uneasy about almost everything in his life.

In this case, Stan had good reason to be uneasy. What John soon discovered made him uneasy as well. As he began to clean up the dirty dishes and straighten out the kitchen, he spotted a pile of unopened envelopes. Next to it was his father's special bill basket that was full to overflowing. He looked through the envelopes, and was shocked by what he found. There were unopened bills from all of his creditors, receipts, and papers of all sorts. It was a mess. His father had always been a fanatic at paying bills on time, preferably the day they came in. Now this?

John picked up his cell phone to call Jenny.

"Hi, John...what's up," answered Jenny in her usual cheery voice. "Left Stan Junior off at the nature center, and he's in heaven. Probably won't hear from him till after lunch," she laughed.

"That's good, Jenny. Listen. I think we have a little situation over here at Dad's. You think you could squeeze in some time to run by before you have to get Stan Junior again?"

"Well, that doesn't sound good; yeah, probably. What's up?" she asked in a concerned voice.

"Well, I'd rather not try to explain over the phone. It's something you should probably see rather than hear about. How long before you could be here?"

"Holy cow, this must be serious if you want me there that fast. OK...fifteen, maybe twenty minutes? I need to stop for gas at Weigels first."

"Perfect. See you then. No need for alarm, just something I want to show you," John said, trying to lower Jenny's level of concern.

Jenny arrived as she had predicted, about twenty minutes later. Sandy ran to the door, and started jumping with her leash. Usually Jenny took her out, so Sandy was thrilled to see her.

"OK girl, OOOOOOO KKKKKKK...just let me get in the door, please. Noooooooooo, not now. Later. Later. I'll take you out in a bit. Jeez, you'd think that dog hasn't been out in a week," Jenny laughed.

"Yeah...that's another thing, maybe she hasn't. I found some pee over by the door, as well as a nice present in the mud room. I'm not sure Dad is taking her out enough."

Jenny didn't react to that news; she just wanted to hear what the more important issue might be.

"So, then, what is it you brought me over to see that's so important? Dad's check from the Publisher's Clearing House finally come in?" Jenny joked.

"No. This is serious, I think," John said. "Look at this unopened mail, all these unpaid bills. I mean there are second notices, late payment letters, all kinds of scary shit. I'm not sure what we should do? I mean, if we confront him on this, you just know what kind of nuclear explosion that will cause. But if we do nothing, I mean they could shut off his utilities or something. Should I just pay them and not say anything? Jesus, if he ever found out I snooped through his bills, then went ahead and paid them without telling him? Holy hell, I'd have to leave the country."

Jenny felt her stomach sink. "Shit."

"Yeah, shit; exactly," responded John.

"Well, maybe he's been preoccupied with that murder case, and just let things get behind," Jenny said.

"You really think that, Jenny?"

"No. Not really. John, I don't know what to do. I'm afraid."

"Me too…I know he can be a little forgetful at times, and he's done some crazy shit here and there…but this? This is more serious. I wonder if he would let me handle the bills for him. Maybe I could just say that with this case I'd like to help out. Does that have any chance of working?" John was desperate for an idea, and willing to consider anything.

"Really, John? Knowing Dad, I'm not sure he'd fall for it. But quite honestly, I don't have any better ideas. Could we do it in some non-judgmental way? Perhaps something where we're all having fun? I don't know; confronting him on this would clearly be the *wrong* way. We need something better than that. Hey! Wait a minute," Jenny said excitedly.

"Look, you're the finance guy in this family, right? There's nothing you don't know on that topic. So maybe you can approach this from the position that you are going to help *all of us* out, not just Dad. That way he won't feel so singled out. What do you think? Good idea?"

"Hmmm. Yeah, maybe," John said with some lingering doubt. "OK. Well, I still have concerns, but it's the best bad idea we've got right now," said John, pondering what he might actually say to make this strategy work.

"OK," said Jenny, then we're on the same page. "Look at the time. I have to run. Stan Junior will be boring those people at the center with two hundred thousand bird stories." Jenny had inherited that overestimating thing from her father. "We'll talk more about this, but whatever we're going to do, we need to do it soon."

With that, Jenny left the house and ran out to her car. John decided not to do any more cleaning. If his Dad noticed he had cleaned, he surely would guess he had gone through the bills. No sense tipping their hand at this point.

As John sat in his car, he worried: "What am I going to do? Just what am I really going to do?" He already had doubts about the plan he and Jenny had devised, and he didn't want to even verbalize what he feared was happening.

*****

The briefing was to take place at 8:00 am sharp, and Ted Newsome was to lead the review. To make certain Stan was up to speed, Ted had given him a detailed overview of the case aspects he wanted him to cover. Ordinarily Ted would not have prepped Stan this thoroughly; he would have simply chosen a few topics for Stan to handle. Stan's ability to provide detailed information, answer questions, and lead discussions had always been sharp, perhaps even better than Ted's. Ted, however, suspected something was very wrong. Stan was beginning to forget conversations they had, make mistakes in names, and often seemed unsure of important elements in the investigation.

Even with these lapses, Stan could frequently add insights or ideas that were valuable. He hadn't lost everything. For example, it was Stan who uncovered the fact that Mr. Capobianco had used a throw away phone to make several calls to a New York Italian restaurant at very odd hours. He was pretty certain Mr. Capobianco wasn't ordering pizza. In checking with the NYPD, he had been able to learn that the owners of this restaurant were suspected of laundering money as well as involvement in a number of other organized crime activities. When asked if they knew of Mr. Capobianco, they hadn't heard the name. Not satisfied, Stan had sent Mr. Capobianco's fingerprints and pictures to New York's organized crime unit. That was a breakthrough that moved things considerably forward. Mr. Capobianco was not the man's real name. His real name was Vincent Citerelli, and he was suspected of two homicides involving gang members in Manhattan. Stan had done what he was known for; used his years of experience to uncover a valuable clue.

Today, however, was to be Ted's show. He was going to disclose all the known acquaintances, potential aliases, and a few theories on the reasons why Mr. Citerelli was killed. Witnesses interviewed by Sergeant Krujkhold's officers had allowed them to piece together a fairly complete analysis of where and what Citerelli's movements had been in the days leading up to his murder.

Stan was supposed to go over the information from the results of those interviews, what was relevant, and what pieces were still missing, as well as evidence collected at the scene. It was to be a short segment, one handled by him dozens of times in the past. To prepare for this, Stan had written down almost everything he needed to say, and the way he wanted to say it. In fact, it was nearly a script. No longer could he rely on bullet points and his memory. That was too risky, and he certainly didn't want to appear unprepared in front of the entire department. To say the least, he was nervous. Ted was nervous as well.

The briefing room was full, and the officers shuffled about in their seats as they awaited Stan's overview. A few officers who had arrived late were standing in the rear of the room as Stan began his talk.

"It's pretty obvious," Stan opened, "this was not a robbery. Nothing of value was taken. Mr. Citerelli's wallet was still in the room, his money still in the billfold. Witnesses tell us, Mr. Citerelli had been in and out of his apartment several times during the day, and he had been carrying a black leather briefcase at all times. That briefcase has yet to be discovered. The building superintendent told us Mr. Citerelli had paid his rent through the end of this month; all transactions were in cash. No checkbook or credit cards were found on the body, or in the apartment. When potential witnesses were asked what they had heard, the two parties in adjacent apartments said they had heard a lot of yelling and loud noise coming from the apartment. When asked why they hadn't called the police, one of them said, 'If we call the police every time we hear an argument or loud noise from an apartment, you guys will have to open a substation down here.' No one heard any shots, which is not surprising since Mr. Citerelli died of seven stab wounds to the chest and torso. The murder weapon was a knife having an approximate five to six inch blade. That weapon has also not been recovered."

Stan was relieved by the way this was going. His notes were just what he needed, and he picked up confidence as he went along. Ted was also breathing a sigh of relief. But the smooth seas were not to continue.

"Uhhh, Stan," one officer yelled from the back. "Didn't you say a few days ago, that one of the witnesses said they saw our man traveling with another man in a yellow van? Did you follow up on that? Where is that part of the investigation?"

"Uhhhhhhhhh....yes. Yes. I think I did mention that officer... uhhh." Stan knew the man as well as knew his own family, but the suddenness of the question made his mind go completely blank. He had done a lot of research on that van, but now he couldn't remember what he had found. Sure, it was in his notes, he knew that; but they were on his desk somewhere. Stan just stood in awkward silence, blankly staring in the officer's direction. An uncomfortable silence followed.

The officer who had asked the question looked about at his fellow officers, then back at Stan when he offered,

"Towne, sir - remember me? We worked out of the same unit back when you were in uniform?"

Uneasiness filled the room at this awkward exchange, and Ted could see the look of bewilderment on Stan's face. He knew Stan was in trouble, and had no clue as to this man's name. He jumped in to save what he could of Stan's dignity.

"Yes, Gus. Thank you so much for that little reminder." Ted deliberately used the man's first name to help jog Stan's memory, and save any further embarrassment. "Stan and I are still running that lead down. We'll get back to you the moment we have something definitive. If there's nothing more, that concludes what we have for this morning. Everyone has their assignments in the packets we distributed. I think we are finally making some progress, so good hunting and stay safe."

With that, the room emptied, leaving just Stan and a worried Ted. Ted knew what he had to do.

"Stan, why don't we get a cup of coffee, and go sit in my office? It's more comfortable in there."

"Yes, Ted...good idea. Let me just freshen this cup, and I'll be right in."

As head of the Crimes Against Persons Unit, Ted was feeling as low as he had ever been about what was to come next. Stan and he had joined the police force when they were just kids. He remembered how Stan's father objected when Stan told him he was becoming a police officer with Ted. First the father reprimanded Stan about abandoning a solid career, and then turned his wrath on Ted. It was Ted he blamed for leading his son away from a promising place in the publishing business.

He and Stan went through the police academy together, walked the beat together, backed one another up on countless domestic quarrel calls; they stuck together through everything the street could throw at them. They were more than just colleagues, they were lifelong friends. "But now look where we are," thought Ted. He was sick to his stomach.

Stan finally came back in, and sat across from Ted. No coffee cup. Ted noticed immediately; probably forgot it by the coffee maker. It didn't matter. That was a non-issue compared to what was coming next. Ted began.

"Stan, I need to ask you…are you feeling OK? I know you and I've had a lot on our plate with this investigation, and to be honest, you've done a fine job on some of it. But…well frankly…well, you just seem way off your game of late. You are forgetting key elements of the investigation, misplacing reports and papers. I mean you totally lost all of Krujkhold's inquiry reports for two days until you found them in the junk drawer of your filing cabinet. You came to work without your wallet and badge one day, and worse, didn't have your service revolver on another. Now today - did you actually follow up on that car report?"

Actually, Stan had, but just couldn't remember the details. He was sure he would have remembered at some point, but in fact might never have gotten back to it.

"I know, Ted. I'm sorry. I think I'm letting you down, and you know I would never do that. I'll take better notes, keep more on top of things, I promise. Just a little setback is all."

Stan knew he was on thin ice; he was doing anything he could to keep that other shoe from dropping. It was not to be.

"No, Stan. I'm sorry to say it, but this is not just a 'little setback.'" Ted said. "No, there is something much more serious happening here. I don't know what it is, but I think you should get checked by the staff doctors. In the meantime, I'm going to have to ask that you take a leave of absence. Let's try to get things right for you. You know we are best friends…I will go to the wall for you any time, any place. But right now, for you, this is the best."

Stan sat in stunned silence. A leave of absence! Off the case. Off the force! And for how long? He felt the pain in his very core. He could feel the tears welling up in his eyes. He couldn't let Ted see that he was on the verge of tears. He couldn't. But as he looked across the desk, totally silent, he could see how Ted's eyes were a bit misty as well.

"OK, Ted," Stan said in a barely audible voice. "I'll go get checked out. But if I'm OK, promise you'll let me back in. Promise me."

"Absolutely, Stan. Absolutely. This joint wouldn't be the same without Stan Beecher. Besides, where would we go for the worst jokes known to mankind," he said with the best smile he could muster.

Stan, in a hurry to leave before losing his composure, said in a dejected voice,

"Yeah...give me time to get some new material." He added, "OK...I'll just go home then, and make arrangements for the checkup from the med people as soon as I can," continuing to mutter, almost in a daydream.

As he started to leave, Ted stopped him. "Stan. I'm afraid I have to ask that you leave your badge and service revolver with me. Just for the time being, understand."

Stan took out his badge and gun, placing them on Ted's desk. "Right; proper procedure," he added as he slowly walked out of Ted's office, and proceeded toward the door.

Stan was leaving the building he loved as a beaten man. He didn't know what step would be next. "How have things gone downhill so fast?"

*****

Depression, when it comes, is perhaps one of the most debilitating diseases in a human being's life. Stan was finding that out again. He was starting to become genuinely angry about his situation. He was angry with the forgetfulness, he was angry with the suspension, he was angry with the entire world. About the only thing he wasn't angry with was what seemed like his only true companion, the only one who didn't care about what job he had lost, or what he forgot, or how messy the house had become. Sandy wanted to be near Stan. She could sense something was wrong. She could see how sad Stan was, and tried to make things better. As Stan came to sit in his favorite easy chair, Sandy came over, licked his hand, and sat with her head in his lap. She was looking up at him, the whites of her eyes showing at the bottom. Stan thought, now there is the cutest face he'd ever seen. He needed a friend who cared right at that moment. He needed her, badly.

"That's right girl. You still love me the same now as you did when I left this morning, right? You don't care anything about what happened today. Know what that calls for? That's right! Some treats! Then a good dinner, and a nice long walk!"

That got Sandy's attention. She jumped up and ran into the kitchen near the pantry where the treats were kept. Stan laughed to himself and thought, "If there's one word in the English language dogs understand, it's the word, 'treats.'"

Stan made her a good dinner, opened up a can of Chef Boyardee Stuffed Ravioli that he ate straight out of the can for his dinner, and sat at the kitchen table wondering what he was going to do with himself tomorrow. How was he going to tell his children? Stan was sinking into the depth of a depression unlike any he had known since his wife died. Even he knew he needed some help to get his life back.

Just as he was thinking about this, the phone rang. He looked at the caller ID, it was Jenny. "Oh no," he thought. "I really can't go through this right now. I really can't." He debated with himself so long the phone went to voicemail. He looked as his voicemail message light came on, and wondered if he even had the strength to listen. What he really wanted to do was just go to bed, pull the covers over his head, and somehow make it all go away. Of course, it wasn't going away.

*****

When Jenny arrived at Saint John's Cathedral, it was dimly lit. The street was still damp from an afternoon thundershower, and the unique smell of city streets after a rain was in the air. There was a disquieting silence to the night. Even the ordinarily raucous cicada who had taken up convenient residence in the many oaks lining the boulevard had been quieted by the summer storm. Darkness filled her mind. It was a week night, no masses or other functions were scheduled. The only thing on Father Joseph's docket for the evening was to meet Jenny Beecher.

Father Joseph was Jenny's favorite priest. He was a tall man, a little over six feet, somewhere in his 50's. He was thinly built with blondish, graying hair, and his smile had a certain warmth that seemed to exude kindness. His sermons nearly always managed to resonate with Jenny, sounding as if they were directed at her. Now, in this terrible time, she needed someone to whom she could talk. She felt she needed God's help.

When the Father came out of his office to meet her, Jenny wanted to start things off with honesty about her spiritualism, or perhaps lack of spiritualism to be more accurate.

"Good evening, Father, thank you so much for taking time to see me, I didn't know where else to turn," she began.

"Now, what's troubling you? And, by the way, you can just call me Joe. Treat me as your friend."

"Thank you, Father…I mean Joe. But you know, I haven't been a very spiritual person during my life, I mean, I know I come to church and all, but that's about it. Sometimes I think it's more out of habit than anything else. I mean, I never get involved with *anything* here at the church; nothing. I just come and…I don't know, sit there."

Joseph stopped her again. "I understand…that would be you, and perhaps three or four hundred others who call Saint John's home. Yet, here you are. So perhaps you have deeper spiritual roots than you realize. You don't have to be on the vestry, or run the church socials to have strong ties to God. The fact is, you don't even have to come to church…God doesn't only exist here. So, you just go ahead with why you're here, and let's see if we can somehow help."

Already Jenny felt a little more at ease. The trouble was she just didn't know where to begin. She told Joseph about the growing concerns with her father, how she and her brother were at her Dad's house, what they had found, and the sense that something was terribly wrong. She went on to discuss their strategy to have her brother do the bills, how worried she was that her father would take it the wrong way, and how upset they expected he might become.

Father Joseph never interrupted, even though Jenny's explanation went on for quite some time. When it seemed she had run out of things to say, Joseph started with the simplest of questions.

"Do you believe your father is in trouble, perhaps having some issues with which you and your brother can help?"

"Yes. Of course. That's why I'm here," Jenny added immediately.

Then Father Joseph continued. "Yes, Jenny, I do know. But you see, that's the most important piece of why you are here, and I need *you* to see that. It is the love of your father, and the hope that you can help that brings you tonight to God. And I will assure you of something… God will answer. He will be there for you, and with you. You and your brother, John, will not be traveling this road by yourselves."

"So, Father, I mean Joe, you think we're doing the right thing here? You think we might have a good plan?" Jenny was feeling a little reassured, but somehow, Father Joseph wasn't really validating her course of action.

"If you are asking, do I think you are doing the right thing to try and help, then yes, absolutely; you are doing the right thing. If you are asking, will your idea work, then I have to tell you, I don't know. I just know that if your father is the loving family man I think he is, then at some point he is going to see your ideas are born out of love and not judgment. Whenever that time comes, and whatever pain or temporary disharmony has occurred, it will have been worth it to see your Dad in a better place. Have a little trust that God will see you through this… perhaps even a little prayer asking Him directly for His help would not be out of order. If you like, I will pray with you, or if you prefer to do that in private, that's fine as well."

"Oh, thank you Father. I do feel a little better. I think I'll pray by myself, but if you would pray for us as well, I would be so thankful."

Father Joseph looked at Jenny, and took her hand in his.

"I know that right now, it is very hard for you to see the way forward...to know if you're going in the right direction. But be sure, God knows the way forward. He will help lead you in the right direction if you will listen to His voice. He'll be right there in your heart. And even if it seems you're going in the wrong direction, move ahead in the knowledge that God has His own plan. I'm glad you came tonight. But I would like your promise on something."

Jenny was almost afraid to ask what that might be, but she was too far along to refuse. "Yes, certainly; what would you like?"

"You'll let me know how this goes, and most of all, if there is anything else we can do to help? I don't know how your father feels about these things, but if one of us coming out to the house at some point would help, you have only to ask."

"Yes, thank you Father. I will be sure to tell you. I'll let you know if there's anything else. I think I'll go home now. You've been a big help."

"I'm glad you feel a little better. Hope to see you Sunday."

With Father Joseph's words still echoing in her ears, Jenny left the church, and walked to her car parked on Main Street. It was late, it was dark, and clouds of doubt continued to hang in the air. She wasn't sure if she was actually walking out with answers, but then what she probably needed most was reassurance that she and John were doing the right thing. Perhaps she had that; perhaps.

*****

It was early, and Sandy had already administered her usual wakeup call. Stan slowly rolled over, looked at the clock, and felt a total sense of loss. It was his first day off the job, and his mind was totally absent of any ideas as to what to do. He had no place to go, no reason to get up, no reason to go on. A feeling of complete depression had set in. He went to the bathroom, and what he saw in the mirror was a shock. His hair looked like it had been styled by Mixmaster, he had at least a two day beard on his face, and he was still in his t-shirt and dress pants from the previous day. His entire appearance made him look like a homeless person.

He reached over, turned on the shower, and got undressed. As he threw the clothes into the overflowing laundry basket, he looked around at the piles of shoes, dirty shirts, wrinkled pants, and dirty socks just long enough to get a sense of how low he had gotten.

"Jesus, look at this place. I'd call a cleaning service if it wasn't too embarrassing to have anyone *see* this rat hole," he thought out loud. He just sighed, opened the shower door and stepped in. The hot water running over his body felt good. He stood there letting the soothing water cascade over him. He reached over, and grabbed the shampoo. He wondered just when it was that he last washed his hair. For the life of him, he couldn't really remember... "a while he thought, a while." Stan then proceeded to wash and scrub every inch of his body. It felt so good he wondered why he hadn't been taking better care of himself. He turned off the water, stepped out and looked for a towel.

"Oh just great!" he said with exasperation. "No freaking clean towel."

He went to the closet. There among the piles of clothes was a used yellow towel. He grabbed it and started drying off.

"Any port in a storm big boy, any port in storm," Stan muttered aloud.

After he shaved, combed his hair, and brushed his teeth, he went to the closet to get something clean to wear. There were thin pickings to be sure, but he finally found a pair of pants and clean shirt buried in the back of the closet. He put them on along with his last pair of clean socks; he was ready to go for the day. Just why he needed to be so ready, he wasn't sure, but it did feel good to be in clean clothes and look a little more human.

Stan went to the kitchen, on the refrigerator door was a note.

"Feed Sandy."

He had some time ago begun writing these little "housekeeping" notes to remind himself to do things. Often he would have to ask himself, "Did I have breakfast, did I walk Sandy, did she eat?" Fact was, too often he just didn't know. Now, reminder notes were all over the house. The pantry had notes on meal times; "breakfast, lunch, dinner." In addition to the "Walk Sandy" note, there were others that seemed almost humorous. On his easy chair was one that read, "Take off coat." It wasn't hard to see, Stan's memory had been slowly worsening.

As Stan stood at the pantry looking for Sandy's dog food, the phone rang. He looked at the caller ID, "Jenny."

"Dammit, dammit, dammit!" he said to himself. He had forgotten to call her back. In fact, had he even listened to the message? "Oh well, let's see what's going on," he thought, and picked up.

"Hi, Sweetheart, what's cooking?"

"Jeez, Dad...I was worried about you. Are you OK?"

"Oh yeah...I'm ok," Stan lied as he placed the cereal box on the table, and pulled out a chair in which to sit. "Sorry I didn't call back. I just kind of collapsed into bed and fell asleep. Hope it wasn't important," Stan said, trying to sound as upbeat as possible.

"Oh, OK. Well, that's fine; you must have needed the rest." Jenny then took a big breath and said to herself, "Oh well, here we go."

"Are you working today Dad? What time do you have to go in, because John and I were thinking of stopping by to visit."

Stan rose from the chair and stood for a second, not quite knowing how he should respond, then said, "No, no. I'll be home today. What time did you want to come over? I was going to do some laundry and housecleaning; I should be here all day."

"Oh good, Daddy. Well, how about lunch time? We'll bring subs and have a nice time."

Hmmmmm, thought, Stan. "Daddy?" "Bring subs?" These two were up to something. "I didn't spend 40+ years on the job not to smell a rat," Stan thought.

"Gee, subs would be great. Don't make mine Italian, though. I have enough Italian in my life to last a while with that Citerelli case. Get me a roast beef; extra meat and provolone cheese. Wait, provolone;

- 74 -

that's Italian too…change it to Swiss. I'll see you guys at lunch. Gotta run, Sandy's hopping on one leg at the door, and we all know what that means," Stan laughed as he tried to ring off before any further questions could be asked.

"Uh oh," thought Jenny. "This is going too smoothly. He was entirely too happy, and too compliant on that call. He suspects something. I know it. This is going to be a disaster. I'm already nervous." Then she thought, "I better call John, and give him a heads up. I think today is going to be bad, bad, bad." She dialed his number, almost hoping she would just get his voice mail. No such luck.

"Hi Jenny. Did you talk to Dad? Are we on?"

"Uhhhhh, yeah. That's the problem."

John was confused. "What do you mean, that's the problem. Don't you want to go get this over with? We gotta do something." John was now worried she was getting cold feet.

"No. No. We're going for lunch and bringing subs. It's just that… well…he was waay to cheery. He had this strange tone in his voice, you know? Everything just went too smoothly. I think he knows something is up." Of course, Jenny was right, but then what was she to do?

"Oh, I don't think so. You're probably just reading things into it because you're nervous. Look, I'll pick you up at noon, we'll go get the subs, and do what we have to do. We'll be fine. I'll make sure to hide his gun before we start talking," John quipped trying to make things a little less frightening.

John and Jenny showed up at Gill Avenue right on schedule. Stan was waiting, looking out the front window. He crumpled up his reminder note, and stuffed it in his pocket. Jenny's nerves were so tight she thought she'd have a nervous breakdown if this wasn't over soon. She hadn't had a peaceful night's sleep since this decision had been made.

Stan had done his best to clean up the kitchen, and make enough room on the table for them to eat. It was perhaps not great, but much better. The three of them sat down, and opened their sandwiches. John looked at Jenny, Jenny looked at John. Jenny had this, "you better start" look on her face.

John took a deep breath and began.

"So then Dad…Jenny, Stan Junior, and I were trying to put together a little family plan on how we might all work together. You know, each of us kind of tapping into our skills, and trying to make things easier for one another. For example, Jenny and Jimmy are going to let me work with them to put together a good budget, handle some finances, work with the bank on bill pay, things like that. I'm working on things for Stan Junior as well; like, you know, establishing a bank account… things like that. Anyway, we're trying to take seriously that thing you have always told us about living below your means. Jenny, on the other hand, is going to help me and Stan Junior get all our projects and household items together. You know, organize paper work, develop filling systems, and, you know, organize stuff, things like that - you know, stuff she does on a regular basis at the hospital."

John was saying to himself, "Jesus, just listen to yourself here… you're babbling like an idiot. You ever do this at work, and you'll be out on your ass in a week."

John took another breath and continued, "Jenny and I thought maybe it would be good to include you on this, maybe help get some of this everyday stuff off your back as well. What do you think?"

The plan was met with stone silence from Stan. Jenny looked at John, and he back at her. "Oh please," she thought, Father Joseph, you better have been right, and God better be sitting right here with us. If ever we needed divine intervention, it is now!"

After what seemed an eternity, Stan finally spoke. "Yeah, really, John? That's probably not a bad idea. Do you guys feel OK about taking all that stuff on? It seems like a hell of a lot of work. But, I do like the idea of our family working together. I think that's great."

What Stan was really thinking was, "You two little bastards. You hatch this plan to take over my life, then cloak it in some kind of, this is just a family unity deal? You couldn't walk that con past a blind man's dog without being found out. You guys must think I'm the dumbest jackass on planet earth to fall for that one."

Stan also knew he was in real trouble. He knew he could no longer manage everything in his life, or even his house. Hell, he even had trouble keeping up with Sandy's needs. So as bitter as it was to admit, this was actually a way out that let him preserve some dignity.

Jenny looked at John, and said to herself, "No way! No damn way, could this be that easy. No sir, in two seconds the roof is blowing off of this house, and we are both getting thrown out."

John was stunned into silence. He wasn't sure where to go next. In his mind, he had planned for every eventuality; what he might say, or how he might advance a more convincing argument. But this? A cave in? No, chance. *This*, he hadn't planned for. Just the same, John forged ahead.

"Oh great... Great! Well. Uhhhh...how about I come over some time, and I just sit down with you, and we organize a little game plan. The two of us can gather up some of the paperwork, and really put things together. You want to help on the organizing part, Jenny?"

"Me?" Jenny said, almost caught by surprise. "Oh...yeah...sure. Absolutely, I'll come and we'll get started."

"Oh wait. Dad, are you working late or anything this week? I mean, is this week OK?"

In her excitement, she hadn't even thought about what would be a good day.

Stan thought a second, and decided that this was as good a time as any to get his situation out in the open. He was going to have to tell them sometime.

"Yes, kids. Well, that's something else I have to tell you." His emotions began to well up. He had this awful feeling that he had let everyone down; he had totally screwed up everything in his life. He had somehow wound up as something he had always held as one of his worst fears...*a failure.* He was so dejected by these thoughts, he wasn't actually sure he could get this out without his voice breaking. Better be quick, he thought. Suck it up, boy. Be strong and just say it!

"Fact is;" he paused to collect himself. "Ted asked me take a little leave of absence from the force. I guess this case was just a bit more than I thought, and…well, to be honest, I haven't really been myself lately. I know; I'm not telling you any news, am I? I mean, you can see I've been struggling…sooooo," Stan paused to take a breath, and think was there anything else he could possibly say at this point. There wasn't. "Yep, there you have it. For right now, I'm kind of out of work. So, tomorrow's fine. In fact, any day is fine." He finished, but he knew this was not the end of it.

Stan looked around the table. Both his children, the ones he loved so much at this moment that his heart physically ached, sat in stunned silence. To break the uncomfortable air, Stan continued.

"You guys will come over when you want, and we will all just get started trying to pull things together. That's good, that's good," Stan said softly.

Jenny could not hold her emotions in check another moment. She knew what being put on leave must have done to her father. Now she understood why he just caved in to their suggestions without even a whimper. She was sitting across from an utterly shattered man, her father. As those thoughts crossed her mind, and she tried to keep herself from crying, she rose from her chair, and went over to hug her father.

"It's OK, Daddy. It's OK. We're all going to help. We're all going to be here for you every day. You'll come back. You wait and see. We're Beechers…no one gets us down!"

But Stan pretty much knew. There was no come back. It was unlikely he'd return to police work from here. His next step was medical, and the sooner he faced that fact, the sooner he would get some necessary help. No one was saying it, but everyone was thinking it. There wasn't much room for doubt. Just the formal diagnosis was missing.

Stan Beecher was almost sure he had Alzheimer's.

4

Discoveries

N o one should have to reinvent their existence on this earth twice! When your life literally comes to a halt, and you must immediately decide what and how your entire way of living must change from this day forward, it is a painful, arduous task. That was exactly what confronted Stanton Beecher at this point; and it wasn't the first time.

Fate had already visited on him the egregious task of reassembling his life after the loss of his life's partner. Marilyn was not simply his wife; she was his best friend, his other half, his world. Answering the door at 12:15 AM to see a uniformed police officer with his detective partner, Ted Newsome was an image he could never wipe away. Stan was devastated by Marilyn's death in that car accident; he thought he would never be the same. He was correct; he never was the same. In a single moment, on a snow covered back road, a small pickup truck lost control, veered across the white line, and struck Marilyn's Chevy Cavalier head on; she never had a chance. In that tragic moment, Stan's first journey of reinvention began. He had no idea how he would survive. He had that same feeling now.

Of course, Stan did survive; he knew he had to somehow hold his life together. The tears, the anger, the rage, the uncontrollable grief, the depression, all of it slowly subsided, and a new life emerged. Stan always believed were it not for his three children, he might never have come this far. Even in the darkest hours of those days, Stan knew he had to somehow find a way forward, to hold this family together. The slow agonizing task of rearranging daily routines, comforting three grieving children, maintaining a focus at work, and confronting all those decisions without Marilyn's voice was overwhelming. He was convinced a loving God would not have done this to him and his children.

Stan wanted to be angry with Curtis Young, too. Curtis was the other driver, a young man of only 23, just returning from visiting his girlfriend, and thinking of marriage. Stan wanted to blame him for *everything*. He was denied even that. Curtis had not been drinking, he was not speeding, and he was not distracted. He simply had come into a curve with layer of black ice, his truck sliding into the oncoming lane, and Marilyn sadly coming from the other direction. Ultimately, Stan even felt sorry for young Curtis. From that day forward, Curtis Young's seeming idyllic life had changed as well. At the funeral, there wasn't anyone more sorrowful than Curtis. As he tried to apologize yet again to John, Jenny, and Stan Junior, he broke down and wept like a child; they all wept together.

Sleeping with that empty space next to him, waking up alone, coming home to an empty house; these were all agonies that haunted Stan for a very long time. Yet, he pushed on. Slowly, he adjusted to doing his own cooking, to Marilyn's empty chair at family dinners, and to handling the day to day decisions thrust upon him as a man living virtually alone; there was no one else. Household chores previously taken for granted were a challenge. It seemed he had to somehow fill that empty space in his life called Marilyn. This reinvention was not pleasant, and it was not easy, but it was necessary.

Now, Stan was faced with the task a second time. This time, however, was different. This time he felt totally alone; on an island only he inhabited. This time, the road ahead was bleak. People around him, especially his children, all pledged they would "be there" for him. In their way, they were. Nonetheless; the unfortunate fact of life is, you don't need to be by yourself to feel alone. You can be surrounded by people, and have never felt so alone in your life. When you come to realize no one can really empathize with your circumstance, and no one has the ability to change *anything* regarding the demons with which you're struggling, it is then you feel most alone. It is a battle being waged against yourself, and one where no clear victor is ever likely to emerge. Stan no longer had his work to occupy his thinking or time, and his mind was getting weaker, not stronger. Worst of all, he saw no avenue to regain his self respect. No; this time things were totally different.

*****

As Stan pulled himself from under the covers, out onto the floor, he began talking to himself. "Nowhere to go, nothing to do – Sandy, if it weren't for you I could just stay in bed forever." But habit forced him up and out.

Once Stan finished his morning personal maintenance, something he had promised Jenny he would try to do, he padded his way out to the kitchen in his dress suit and slippers. Stan had decided one way to keep things from changing too much was to dress as if he were going to work. Maybe he would even drive by the office, see which cars were there. He rejected that idea almost immediately; no sense aggravating a still open wound.

He opened the pantry to take out a box of cereal for his breakfast, and was faced with four boxes of Honey Nut Cheerios. He made out meticulous shopping lists each day so he could get only the things he needed. When he got to the supermarket, however, he would see things he *thought* he might need, and just add them to the cart.

As he closed the door to the pantry, he saw the note: "Feed Sandy."

"Oh my poor girl. You see me making breakfast, and you haven't had yours."

Sandy's mouth was watering, her tail wagging as she went over and stood by her bowl. "Dogs know exactly when you're talking about filling that dish," Stan thought. "Here," he said to himself, "was at least *one* blessing." Having Sandy in the house occupied a portion of his daily thoughts, plus she was someone to talk to. Her walks were now the highlight of his day. Sandy had become the primary beneficiary of Stan's "retirement status." There were more feedings, more walks, and more attention. Sandy could not have felt better about this turn of events. Stan was not *quite* as happy, but the two of them were doing most everything together now.

Once Stan finished his Cheerios, he looked out the window onto the bright sunny morning. An idea came into his head as to how he would spend the morning.

"Sandy girl, what do you say; should the two of us go over to the Park and Bark?"

The Park and Bark was a favorite dog-run where people brought their pets for exercise and a chance to play. It was six miles from Stan's house, too far to walk, so Stan had to drive. Sandy loved the park, and she knew it by name. As soon as Stan said, "Park and Bark," Sandy ran for her leash, and then began her famous standing on hind legs while hopping forward.

"Oh, ho ho ho…I see someone thinks that's a great idea," Stan chuckled. "OK, let's go get in the car, and we'll ride over."

A ride in the car! That was one of Sandy's other favorite treats. Without further invitation required, it was into the backseat, and Stan backed the Impala down the drive.

When they arrived, there were only two other dogs in the fenced area. Stan went over, unhooked Sandy from her leash, and took up residence on an empty bench to enjoy the sun. A few moments later, a woman arrived in a grey SUV with a black Labrador retriever. The Lab ran right over to Sandy, and the two of them became immediate friends; jumping, biting, and chasing one another around the grassy park.

Stan smiled as the woman came over to sit on the other end of the bench.

"Looks like two new friends have found one another," Stan said.

She laughed, and said, "Wouldn't it be nice if people could make friends that easily...make life a lot more fun."

She was a nice looking woman of about 60, just a hint of makeup, and a friendly demeanor. She was dressed in a jogging outfit, with new running shoes, and had one of those pedometers on her arm. Stan assumed she must be someone who took her health and conditioning seriously. She sat with her back against the bench, and head slightly tilted upward toward the warm sun, seemingly soaking in everything the day was offering. A light breeze was tossing at the locks of her slightly graying, auburn hair.

"You are so right...so right," Stan answered with a smile.

"My name is Stan Beecher; what's your dog's name?" asked Stan.

"Cruiser; and my name's Ann," the lady answered without turning toward Stan, or providing her last name.

"Do you come here often," Stan asked.

"No, not too often; if it's a nice day, I might try to make it. Cruiser loves it here," she said sitting back straight. She looked over, and gently smiled in Stan's direction.

"I don't get here very often, either," Stan added. "Sandy, that's my dog, would come every day if she had her way. Until lately, I just didn't have much time. I worked in the police department, and well, the hours were a bit unpredictable, if you know what I mean."

Ann smiled again as she returned to her position with closed eyes and head tilted back toward the sun.

"I do understand," she said, speaking upward toward the sky. "I was in the military...Army Nurse Corps. But as you get near 60, the Army tends to show you the door. So, here I am; filling my days off by going to the dog park," she laughed.

To Stan, this revelation wasn't as funny as it was ironic. He realized she was trying to occupy some of her days, just as he was trying to occupy some of his.

"Me too," Stan said, placing his hands in his pocket, and assuming a mirrored position to Ann's. "I recently..." and he paused trying to decide how he wanted to phrase the rest of the statement, then let out a somewhat longer sigh than intended as he continued, "I recently took leave, and am considering retirement."

"Well, I am what I guess they call, 'semi-retired,'" Ann said. "To be honest, I'm not so sure I'd like a full retirement quite yet. Just being out of the Army is taking some getting used to," she said rising from the bench for the moment, and walking toward the fenced area where her dog had come to inspect if she was still watching.

This conversation went on for some time, and Stan learned she had retired to this area to be near her brother. The two had never been that close, but as she had no other family, moving here seemed a better idea than some of the others. She was now involved with the VA, where she was working in the geriatric care unit.

Ann confided, "I've always worked in the medical field, but working at the VA has been an eye-opening experience. I find so many vets dealing with issues far beyond just declining physical health... depression, loss of family, memory, alcoholism, even some drug issues; they all present real challenges."

Although he had never served in the military, this was all resonating close to home with Stan. He briefly thought about mentioning what he was going through; then dismissed it.

After a time, Stan decided to approach things from a different direction. "I'm not that old, but to tell you the truth - Ann, right? - To tell you the truth, Ann, I can see how every one of those issues could be a problem. I even worry that could be me down the road. I guess we all have a healthy fear of how age might affect us," he said, slowly rising to his feet, stretching, and watching carefully for her reaction.

"You would be surprised some of the things people go through," Ann said. "And I'm not talking about just 80 and 90 year olds, either. Not at all; many people our age have major issues as well. Luckily for me, my work here has provided me with contacts and information for these problems, which is a good thing," Ann hastily tacked on. "It seems that the older I get, the more I've come to realize how uncertain life can be. When I was younger, I never thought of anything going wrong. But now? Well...you just never know. You just never know."

Stan thought to himself, "Lady, you have no idea."

In the meantime, Sandy seemed played out, and was now at the fence. That always signaled it was time to go home, and do her other favorite thing - eat.

Stan stood and walked toward the fence where now both dogs stood waiting for their owners. As he passed where Ann was sitting, he reached out his hand to shake hers and say goodbye.

"Well, Ann, I've enjoyed our little chat. Do you happen to have a card? I mean, you never know when I might need one of those many contacts you have," Stan laughed, trying to make it sound like a joke.

He was quite pleased with himself as to how sly he had been getting this information. He also knew, without a card, there was every possibility he would forget her name, and lose this contact forever.

"Yes, as a matter of fact I do. It's an old military card, so let me write my current information on the back."

Stan was happy about this chance meeting. Nothing might come of it, but just the few minutes talking to someone had been nice.

Ann gave him the card. It read:

Ann S. Peterson
Walter Reed Army Medical Center
Washington, DC

Her VA phone number was hand written on the back. Stan had what he wanted. They bid one another goodbye as Sandy hopped up in the back seat of the Impala, and Cruiser jumped in the SUV. This had been a lucky meeting for Stan, but for this day his luck was about to run out.

*****

With Sandy safely in the car, Stan drove off toward home. The radio was on, Sandy was looking out the window thinking happy dog thoughts; all seemed fine. Ten minutes had gone by when Stan noticed he was on a road he didn't recognize as one leading home. He looked to find a street sign, or at least a landmark, but nothing seemed right. "Where the hell am I?" he thought. Sweat started to break out across his forehead. As he looked at buildings and stores along the road, he could sense he'd seen them before, he knew he had; but nothing was making sense. "I'll just continue a bit further until I see something I recognize," he thought. Five minutes later he felt completely lost. "This is crazy," he said to himself. "I've lived here all my life, how can I not know these places?" Fear was settling in, and his heart was racing. Stan was beginning to panic. He looked everywhere for help, but there was none.

"Now what the hell did I do," Stan muttered aloud.

He looked ahead and, seeing a large sign, drove into the Agri-Feed parking lot. Stan just sat in the car a few moments gazing out the front window, and trying to think of what to do next. He was sweating; now a jumbled mass of nerves and fear.

Finally Stan said aloud, "I must have made some kind of wrong turn somewhere, but where? Where the hell am I?" he repeated to himself.

For some time now, whenever he came under stress, his mind seemed to freeze up. To be sure, this was one of those times. He sat and thought. As he saw it, he had only two bad options. One; he could continue to drive around until he recognized something, then maybe he could navigate his way home. Or two, he could call Jenny for help. He certainly wasn't calling John because that would just start an unpleasant argument about why he was out there in the first place. Stan decided to call his daughter. God, he hated to do it. He detested looking like some doddering old fool. There was no choice. He had to do it.

Jenny had the cell phone ringer turned off at work, but she could hear it vibrating in her pocketbook. As she was free for the moment, she looked at who it was, and immediately picked up.

"Hi Dad, what's up? You hardly ever call me at work," she said, hoping it was nothing too serious.

"Hey Sweetie. Well…you'll never guess what your dopey Dad did this morning. I took Sandy over to Park and Bark, but on the way home, I guess I was daydreaming, and must have made a wrong turn. Anyway, I'm out here in the Knoxville boondocks somewhere, and I don't know the best way home. You think you could give me some fast directions if I tell you where I am?" Stan was careful not to use the word, "lost." That's the last impression he wanted to make.

Unfortunately, "lost" was the very first impression that jumped into Jenny's mind. She didn't want to make her father nervous or annoyed, so her next words were carefully chosen.

"Sure Dad, tell me where you are, let me see if I can give you a fast way home."

"Well, I'm not sure of the road, but there's an Agri Feed here. I think it's out toward the west somewhere. Like I said, I've got to learn not to sing along with the radio and daydream when I drive. I asked Sandy if she knew, but no help there at all," he joked, trying to make light of his situation.

"Agri Feed! How the heck did he get out there? That's way out on Middlebrook Pike somewhere," Jenny said to herself. In her mind, she was thinking, "No way I can give him easy directions from there to his house. I better just go get him, he can follow me home."

"Oh, OK Dad, no problem," Jenny lied. "Listen, it's almost lunch and I was going out anyway. That's not too far from where I am, so I'll just run over, and you can follow me back to the house. Is that OK with you?"

"Can't you just give me directions?" The last thing Stan wanted was a "rescue party" to be dispatched.

"Truth is Dad, I know the way from where you are, but I don't really know the names of all the streets. It will be a lot easier for me to just let you follow. It's no problem. Just stay where you are, and I'll be there right away."

"OK...if that's what you think. Sandy and I will wait. How long you think before you'll be here?"

"Like 15 minutes, Dad. You just stay put." Jenny rang off, told her supervisor she had a little family situation, and would return after lunch. She did a quick search for Agri Feed directions on the internet just to be certain she knew where she was going.

When she arrived at the Agri Feed she spotted her father's car parked on the side. Her Dad was out of the car walking Sandy. As she pulled up, her father just stood there looking off into space. Curiously, he didn't even recognize Jenny's van or Jenny until she got out of the car and approached him.

"Oh...goodness, there you are," Stan painfully smiled in his surprise. "Thanks so much for coming out. I feel like an idiot."

"No problem, Dad. You can just follow me. We're actually not that far from home." Jenny lied again. Her Dad was way off base.

Once they got to the house, Stan was happy to be home. He thanked Jenny again as she returned to her car for the drive back to Parkwest Hospital. While driving back, she dialed John's number to alert him to today's little drama. He wasn't going to believe it.

But John did believe it. It added to his worries, and reinforced his growing sense that something more substantial would soon have to be done.

*****

At 10:10, Monday morning, Stan was in his usual position looking out his front window, waiting for Jenny to arrive for their drive to Gatlinburg. As Jenny's red minivan pulled in the drive, Stan said to himself, "Humph, ten minutes late. How many times have I told these three to be better than just on time?"

Stan Junior was out of the car first, bounding up the steps. Sandy gave him the usual twelve lick greeting as he came in.

"Hi Dad," Stan Junior exploded. "Are you excited? Did Jenny tell you? We're going up to Gatlinburg, and the nature center, and maybe play miniature golf...."

Stan cut him off before he could schedule enough things they would have to stay for the week. "Yesss...yes. She told me; exciting stuff here Stan Junior; exciting stuff. You ready?"

Without further discussion, everyone piled into the van, and they were off on their little day trip.

"I'm just going to call John, and tell him we're leaving...just be a sec'," Jenny all too cheerily said.

Stan wondered why John would need to know when they were leaving but quickly dismissed the thought.

After receiving Jenny's call, John left the office, and drove directly over to Gill Avenue. As he went in, he had this sense of relief and purpose. Finally, he was going to be able to do something worthwhile for his Dad.

John took everything off the kitchen table then organized what was there in separate piles.

"Unopened letters"

"Late notices"

"Current bills"

"Bank statements"

"Receipts"

"Miscellaneous"

From there, he searched for his father's bankbook, checkbook, savings passbooks, IRS returns, anything that might be of financial concern. He was going to need that checkbook. He could write the checks out, but his Dad would still have to sign them. It would be a lot easier if he could get his father to sign off on a limited power of attorney, but knew that was going to be a battle. Maybe something for another day, he thought.

He decided to attack the "unopened letters" before the bills, that way he would be dealing with the most current bill first. John found what he had expected; unpaid bills, unfulfilled pledge requests, and notices from organizations he had previously supported.

"Simple things," John said to himself. "Aren't there any larger bills than these?" Noticeably absent were things like loan payments and credit card statements. The only indication his Dad even owned a credit card was a statement linked to a Fidelity American Express Gold Card that indicated a zero balance. John continued looking for bigger ticket items, something like property taxes. He wasn't totally surprised. Dad was the original, "pay as you go, and if you don't have the money, you can't afford it," poster child.

John thought to himself, "This is why whenever any of us asked for something, he always seemed to have the money to pay for it. He *never* spent money on himself."

John opened his father's checkbook to write out the checks, but couldn't find the ledger? How did Dad keep track of what checks he wrote without the little check register? "Jeez, Dad," he thought. "How tough could it be to just fill in the register when you write a check? It isn't like you have a ton of them to make out. Better yet, has anyone ever mentioned online banking to you?" Whatever, he would just double check the latest bank statement to make certain there was enough cash on hand before having his Dad sign the checks.

From what John could see, his father used two different banks; Fidelity Investments and FSG Bank. He began with FSG since that was where it seemed he paid his ordinary bills. He opened all the statements, and laid them out into a savings pile and a checking pile. As he was pouring over the FSG statements, his eyes began to widen.

SAVINGS ACCOUNT BALANCE: $23,206
BUSINESS ACCOUNT BALANCE: $8,113
CHECKING ACCOUNT BALANCE: $14,971

"Holy cow, Dad! Really? These savings accounts are paying like a quarter of one percent interest, and you're letting them hold over thirty grand? Why the heck don't you talk to *me* a little? You obviously have no clue about investments and how to make your money work. They must love you down at ole FSG. And a checking balance of 15 grand? Given your meager expenses, that's way too big a balance. It's not like you're raking in the dividends on *that* account either!"

At least John's mind was clear on one thing; his Dad was not in financial trouble. When he saw all those unpaid bills, he had feared his father had given money away to bogus charities. Now, he knew it was just neglect. Not that neglect made him feel good, it didn't. Overlooking all these bills was the sign of something else, something that could not be solved by money.

He finished writing out the few checks needed to bring his Dad current, then decided to see what the Fidelity account held. At least the credit card was a zero balance, so he assumed his father was in good shape on that account as well. As he opened the thick statement, he just stared at it in disbelief. John leaned back in his chair and uttered a loud,

"HOOOOOOOOOOOLY SHIT!"

He couldn't believe what his eyes saw, thinking there must be something I'm overlooking; there must be some kind of mistake I'm missing. But there wasn't. He knew financial statements inside out, and he knew what this statement was telling him.

Balance as of 6/2/2010

Total Equity Investment Portfolio: $101,211
Total Cash to Invest: $16,307
Total Fidelity Funds: $244,980

Total Fidelity Account Balance: $362,498

John sat in his chair in stunned silence. His father was much better off than anyone ever suspected. The entire family knew his father had always been a bit of a saver; but this! He had to have been putting money aside since his twenties to amass this retirement portfolio. And who the hell was advising him on this stuff? John looked over his father's equity portfolio. It held a number of solid, high growth and dividend investments like Exxon, J & J, Aetna Insurance, and several bank preferred stocks, all good companies. John also noticed, if this statement was the norm, his Dad was getting a solid dividend return which was what he assumed accounted for that $16,000 cash balance. He thought to himself, "Jesus, Dad; did no one ever mention 'dividend reinvestment' to you? Better yet, I could put you in a high yield annuity, and you could be getting a nice check every month. Just talk to me!"

John didn't know whether to be excited, shocked, upset, or just how to feel. He did know one thing that made him feel good; his father was in excellent financial shape moving forward. Between his police pension and benefits, plus these accounts, his father would have a solid financial future no matter what happened! John saw new options opening, and felt a lot better.

*****

The Rest A-Bit Motor Lodge was a run-down motel located out between the Interstate and Broadway, not far from the old Regas Restaurant; a section of town Stan referred to as, "a sketchy neighborhood." It catered to a class of patrons that included the homeless, prostitutes, and individuals looking for low profile, inexpensive lodging.

Disturbances and police calls to this location were a routine occurrence, so when Officer Towne's scanner sounded, he wasn't surprised to see The Rest A-Bit show up on the screen. The radio call advised;

"Car 49... Respond to Rest A-Bit Motel on a 10-26, possible 10-31. Advise: proceed Code 8." This meant there was a disorderly person, and possible stabbing incident. He was to proceed without lights or siren. "Typical," thought Gus. "Just another night of fun and frolic at the 'Ole Rest A-Bit.'" This, however, was not to be a routine call.

As Gus pulled up, an African-American male was in the parking lot yelling toward an open door where a large, white male in a pair of pants and no shirt was standing. Behind the man was a woman screaming obscenities and threats. Gus called for backup; then exited his car to deal with the man in the parking lot trying to enter a parked vehicle. There was a small amount of blood on the ground near the man, his black hoodie was beginning to soak with blood stains, and the individual was unsteady on his feet. As Gus approached the man, he shouted to him;

"Just lie down on the pavement, and let me see your hands...NOW. I have an ambulance on the way, so just lie down."

As he approached, Gus unfastened his service revolver, and kept his hand on the butt of his gun just in case. The man was yelling back at him, but Gus just repeated his command louder. The man slumped down onto the rocker panel of the car. Officer Towne briefly looked toward the motel room where the second man was furiously gathering up things, and appeared ready to run.

Almost simultaneously, two more KPD cars rolled into the parking lot; this time with sirens and lights flashing. Gus yelled for the newly arrived officers to secure the room, and call in a 10-47, which would bring an ambulance to the scene. He cautiously approached the man by the car, still wary if this man had a weapon.

The two new officers rushed the door, kept both parties in the room, and began to secure the area. As expected, a large crowd was gathering as more police cars arrived on the scene. In less than five minutes, the police had all the individuals secured, and the room sealed off. Now, it was time to unravel just what was going on.

Walking toward the room to question the unidentified man and woman, Gus Towne noticed something that made him stop. Parked just a few feet from the door was a yellow van. Ordinarily this would not have attracted him, but he recalled the briefing held a few weeks earlier where he had asked Stan Beecher about just such a vehicle. As it turned out, Beecher actually had done a little work on this lead, and obtained a partial description of the license plate. It was reportedly an out of state plate, possibly New York, with a 12 in the number. Gus walked over to the van, and there it was; New York plates, license number; ADL 4612! This was more than coincidence. Gus placed an immediate call back to the station to alert them of this discovery.

Speaking with the room occupants, Gus learned that the woman was a 24 year old, Crystal Smelcer of Newport, Tennessee. She was well known as a working girl with three priors including a still outstanding shop-lifting charge. As soon as the officers entered the motel room, Crystal began screaming.

"This low life bastard invited me over here for a party, then tried to stiff me on the fifty bucks he owed me. It's not bad enough he threw me around, but he wouldn't pay either, so I texted my boyfriend," Crystal shouted.

The other man tried to rebut what the girl was alleging, but Gus cut him off, he wanted to hear more of this story; like how did the man in the parking lot come to be bleeding all over the pavement.

"OK, sir...you need to just stay quiet right now. I'll give you a chance to speak in a moment, but now you just sit there and wait your turn."

"Now then, Crystal...He didn't pay you, so you called your friend. What happened then?"

Crystal couldn't wait to answer. "Jeron came in, and this guy pulled a knife from somewhere and stabbed him...just stabbed him with no warning, no reason...nothing!"

"Now," Towne thought, "we need to find that knife. It couldn't be far." He went on questioning the girl. "So Crystal, if he stabbed him, where is this knife? Did you see it?"

Still yelling, Crystal said, "Fuck yeah, I saw it. He threw it under the bed; or somewhere over there," she said pointing to the nightstand.

One of the officers in the room went over and began to search the area.

"Got it," as he slowly pulled the knife from under the bed, scooping it with his pen. "I'll bag it for the forensic guys, OK, Gus?"

Gus turned his attention back to the man, who had now become the main character in this little scenario. "So, what is your story then sir?"

"Look. I was just in town for a little while; I thought I'd have a bit of fun, maybe party a little. I invite this girl over here, and she starts going crazy that I owe her money. She never told me she was a whore…"

"Oh yes, I fucking well did you bastard. We even settled on a price, and th…" Gus then put up a hand to cut her short. "Ma'am, you have to stay quiet now. You had a turn, now this gentleman is speaking. "OK…. go on with your story. So you were staying in town for a while to party, then somehow it blew up into this? Tell me about that."

"Right, so the next thing I know, this big black dude comes in the room, starts shoving me around, threatening to shoot me if I don't pay, so I defended myself."

"Oh, that is such bull s…." Crystal started to yell, until the other officer silenced her.

"Right, ok then. Well, we are all going to have a ride downtown right now, where we will sort this out as to who did what and to whom," said Gus. As Gus looked at one of the other officers, he noticed on the other side of the bureau was a black briefcase.

Gus was already fairly certain this could be their man from the Citerelli case, so this had now become deadly serious. Gus began to advise the man of his rights, when he began yelling, and trying to run out of the room. He was immediately subdued, put onto the floor by the other officers, and handcuffed. Now, everybody was under arrest. Crystal was being arrested for prostitution; the other man for assault with a deadly weapon.

The room was sealed off as a crime scene, and the individual from the parking lot was arrested at the hospital. It took twenty minutes, but Ted Newsome arrived with a complete forensics team, as the investigation of a possible link to the Citerelli murder was underway.

Inside the room, under the bed, a large, bloodstained knife had been found and bagged. The black briefcase was removed by the forensics team, and taken to the lab. In it, they found a large amount of cash, several ledgers, a set of papers with the name Citerelli, and a plane confirmation for the following week. It was a flight scheduled to leave Dallas with a final destination of Buenos Aires, Argentina. The yellow van was impounded, and later found to have Mr. Citerelli's finger prints on numerous surfaces.

Ted Newsome was pleased. He complimented officer Towne on the excellent work, and told him he would put his name in for a commendation. It seemed once again, that something Stan Beecher had uncovered, led to an arrest in a major case. Ted was eager to share this with his friend. He knew Stan could use a little good news.

The case appeared solved except for a few details. Ted Newsome would fill in most of the blanks through the interrogation process.

The final step Ted wanted to take was to see to it that Stan Beecher and Gus Towne be given proper credit for their roles in helping solve this crime.

*****

Even with the little mishap returning from the Park and Bark, Stan continued to take Sandy for occasional rendezvous with his new friend Cruiser. In addition, he and Ann were becoming good friends. Over the course of a few weeks, Stan had broached the subject of his "occasional forgetfulness," and wondered if in her time at the VA she had dealt with such issues. Of course, she had, often. Ann suggested the best way for Stan to put his mind at ease would be to simply have some neurological and genetic testing completed. Those would supply necessary information on exactly what might be causing Stan's memory problem. It might even rule out anything serious.

Stan didn't respond with any further information on his own situation, but did ask if she knew of a good place to have those tests done. Absolutely, she knew, but Ann was careful to avoid raising any red flags. She simply said,

"Here, let me write down the name of someplace I think I might go if I wanted to check something like this."

She took out a piece of paper, and wrote down the name of a hospital. Stan had no idea if this would be useful, but as it seemed to be continuously on his mind, he thought it best to at least get the information. Ann had written;

Memory and Alzheimer's Treatment Center
The Johns Hopkins Bayview Medical Center
5300 Alpha Commons Dr., Floor 4
Baltimore, MD 21224
410-550-6337

What Stan did not know was that John had already decided to make an appointment for a medical evaluation.

The day had come for Stan to move to the next step.

5

The Diagnosis

Ted arrived exactly on time at 8:00 AM to take Stan for a "surprise breakfast." A surprise it was, too. Stan hadn't spoken to Ted since the day he walked out of his office to begin his "leave." Stan thought back to what a devastatingly bad day that was. He never saw it coming; he had no idea how much his forgetfulness had been affecting his work. But that was water under the bridge. Today he was excited to be going out with Ted. It was like old times, and Stan was feeling better than he had in some time.

As Ted pulled into his driveway, Stan was out the door, walking toward the car and waving. Ted looked genuinely happy to see his old friend. He opened the door for Stan, and apologized for not having called before. Stan simply waved a hand as if to say, "forget it."

"Stan, I don't know why I didn't call sooner, I hope you're doing OK," Ted started the conversation.

"Oh, not too bad. It takes some getting used to, though. You spend that many years doing something, you're at a loss when you have to figure some other way to fill your days, know what I mean, Ted?"

Stan tried to sound cheerful, but Ted knew Stan was having a difficult time with the adjustment. Who wouldn't?

"Well, what'll it be for breakfast? You pick the place," Ted offered, although he knew exactly where Stan was going to choose.

"Only one place worth going, Ted, only one place worth going. You know where it is," Stan laughed.

"Indeed I do, young man, indeed I do," Ted said, as they rolled off toward Pete's Café.

As the two entered, Pete waved hello from the back, while they stood in a line of about four small groups. Pete's was a seat yourself arrangement; when you saw a booth open, you just went and took up residence. Stan looked over at the full counter, and they decided to wait for a booth.

Five minutes later, Ted and Stan were seated near the window. The fact was, all the booths were near the window because Pete's was a fairly narrow but long café. Pictures of Tennessee athletes, memorabilia, and local color adorned the vacant wall space. Waitresses and bus people scurried back and forth trying to make sure the tables were served and cleared. It was busy, full of happy noise, conversation, and a friendly staff - perfect for a morning meal.

Ted began. "So Stan, I have some really good news for you today."

"And what might that be? I was wondering what the occasion was that you were inviting me out? And you're paying, right? Remember, I'm out of work, flat on my ass broke. In fact, I'm looking under the Henley Street Bridge to see if there's anything available for my dresser drawers in case I'm tossed out of the Gill Avenue Estates," Stan joked.

"No, no. Today is entirely on me."

"So...what's the big news?" Stan was hoping perhaps Ted was going to say they had found another spot in the department where he could come back.

"You know that Riverside case you and I were working about that Citerelli guy? We have it just about wrapped up. Most importantly, the reason it cleared up this fast is due to the good work *you* did. Had you not turned up the key links in this case, this perp might have skipped town, and we would have never solved it."

"Really?" Stan asked, almost at a loss as to how that could be. "How so?"

Before Ted could go any further, their favorite waitress, Louise, showed up at the table.

"Oh my goodness…look whose presence we're blessed with today! Why if it isn't Mr. Joke Machine of the Long Blue Line. Where ya been, Sweetie? I thought y'all won the lottery, and flew off to Vegas without poor little me. But I guess not, 'cause here y'all are, and in the presence of the one and only Detective Lieutenant Newsome."

Stan looked up at her and said, "Oh good morning, Stella."

Ted shuffled uncomfortably, looking for some way to bail his friend out of this embarrassment.

"Yes, sir; Stella by Starlight, that's our girl," Ted tacked on.

Louise wasn't buying it. "What happened, Stan? You fall on your noggin' getting out of that squad car this mornin'? It's Louise, remember me," she said, tapping on her nametag with her pen.

Stan just looked at her and smiled.

"That's OK, Sweetie, as long as you keep leaving me those nice little love notes when you leave, you call me whatever you like - except Ted's ex-wife's name," she added as she laughed at her own joke. "Anyway, what's it going to be for you two? Let me guess, there Ted…blueberry pancake special with sausage and scrambled egg?"

"Yes, Louise, that would be fine," said Ted. He loved Pete's pancakes, and whichever one was on special, that was for him.

"Stan? You changing your order, perhaps something a little more special today?" Louise stood looking at Stan, but nothing was coming back; not a sound. He just sat there, looking at her with a somewhat vacant smile.

Ted rescued the situation. "Louise, he's having his usual as well. Now stop confusing him with hard questions. The man doesn't even have a menu."

"Oh yeah," Louise answered. "Like he doesn't have that menu memorized at this point. All you 'bluebloods' know Pete's menu better than Pete does. Anyway, the Stan special it is."

"And keep these cups filled!"

Louise looked back at him with that, "You've got to be kidding me" stare.

"You know Ted, I'm beginning to see why you never remarried. No one could put up with y'all's sense of humor," Louise said in her southern accent. "And what about you Bob Hope? No bad jokes from you today? Ted, you better check his temperature, because he's waaaay off his feed this morning." With that she walked off to get the food.

Stan was still sitting with a bit of a stunned look on his face; Ted thought it best to just pick up the conversation where he had left off.

"Anyway, where was I? Oh yeah, this case turned on the stuff you uncovered. Remember that yellow van you reported with the out of state plates?"

The actual answer was, "vaguely," but Stan stayed quiet. He realized this conversation was one Ted should lead, and he didn't want to make any more mistakes.

"Towne, that guy you worked with way back when, well he gets a call out to that sleazy Rest A' Bit Motel, and what do you think?" Stan had no idea.

"There… big as life, is the yellow van! Plus, we find the missing briefcase, the knife, the works! Then, there was some lowlife hood from Manhattan that worked at the *same damn restaurant* you uncovered in your preliminary investigation! I interrogated that moron for six hours before I started pulling stuff loose. Of course, he was getting charged either way; I was just trying to pyramid off your good work. So Stan, once again, you were the star of the case. Good going, my friend. Good going!"

Perhaps Ted was overstating things a bit, but he was right about one thing: without Stan uncovering that van and partial plate, this could have just gone down as assault with a deadly, and been left at that.

Stan smiled and thanked Ted for the kind words. He remembered much of what Ted was saying, but he was glad he didn't have to recount those details on his own.

Once the breakfasts came, Ted and Stan resorted to small talk about families, department gossip, and UT sports. Like Stan, and just about everyone else in town, Ted was big on sports. They finished their breakfast and stood to leave. Ted left a much bigger tip than usual, hoping it would take Louise's mind off Stan's lapse. Pete yelled good bye as they went out the door, and they both waved.

On the way back to the house, Stan said, "I hope you'll still be coming by to say hi once in a while, Ted. This was a lot of fun."

Stan thought to himself, "Why did I make a mistake with that woman's name." It was frustrating!

"Oh, no no. No problem, Stan. I'm just going to drop you off in the front, if that's OK. I've got a 10 o'clock briefing."

"That's fine. I really had a good time. I miss our breakfasts. Those two kids of mine work, so we never get out these days. I could go with Sandy, but I'm no fan of Milk Bone Biscuits over easy."

"There's the Stan I know," thought Ted.

"OK...buddy. Have a good day. And don't worry; your name *headlines* my report!" Ted said with extra emphasis on the word, "headlines."

"Thanks, Ted; thanks so much. It means a lot."

*****

Since Stan's untimely leave of absence from the police force, Jenny and John took turns having him over for Sunday dinner. Tonight was Jenny and Jimmy's turn. Even though Jenny and Jimmy's dining room was small, she insisted on keeping the Sunday Dinners alive. She felt it gave everyone an opportunity to visit, talk about their week, and see how Dad was making out on his own. On this occasion, however, John had an agenda. He and his wife Linda had talked about Stan's memory issues which had now escalated to the point where it was necessary to make arrangements with a neurologist for his father's review. As far as John and Linda were concerned, the memory lapses had gone on long enough. Tonight John would announce how things were to go forward. Jenny, on the other hand, had no idea this was to be unveiled.

Jenny and Linda worked in the kitchen until the evening meal was ready for the joint announcement, "Dinner is ready, so everybody come sit down at the table. It's a delicious pork roast and gravy, with new potatoes, carrots, baked beans, apple sauce...the works, Dad."

This was a meal Jenny's mom had prepared for the family many times, and she knew it to be one of her Dad's favorites. Whenever he found baked beans on the menu, he would always announce the same thing.

"Mmmmmm, baked beans; you know I'm a baked bean junkie. I loooooove my home baked beans," he would laugh.

Of course, this was in addition to his being a chili junkie, hot dog aficionado, sloppy joe fan, and any of a dozen other favorite foods. In short...her father enjoyed eating.

As Stan got up to move toward the table, he inexplicably sat right back down, and stayed there.

"You OK, Dad?" John asked.

"Oh yeah, no problem. I just sort of lost my balance a second. Come over and help get me out of this chair. I feel like I'm sitting in the basement here," he laughed.

Over the last month, Stan had noticed he was having more and more difficulty moving around. He would sometimes trip or lose his balance, often using a wall or table to steady himself. He wasn't sure if this was linked to his memory issues, or was just a sign he was moving closer to seventy than sixty. On the other hand, nothing was going to keep him from that dinner table!

John helped him up. They walked over to the table and sat down.

Her Dad then looked up at his daughter with a big smile and said, "So Jenny. What's on the menu tonight?"

Jenny looked over at her brother, and he looked back at her, then over at his wife Linda who was sitting with her head down. Jenny was saddened that her father had already forgotten what was for dinner. It had the opposite effect on her brother. He was now more certain than ever his evening's agenda was the right path.

As they passed around the dishes and serving plates, Jenny was putting things onto her father's dish. Stan just smiled at her as small talk continued around the table. He was enjoying this. It reminded him of the many times Marilyn had set the family table, and all that happy conversation going back and forth. Family dinners had always been special at the Beecher house. Tonight felt like one of those times. Stan felt "at home."

Linda looked over at John with that "well?" look on her face as John began: "So Dad, how are things going with you this week? You go down to Park and Bark, see that lady?"

Stan looked over at John, and answered. "Well, as you well know, I'm not supposed to go there on my own any more, by order of Herr Reich marshal Beecher over here. But yes, I did get down there a couple of times this week." Once was the actual number. "Other than that, son, you will be pleased to know I am right as rain. Whatever it is that's so right with rain - never quite understood that saying," Stan concluded, drifting off in his speech.

John was moving forward. "Well, you know, I was thinking; remember that card the lady gave you with the address of that hospital up in Baltimore? I know you were worried about this, so I took it on myself to make us an appointment there. We are all set for next week."

Jenny's head shot up, and she looked at John in total amazement and displeasure. John had never mentioned a word to her. Jimmy looked over at his wife, wondering if she knew this was coming. If so, she hadn't mentioned it to him.

Jenny was thinking, "You jerk! You go ahead and make these plans, and you don't think to bring me in on the discussion or decision? You are so callous that you don't even talk to Dad about this...you just announce?!" Jenny was furious.

Stan remained calm, seemingly unmoved by what had just been said. "Oh you did? How wonderful," Stan said, sounding to everyone as if he didn't fully grasp the plan John had just laid out. "Well, I guess that's fine. What did you just say? We're going to a doctor?" Stan paused and looked about, processing John's announcement about a doctor. He wondered if he had already agreed to go for some kind of exam. He decided he probably had, and continued:

"OK, let's go speak to these people, and everyone can get off my back about this forgetting crap. You're taking me, right John? Is that what I'm hearing?"

John had feared his father might blow up when informed of these arrangements, but it never came. Linda looked at her husband with that, "See, I told you so" look. Feeling a sense of relief, John said, "Actually we are flying out of Knoxville to Washington on Wednesday next week. Flights are cheap, and when you figure in time and gas, it's better to just fly."

"Oh," Jenny thought. "You just wait till I get you alone, buster! Not only do you make the appointment without consulting me, you book flight arrangements as well? I'm not supposed to go? Stan Junior isn't included? Everything here is about you?!!" It was everything Jenny could do to not explode at the table.

Dinner concluded, and Jenny said, "OK, everybody. Everyone go on into the living room and relax. I will clear this off, and later we will have a nice dessert of apple pie and ice cream! That good with you, Dad?"

"Apple pie and ice cream! You bet it is. You know, I'm an apple pie junkie...and make sure it has some cream too. I don't want to get gyped," Stan playfully added.

"Great, it will just be a jiff till I get this cleared off and the coffee ready. John, can you come out here and help me a minute?" Jenny was loaded for bear.

John looked over at Linda, who was already getting up to go with her husband, but he put his hand up to tell her to stay put for now. The last thing he wanted was the two women at one another's throats. No, he would take care of this himself. It was really his idea, and he would take ownership.

Jimmy tried to stay out of family disagreements, but he knew his wife was incensed by her brother's announcement. She rarely got angry, but Jimmy knew her well enough to know she could have an explosive temper, and in this case, she was a walking five-alarm fire. He thought to himself, "If Linda stays out here, I stay out here; Linda goes in there, I go in there. God, what a mess!"

As John entered the kitchen, he could see the anger flashing in his sister's eyes. He knew he was going to get an earful. He had anticipated she would not be pleased, but at this point, John had decided someone had to start making decisions. Everyone had to stop living in denial that Dad might be fine; this was *not* just an aging issue. He was *not* fine, and this was *not* something that 'might get better at some point.'"

Jenny exploded in a raised, angered whisper. "What in hell are you doing? You make all these plans, flight arrangements, who knows what all, and you don't think maybe I would like to have been included? You just go ahead and start acting as if no one else matters? You have pulled some stunts in your day, but this one takes the cake. I am so pissed at you right now that I could absolutely whack you in the head with this pan! Is this your idea or Linda's? I want to know!"

"Mine, but can you just listen to me a sec..." that was all John could get out before Jenny lit into him again.

"No! You listen to me. This is *not all about you!* So, as inconvenient as it might be to actually include others in your little agenda, you better NEVER pull this crap again. I mean it!"

This was a losing battle, and John knew it. He expected Jenny would be annoyed, but he wasn't quite prepared for this level of anger. It was time to retreat and save any further discussion for another day when tempers were less frayed.

"Fine, fine, Jenny," John said with that "you win" tone of voice. "In the future, I will check with you first, OK?"

"You damn well better," Jenny nearly shouted.

From the living room came Stan's voice. "If you two are done talking about me in there, I could go for a cup of coffee. Jenny, you're like a cheerleader with a megaphone when you whisper," Stan laughed.

He knew what the kitchen discussion was about. John had, as usual, gone off and done his own thing. John had always been a bit of a lone wolf, and just move to action independent of everyone else.

"Yes. OK, Dad, coming right up," Jenny called out. "We don't want to keep the coffee waiting, and turn you into a grumpy old bear, do we?" said Jenny as she tried to lighten the mood.

Stan laughed back, "Exactly right. See, you *are* learning after all these years." Stan laughed. He didn't want to see the two of them arguing; especially if the argument was about him.

Shortly, Jenny had the pie and ice cream on the table. Linda helped serve, and said nothing further, but a few icy looks from Jenny let her know she was just as much in the dog house as her husband. Frankly, Linda couldn't care less. She just wanted this situation moved forward at whatever the cost. In a few minutes everyone was seated, and the air somewhat lighter, although it was obvious to Jimmy his wife had not yet gotten her blood pressure back under control.

As they were finishing dessert, John added a final statement.

"So, Dad; I will come over and pick you up Wednesday at 9:00. Our flight isn't until 10:45, so that gives us lots of time." John looked at Jenny, and she was looking down, shaking her head.

She thought, "This boy will never learn…never!"

*****

As the car entered the parking lot of the Memory and Alzheimer's Treatment Center at Johns Hopkins Hospital, Stan was nervous. He had been uneasy since the Sunday dinner where this had been announced. There was something to be said for simply "not knowing." When you aren't certain something is wrong, there is the luxury of believing you are just experiencing temporary confusions. You can try to convince yourself that you are just getting a little older, nothing is critically wrong. After today, Stan thought, any illusions would be gone, and there was the strong possibility this was something serious. He was worried.

Stan looked out the car window as they approached. Before them was a large, modern, red brick building of about six stories. The Bayview Campus of Johns Hopkins had a circular drive, plantings, and an attractive, red covered entranceway. It was not exactly what Stan had expected, but then, he really didn't know what to expect.

As the two of them entered, there was a reception desk where John went to get directions. It wasn't long before they were led into the very well appointed office of a young female doctor named Elizabeth Wu. Dr. Wu was an Associate Head of Geriatric Medicine, specializing in memory problems, particularly those with multiple medical issues surrounding the aging process. She was a small Asian woman, younger than Stan expected. In fact he did not expect a woman.

As the doctor emerged, she said, "Good morning, Mr. Beecher. I'm so pleased to meet you. Your son has told me so much about you and your family. It's nice to actually see you in person."

Stan stood for a moment looking at the doctor. His face had slightly paled, and the smile with which he had entered had now vanished, and been replaced by a furrowed brow of concern. Small beads of perspiration were beginning to appear on his forehead.

Stan thought, "So, you've heard a lot about me and my family? This means John has already been talking to people here on at least one or two occasions; talking behind my back. Just what was it that he said? What does this doctor think? Does she think I'm already incompetent? Does she know any of my history, any of those problems these kids have been constantly throwing in my face? Has she any appreciation at all for what this has been like?"

A thousand questions and concerns were now running at high speed through Stan's mind, and he wished John had given him a little information about what he and this doctor had discussed. He wanted to know what ideas were already in this doctor's mind about him. He was also now afraid. What if he said something wrong, or forgot a detail that John had already told her? No, this was not what Stan had thought this meeting would be like. He would return to the car right now if that were an option.

"My name is Doctor Wu, I'm a neurologist here at the clinic, and what we are going to do today is just a few tests to see what kinds of issues you might be having. When we are done here, I am going to send you off to have some additional, more general health tests completed. What I hope to get over our time together is a complete picture of your overall health. Many times, when people are having troubles such as yours, it can be due to other more physically related items as opposed to something with the brain alone. We will want to rule out any of those other factors. Do you have any questions for me? Any concerns?"

"Any questions or concerns," Stan thought. "Are you kidding? I have a thousand questions and concerns! Just none that I can actually put into words; not that I would ask even if I could." So Stan gave what he thought was the usual answer; "No. I don't think so. If I think of something, I'll ask."

"OK, great. You're probably thinking most people don't know what to ask at this point anyway. We'll get started and just see how things go, OK?"

"Oh great," thought Stan. "The woman's a bloody mind reader as well. I better watch what the hell I even think around this joint."

Doctor Wu looked at John and said, "Mr. Beecher, you can leave now. Did you bring that list of all your father's medications and prescriptions I asked for? I'll need them. If you have your cell phone, just leave the number at the desk, and we'll give you a call when we're all wrapped up. I'll meet with you and your father again to go over where we stand. Do you have any questions for me before you leave?"

"No, I'm fine for now. I'll just leave you to it, and wait for a call. It was nice meeting you." John left, thinking to himself; finally. Finally we begin to get some answers.

Once John had left, Doctor Wu looked at Stan, smiled, and said, "In your own words, Stan, why don't you just tell me as best you can what it is you've been experiencing, and how that has been affecting your daily living."

"Jesus, where do I even begin," thought Stan; but begin he did. He related the way he lost his job, getting lost, and forgetting people's names. He said he had been having some balance issues, and didn't know if that had anything to do with it. He talked about his sleep problems, occasional disorientation, and periodic confusion.

Stan was asked about his diet, appetite, how much alcohol he drank, did he take any drugs or narcotic prescriptions; in other words, everything about his life.

Doctor Wu listened patiently. When Stan seemed to slow down, she said, "Tell me about your sleeplessness. Is that every night? Do you get up or just stay in bed? How long does it usually take before you can return to sleep?"

"No, not every night...but a lot of them. Sometimes I wake up several times. I have to use the bathroom, get a drink, look out the window, let Sandy out back - Sandy's my dog. I don't know how long it takes to get back to sleep. It varies I guess. Sometimes I don't seem to get back to sleep at all."

"I see. OK. Well, these issues have been going on how long?" Doctor Wu asked.

"I honestly don't know when they began. Like I said before, time is becoming a bit of an issue."

"Yes, of course. I understand. Well, what I want to do is conduct a few neurological tests, and see how we are doing there."

She went on to conduct some tests on balance, reflex action, coordination, and continued her exam with an MMSE, a Mini Mental State Exam. Stan answered a series of questions designed to provide a numeric assessment of his range of mental skills. He was asked to spell words backwards, count backwards by seven, name his children, tell her the date, and numerous others. Then Doctor Wu performed what she told Stan was, "a mini-cog; a brief test of some of his cognitive abilities." Those results would give her an idea of his memory ability.

"Mr. Beecher, I'm going to give the names of three fairly common things, then a little later, we will come back to them, and I'll ask you to give them back to me. Is that OK?"

"Of course it's OK." Stan did not think he was doing well at all. His initial fears were getting stronger. He decided to mask his fear through an attempt at humor.

"You do realize that my son never told me there was going to be a quiz today, so I haven't studied. Perhaps you should have sent out a little study guide to help me get ready."

Doctor Wu laughed. She knew these tests could be stressful. She had had patients who became angry, and sometimes even refused to take the tests. Stan was doing well, she thought.

"That's funny, Mr. Beecher. Your son told me you had a sense of humor, and you do." On she went with the tests. She asked Stan to remember, "The Washington Monument, 50 Chestnut Street, and guitar." She proceeded with a variety of other comments and information; then came back to the original three questions.

"Can you tell me back the things I asked you to remember, Stan?"

Stan said to himself, "no problem." But, as he started, he suddenly realized he wasn't sure. Panic. "Oh Jesus, Stan; come on!" he said to himself. "Uhhhhhh...let's see, then. There was something street. Chestnut, right? Yes...I'm pretty sure of that one."

"Do you remember the number, Stan?" Dr. Wu asked.

"Right. The number. Hmmm; to be honest, I'm not sure of that."

"OK," said Dr. Wu. "What about the other items? What do you remember of those?"

"OK...oh...wait. There was the Washington Monument. That was in there. Uhhhh...what else." Stan couldn't come up with the last one.

Doctor Wu stepped in to help. "Was it a flute, or a drum, or a guitar, or a piano?"

Still struggling, Stan said, Oh, right. Sure. "IIIIII think it was drum. Yes, drum."

"OK, then. We are getting to the end, Stan. You're doing fine. Just one more little item, and we're done here."

"Fine, my ass," said Stan to himself. "Total screw-up would be more like it."

"Stan, on this piece of paper, I just want you to draw me the face of a clock, and put the hands at 10:20. You think you can do that for me?"

"Thank God," Stan said to himself. "That's something I should be able to handle."

He sat down at a small table and began to draw. When he finished, he handed the paper over to the doctor, feeling fairly pleased, although the task hadn't been as easy as he had first imagined.

Dr. Wu looked at the clock he had drawn. Without saying a word, she looked back at Stan, and said, "OK, I'm going to have someone come up and get you so they can do the physical exam workup. That won't take too long, then we should be done for today."

Stan's clock was unusual. The face was close to a circle, but the numbers going around broke down when he got to 8 through 10. The numbers were there, but crowded, ill formed, and out of position. The hour hand was pointed correctly, but the minute hand was just a line that didn't reach the numbers. The doctor put Stan's drawing in her folder. She was eager to see the results of the physical exam, but she was going to want to do a brain MRI; or possibly even a PET scan before she reached any final conclusions. What she most wanted to see were the results of the genetic testing, but they wouldn't be available for a few days.

At the meeting later that day, John sat next to his father, as Doctor Wu unveiled her preliminary findings.

"Well, initially, we see some definite issues with Stan's memory function. He did well on some of the tests, but struggled with some of the others. I think we all expected that, or you probably wouldn't have come to see me. I am going to want to see the results of the other tests we did before I make any final diagnosis. We will also want to do some scans of Stan's brain which we can do fairly soon, so it won't delay things much longer."

She continued, "But, there are some other issues that seem to be present that I want to talk about today. Were you aware of the very high blood sugar you have, Stan? Your daily reading was 245 with an A1C at 8.6. Those are quite high."

"Not really. Never really thought about it."

"Yes, well, I'm a little surprised you are not experiencing more symptoms than you are. I'm also afraid that is not the only issue. We will of course have to do more tests, but initially it appears you might also have the onset of some early stage Parkinson's disease. That may be why you are having those balance issues and your gait is somewhat altered. My concern here is that between the Parkinson's and high blood sugars, is there any liver or kidney damage? Again, we need to do more tests, but these are all things about which we need a better understanding before we can move forward with any final conclusions."

John and Stan both sat in their chairs somewhat stunned by everything Doctor Wu was telling them. Finally, John asked a question. "What about the memory? Does my father have Alzheimer's or not?"

"As of today, I can't really answer that question. He clearly has some memory issues, but to make a final decision we need to have Stan come back to us in a few months so we can repeat our tests. We will then look at those results, and compare them with today. We will also have the genetic and scan results analyzed by that time. With everything, that will give us a more complete picture."

"In the meantime, I am going to give you a list of names of doctors in your area who can deal with the possible diabetes. Whomever you choose, they will want to do a glucose tolerance test, decide on what medications to prescribe, provide a nutrition plan, and then see your father on a regular basis. The doctors downstairs have already started your father on some medication to lower his current blood sugar, and we have a prescription you should fill right now. Stan, you know you need to get started on the sugar problem before you leave, right?"

Before his Dad could answer, John asked, "Is there a test for this Parkinson's you can give that will tell us if he has it or not?"

"Unfortunately, there is no conclusive lab test. I am recommending a local neurologist in Knoxville with whom you can follow up when you arrive back home. I want to reiterate, we are not certain Parkinson's is at issue here. At this point, it is just something I think should be further examined. The Knoxville neurologist and I will be in contact to coordinate everything we do."

"I know this is a lot to digest in one visit, and I wish I had better things to say, however, the good news is we are going to do what's best for Stan, and *we will* get things going in a better direction. You were wise to come; I think we all have some important, much needed information. I am going to make an appointment for you to see me again in six months. By that time, Mr. Beecher, we will have everything we need to give you some definitive answers." Dr. Wu was looking directly at Stan during this discussion to see if what she was saying seemed to be understood. Stan was nodding, but Dr. Wu was reasonably certain that at least some of her commentary had not really reached him.

As Doctor Wu concluded, Stan again had that feeling of total defeat. He wanted to keep a positive outlook, but at this point, there was very little sunshine. He wished Jenny had come. He didn't think it fair that she was not able to hear this from the doctor; maybe ask some questions she might have. She was going to be disappointed and angry.

Once the scans and other tests were completed over the following days, John and Stan drove to the airport for the trip back to Knoxville. Stan was not so worried about whatever the doctor had said about his blood sugar; he knew lots of people with sugar problems, and they functioned just fine. As for the other thing they were talking about, well, he guessed that was a bridge to be crossed later. As far as Stan was concerned, he had a little sugar problem and a memory problem. He would deal with it. He would be fine; and the family would be fine. As for now, he would just go back to his house, and life would go on.

6

Troubled Times

Jenny sat at her kitchen table, alone, angry, and afraid. Ever since John's first call from Baltimore, she had felt remorse that she had not been there with her father during what she knew was something that must have torn at his insides; it was certainly tearing at hers. She was furious with John for not having had sufficient understanding to know that for this, they all needed to be together. She was even angrier with herself for not simply going to the airport, purchasing a ticket, and insisting on attending with her father.

"Why didn't I just tell John I was going, and that was that? Why did I let *him* run the show? Am I not just as important a member of this family as he? In fact, isn't Stan Junior an equal member of the family? Why do I allow this?" Jenny almost shouted to herself. Her thoughts went back and forth as to whether she should release this pent up anger by venting it on her brother on his return, or avoid a scene, and simply vow to never again let it happen.

Jenny had come to the frightening realization that her father, at least from a mental standpoint, might not be with them much longer.

She could no longer live in the hope that all of this was temporary. No, the reports from John had brought her worst fears squarely to the fore. Her mind ran rampant with a million thoughts.

As she looked out her window, she recalled so many happy times, so much family history, so much love. She thought to herself that, like everyone, she had taken for granted all the many special times and memories; they were simple but wonderful times. Jenny thought back to when she was a little girl, and had come home to announce she had received a part in the class play. The look of pride on her Dad's face, and the way he and her mother made her feel the achievement was so exceptional. The next day, her mother and she baked a special cake to celebrate the occasion. They wrote, "Congratulations Jenny...Our Favorite Actress" on top. When it was brought to the table, her father made one of his famous announcements.

Tapping his glass with a spoon, he proclaimed, "I hope everyone at this table appreciates what Jenny has accomplished! She has provided an occasion for which a cake has been specially prepared by our *two* master cake-bakers, and now we can all celebrate her marvelous accomplishment. I am especially happy, because as everyone knows, I am a cake eating specialist! So thank you Jenny, you are the best daughter ever."

Jenny also recalled a dinner announcement that did not receive quite as warm a reception. She was 15, and she was in love!

"I just wanted to let everyone know, I have a boyfriend who I just love to pieces!" Jenny announced with fanfare and enthusiasm.

The silence that followed was indelibly marked in her memory. She had expected everyone to be thrilled for her; that did not happen. No, her father and mother simply stared across the table at one another for what seemed a very long time. Jenny smiled at the memory. Finally, her Dad spoke. It was a comment so full of wisdom; so filled with insight, so apropos to the moment, so brilliant a response. Jenny would never forget it.

"Marilyn, I do believe this is *your* department." That was it. That was it?

Her mother looked Jenny in the eye, then said, "Well, dear. Then we shall have to talk about this after dinner, and you will tell me all about this young man."

As it turned out, the romance had a very short life. Within the week, Jenny was in her room crying her eyes out. It seemed the "new boyfriend" had invited one of her girlfriends to a pool party given by a mutual friend. Such betrayal could not, and would not be tolerated. It was over. Her life was over. She would never be happy again.

Luckily, her mother was there to calm the waters. Jenny was once again made assistant chef to help with the dinner arrangements. "And we will say no more about this boy who has given up the most wonderful girl he will ever meet!" announced her mother with finality.

Her father's role in this scenario, and she was certain the two of them had cooked up the entire plot in advance, was to gush over whatever things Jenny had had a hand in making. Nothing was to be said of the aforementioned boyfriend. Her father played his role perfectly, although Jenny always suspected that inside, her father was quite happy the entire thing had ended.

And finally there was the love of her life, Jimmy. She still laughed to herself about announcing he was an African American. Her father's look was absolutely priceless. And Mom had been an absolute jewel. Best of all, her father and mother later took Jimmy into the family like a son. Jimmy came over for meals, allowed himself to be tortured by her brother with stories of school or birds, helped her father and brother assemble a bird feeder for the back yard; it was a special time. These remembrances made Jenny smile.

Jenny had always had a softer, more fragile side to her. Her father catered to that. He might have scolded John for some misdeed, but if Jenny committed the same offense, her father simply spoke with her to "help her understand how to do things better in the future." This seeming "favoritism" made John furious. On the other hand, it was perfectly fine as far as Jenny was concerned.

All these thoughts were running through Jenny's mind this morning. She could not wait to see her father, and give him a big hug. She wanted to make sure he knew she was going to be there for the long term. She would stand with him no matter what came their way. She hoped he knew that already. Jenny was ready for whatever lay ahead. At least, so she thought.

*****

The plane landed on time at 12:15; Jenny and Stan Junior were waiting. Even though John had suggested she simply wait in the car outside the baggage claim area to pick them up, Jenny had parked in short term parking, and went as close to the boarding area as security allowed. She didn't want her father to arrive without family to provide a cheerful welcome home.

Jenny had not told Stan Junior too much about what she knew of her father's declining health. She simply told him the doctors were still working on the report, and they would know more soon. She also mentioned that the trip had been very tiring for their father, and perhaps he could save his questions about the visit to another time. Stan Junior was fine with that idea; he just wanted to see his father.

The two of them stood at the end of the long greenway and waterfall area of McGee Tyson Airport, but Jenny was like a child waiting for Santa. Finally, her father emerged through the security area, and she ran all the way up the corridor to throw her arms around him. Even though it had only been a few days, Jenny was happy to have this behind them, and have her father home again.

Stan, in his usual way of trying to dismiss problems so they wouldn't feel so troublesome to others, said,

"What's all this? Did I miss something? Gracious, it was only a few days up in Baltimore with Dr. Ming."

Dr. Ming. Jenny just laughed to herself at her father's way of renaming people to an uncomplimentary fictional or historical character to amuse himself. In this case, he was referring to an evil villain from one his favorite boyhood TV shows, *Flash Gordon*. In that program, there was a character named, *Ming the Merciless* who ruled some evil planet in the universe. Now, it seemed, that wicked ruler had been reincarnated in the person of poor Doctor Wu. Jenny was secretly smiling.

When they arrived home, everyone got out, and helped Dad get his things into the house. Once everything was settled, they sat in the living room talking a while longer.

"Well, kids. Your Dad is a bit pooped from all this travel. And Dr. Ming really put me through my paces, so if you don't mind, I'd like to have a little nap. I hope no one minds." Stan wasn't all that tired, but he just wanted to be alone.

Jenny wondered if he would be all right by himself, if this was a good time to leave him alone. She thought a second, then said: "Sure, Dad, let me get John and Stan Junior home. You can rest up. I'll go get Sandy, and bring her back. Do you want to have dinner over at my house tonight? I could make meat loaf or something."

"No, no. I'll just make myself some of that vegetable soup I'm trying to get rid of in the cupboard. But yes, bring Sandy back on your next trip. I miss her."

With that Stan got up, and started toward the bedroom. Jenny had not previously noticed, but her father used much of the room furniture and wall to steady himself on the way. Once he got going, he seemed fairly well balanced, but in those first moments after getting up, he seemed to need help. Everyone collected their things, and made their way to the car. As Jenny backed out of the driveway onto the street, she stopped and looked at John.

"Now!" she said with finality; "When we get back to my house, you come in, and we can have a little talk about *everything* that went on up at John's Hopkins. I want to know what Dad said, how he felt, what the doctor said, what's going to happen with the doctors here in Knoxville; EV-ER-Y-THING!" Jenny was in no mood for any nonsense, or vague answers from her brother. She wanted to be part of things going forward, and was not about to take no for an answer. This was to be the beginning of a new era of her involvement in the Beecher family.

*****

Jenny had called her husband, Jimmy, earlier in the day to ask that he come home early. She wanted him present for the discussion she planned to have with John. She trusted his medical expertise, and knew if John related something she didn't understand; it was likely Jimmy could clarify the information. Seeing Jimmy's truck in the driveway gave Jenny a sense of relief.

She alerted John, "I hope you don't mind, but I asked Jimmy to sit in with us because he might be able to add more detail on Dad's condition. I want him to help us understand what we can do to help."

John had no problem with that; in fact he expected Jimmy would be there.

"No, no problem. In fact, I have a few questions for your husband myself. Dr. Wu gave us the big picture, but not a lot of specifics. I was hoping Jimmy could fill in the blanks."

Everyone entered the house, and once they were seated Jenny said, "OK...John; tell us exactly what Dr. Wu said, and where we are with Dad. I know we've already talked a little, but let's go over it again."

"OK," John said. "First and foremost, Dad did not do that well on the neurological and memory tests she performed. I won't bore you with all the names, but it was obvious he had trouble with some of it. Dr. Wu said it was nothing startling, but there is no doubt he is suffering memory loss. She is going to do a follow up with the same tests, then she can tell us exactly where he is. She never used the word, 'Alzheimer's,' and when I tried to pin her down, she dodged the question."

Jimmy was curious about this lack of clarity and asked, "Did she say where Stan is as compared to normal levels right now? Did she talk about whether he is still in position to handle daily living? I know we've all been seeing some indications that he doesn't always take care of everything. Yet, when I talk to him, he seems pretty good for the most part. Actually, his mind seems about the way it's always been some of the time."

"No," John answered. "She didn't seem overly concerned about safety or things like that, or if she was, she didn't mention it."

"OK," Jimmy responded. "I don't know what you see when you go, but I try to stop in over there a few times a week, and to be honest, my biggest concerns are the lack of housekeeping, maybe some of personal hygiene, and his eating habits. I don't think it's so much that he is forgetting, he just doesn't seem to care enough to stay on top of those things. What do you think?"

"I think Jenny and I see the same thing as you, Jimmy. Would you agree, Jenny?"

"Of course, all that stuff has gone noticeably downhill, although, if he thinks someone is coming, or there is some reason to straighten up, then he does it. So, he's capable, but perhaps not very motivated. But, I want to hear about this other stuff, like the diabetes and Parkinson's," Jenny concluded.

"Right," said John. "To be honest, I don't know a lot about it, and frankly, the doctor didn't really say all that much either. She said his A1C was high, and thought he almost definitely has Type II diabetes. She suggested he work with his doctor to get that reviewed with something called a 'glucose tolerance test.'"

Jimmy added, "That's just the measure of long-term sugar levels, Jenny. Anything over about 6.8 is a kind of red flag. Over 8 is a big warning flag."

John added, "Yes, well Dad's was 8.6, so mark that with a big red flag."

John continued, "As for the Parkinson's possibility, well that came out of her neurological tests, and the fact that his gait isn't quite right. He also lost his balance on some of her tests. She did say, those problems could be due to other things, but she thought we should follow up. She *didn't* say he had Parkinson's. I think we should make an appointment for Dad with the neurologist she suggested. What do you guys think?"

John made certain to ask Jenny's opinion this time before making that appointment on his own. He didn't need to have his head bitten off again for failing to include her in the decision.

Jenny looked over at Jimmy and said, "No, I agree. Jimmy can research the doctor, but I'm pretty sure if he works with us, he's good. So, then, we're agreed so far that we are making an appointment with Dad's regular doctor for the sugar, and we are making a neurologist appointment for the Parkinson's. John, if you want, you can make Dad's regular doctor appointment, that would be good. Jimmy and I can make the neurologist appointment at Parkwest. Sometimes, if they see it's a staff member, you get head of the line treatment. That just leaves one other issue."

Jimmy looked at his wife quizzically, "What issue?"

"Do we want to get Dad some help with the daily housekeeping?" Jenny asked, looking directly at her brother. "I'm thinking perhaps someone from 'Home Helping Hands,' or some outfit like that wouldn't be a bad idea. They could come in, and straighten out stuff, maybe once a week."

John heard the magic words for which he had been waiting. He had wanted to get someone in his father's house to help for some time. He was getting worn out going over there four and five times a week to check on things. In addition, he was hearing complaints from Linda about the amount of time spent at his father's. John thought that with a daily person, they could all feel safer, and his personal visits could be substantially reduced. That would make his life considerably more bearable.

"Actually, Jenny, you and I are on the same page with that. Dad needs daily assistance, and this is the perfect time to get that started. Instead of just a cleaning service, however, I think we need a little more."

Jenny sat back in her chair, and tried to slow her brother down. "Wait a second, John. You know something like that is *not* going to fly with Dad. If there is anything he guards more closely than his independence, I don't know what it is. I think he will give that idea thumbs down right from the get-go." She looked at Jimmy with that, "give me some support here" look.

Jimmy took his cue, and joined the debate. "Yeah, John...you know your father better than me, but I don't think he'll go for someone hanging around his house all day, every day. Even the housekeeping might be a hard sell."

John was not about to give up, and tried to salvage the idea, "I know. I know. Dad can be a little difficult on this stuff at times, but suppose you let me float these ideas, and see how things work out. It couldn't hurt, and to be honest, it would take a lot of pressure off the rest of us in making Dad's life better. Can you just let me try?"

Somehow, Jenny felt that she was once again being led down a path she didn't want to take. John was steering this in his own direction, but she didn't see a logical way to just nix the idea out of hand.

"OK, John; but be gentle! Dammit...do not go in there, and steamroll Dad on this. I'm telling you now, tread lightly," Jenny sternly warned, looking at Jimmy for his agreement and support.

John heard his sister, but he had a plan. Now, he had his sister's reluctant agreement to put his plan in action.

*****

Stan was in the backyard playing catch with Sandy when John arrived with Idnama from the Daily Home Care agency. Because her African name was often too hard to pronounce, she went by the name of Edna. Edna had arrived from Nigeria with her husband who was working on temporary assignment with the Alcoa Corporation. She was a pleasant woman in her early 40's, a bit heavy set, and a lilting accent. She understood English fairly well, but the spoken word was a bit more challenging. She wore a plain print housedress, small black hat, no makeup, and her black hair was pulled back into a tight bun. She had a pretty smile she used when she didn't understand what was being said, and she was clearly nervous about making a good impression.

As Stan entered his kitchen from the mud room, he spotted Edna immediately.

"Good morning, John; and just who is this we have here with us to brighten up my day?"

John was nervous, but there was no backing down at this point. "This is Idnama, but she goes by her American name of Edna. I think Jenny called, and told you we would try and get someone to help around the house for you, remember?"

"I do," Stan said with a voice containing just a hint of exasperation. "In fact, I remember very clearly. It was just a 'housekeeping' person, perhaps one day a week, am I right John?"

"Well yes," John said, almost dismissively. "But Edna can do other things as well, and she will be a great ..."

"Like what," Stan angrily blurted, cutting off the end of John's sentence.

"Well...for instance, she can do a bit of cooking, look after Sandy now and again, make sure laundry is up and going - things like that. She could be a big help for you."

"Uh huh...I see. Well, tell you what, son. If and when I *need* someone to come in here, and run my life for me, and be that *big help* you're so anxious to install here, I'll let you know. In the meantime there Edna you can just trot right back down the walk, and I'm sure John will be happy to take you back to wherever it is he got you."

Edna stood still, looking at John for her next set of directions. She was in the middle of a crossfire she wanted no part of. She was frightened and uncomfortable. Edna was afraid of this loud, rough man. Worse, she was afraid she would lose her job before it even started. She could not go home to her husband, and tell him she was fired after only one day. That would be too much shame to bear. She looked at John for any sign of encouragement. None was there.

"Look, Dad. We've already paid for the first month, so could you just work with us a little and try it out? This is really not going to be too much of an inconvenience, is it Dad? I mean, you might even find you like it."

"You what!" Stan fired back. "You prepaid the month?" He looked at John while shaking his head, "And here I thought *you* were the one in this family who was supposed to be so smart with other people's money! Obviously not! You know, John; I'm finding all this crap pretty unbelievable. I'm being pushed and pulled like some kind of five year old, and then you wonder why I get pissed off sometimes. IT'S SHIT LIKE THIS!" Stan screamed at his son.

Edna jumped; then moved another step toward the door. Poor Sandy ran in the kitchen with her tail between her legs, and hid on her bed.

"I hear you, Dad. But it's just a trial. We just want you to see what a help she can be."

Stan sighed a very long sigh, and looked his son straight in the eye. "Have you ever heard the Arab expression; '*The camel's nose under the tent?*' I think the meaning should be self explanatory to anyone with an expensive college education like you; and just by the way, an education I paid good money for! And just so you understand; I *know* what this is, so don't walk out of here thinking you got one over on the old man. Dammit, but you make me mad!" he shouted again as Edna moved even closer toward the door, and Sandy continued hiding but was now shaking as well.

Stan was not done. He now turned his attention and anger onto poor Edna.

"And as for you; we are going to get a few ground rules straight right from the get-go."

"First and foremost, you stay the hell out of my hair. If I'm in the kitchen over here, you *are not* in the kitchen. I like my space, and I don't need you trying to vacuum under my feet, or scare Sandy with some God damned mop routine. Got it?"

Edna thought so, but she looked over at John in case there was a clarification. Clearly, Mr. Stan did not want her scaring the dog. She would be careful.

"Second," Stan continued in his raised, aggravated voice. "You keep your hands off my shit, and don't start moving things around, or trying to find 'better places to put things.' What looks out of place to you is obviously just fine with me...so leave it the hell alone!"

"Yes, Mr. Stan. I not move your shit."

John, just rolled his eyes, and thought, by the time his father finished all the ground rules, Edna would be left sitting on the porch all day because there was nowhere in the house she was allowed to be.

"Good," said Stan. "And you, John...just so you know, this is a sneaky plan you and your sister dreamed up. *Housekeeper, my ass!*"

"You do realize," Stan went on with his rant, "I used to put con artists like you away for a lot less than this shit you're pulling on me."

"Oh no," John thought. "I can't let Dad get rolling on his police stories. I'll never get out of here."

"OK, OK, OK, Dad. I know. But, I have to get going. Edna will be picked up at 5, so you don't need to worry about her getting home."

"Her getting home?" Stan laughed indignantly. "I'm not worried about *her* getting home. I'm worried about *her getting* OUT of *my* home. Jeez, but you are slow on the draw!"

John thanked Edna for coming, and quietly suggested she just take things slowly, and just do what she saw most needed attention. He said goodbye to his father, and quickly retreated down the steps to his car. He looked forward to the safety and peace afforded by his office.

As soon as John was out of the driveway, Stan called his daughter to give her a piece of his mind.

Jenny was at work, so had to let her father's call go to voicemail. It was a wonder the battery didn't melt down.

"Jenny! My favorite daughter," Stan sarcastically began. "Nicely done; sneaking the home care nurse in here. *You* tell me, 'Ohhhh, Daddy, it's just a little housekeeper a couple of days a week,'" Stan mimicked in a little girl's voice. "Next thing I know, I have a wet nurse on a daily basis from 9 – 5 PM putting her nosey-Parker beak into all my business! Thanks you two. Great job, just great. Thanks."

With that, Stan rang off thinking, "I hope those two are happy now. A baby sitter for Dad is obviously just what that damnable Dr. Ming convinced them I needed!"

When Jenny picked up her voicemail, her temper once again went through the roof! She called Jimmy, and begged him to come down to her office before she screamed down the cubicle. Jimmy didn't know what had happened, but whatever it was, he knew he needed to get down there as soon as he could wrap up what he was doing.

Once there, Jimmy listened for a while, then when Jenny began to run out of angry steam, he tried to smooth things over as best he could. Only Jimmy could handle Jenny at times like this, and it was a blessing to everyone he had that ability.

"OK, Jenny. You have every right to feel taken advantage of. Your brother obviously overstepped his authority again. But if we think about it a second, a day time home care person might not be all that bad right now, don't you think? I mean, she can take care of a lot of things that really need to be done, and give you a break. *If* your Dad will accept it, and for right now it seems he has, even though not all that happily, then maybe this can work out. Let's not start any more turmoil over this, all right, Sweetheart?"

As Jenny regained her composure and thought about it, her husband had made some good points. She decided to tell John he overstepped his authority, but not make a federal case of it. Besides, when Jimmy called her "Sweetheart" like that, she was putty in his hands.

The day, it seemed, ended fairly well. The only person unhappy with the situation was Stan Senior. One question remained, however; how long could this arrangement last?

*****

Stan began to mellow somewhat with regard to Edna. She was extraordinarily kind to both him and Sandy, which took the edge off his initial sour demeanor.

"Mr. Stan, you think OK, if maybe I take little Sandy out for walk. She standing by door with rope again; maybe she have to go," Edna would ask.

Stan hated her accent at first, but it was beginning to grow on him. Of course, that did not stop Stan from playing jokes or having fun at Edna's expense.

"Little Sandy, as you like to call her, *always* has to go if there is some *sap* willing to take her out. In this case, that *sap* would be *you*, wouldn't it, Edna?"

"OK, Mr. Stan. I be the sap and take her out; it nice out, anyway."

Stan just chuckled, and went back to his puzzle. Lately, Stan had bought a number of brain work exercises to try and keep his mind alert. He felt if he kept up on those, perhaps when he had to go see Dr. Ming, he would do better than on his last visit. The next visit was not far away. Stan was determined not to let this Alzheimer's, or whatever they decided it was, get the best of him without a fight.

*****

Edna arrived at her usual time, and entered the house to the greeting of Sandy hopping on hind legs near the door, wanting to go out for her walk. Edna called out to alert Stan she had arrived.

"Mr. Stan. Mr. Stan. It's me Edna. I here for you to maybe have breakfast or I take Miss Sandy out for walk," but she heard no answer.

Stan was silent, and not yet out of his room; however, the door was open as Edna walked down the hall toward his bedroom. When she arrived at his door, she saw Stan standing in front of his mirror dressed in a pair of grey sweatpants and a blue tee-shirt with "KPD" in yellow block letters written on the back. This was Stan's normal sleepwear. The lights were out, contributing an air of sadness to the room. Without looking away from the mirror, Stan began to speak in a soft voice that resonated with both dejection and resignation.

Without looking in her direction, but continuing to stare into the mirror, Stan said, "You know, Edna, everywhere I go, I see people - lots of people," he said drawing out the word 'lots.' "All these people just hurrying on by, going places, doing things...having some kind of purpose to their day. All people who have something to do - you know, a future, hopes, a life of some sort."

Stan suddenly stopped and breathed a heavy sigh before he continued. Edna thought to herself, "Mr. Stan so sad today. His spirit is broken."

Stan looked down from the mirror, as he did so a tear fell from his eye onto the dresser top. He looked back up, still never glancing toward Edna as he continued.

"But when I look in this mirror, I don't see someone with hope or a future. I see someone with no future at all...no hope of anything. In fact, I not only have no future, in a little while, it's possible I won't even have a past...at least not one I can remember. That's me. That's what I've become..."

Edna felt an overwhelming sense of grief for him. Was there nothing she could do to bring at least some sense of happiness to Stan's day? Actually, the answer was no. All she could do for him, all anyone could do for him, was to be there to help him cope with whatever the day's next event might be. No matter what anyone else did, it was Stan who had to live with the reality of what he was becoming. In that sad moment, Edna felt her own eyes mist over with tears, her own spirit suffering with Stan's.

*****

The flight was scheduled to leave for Washington at 10:15 AM. This time it would be Jenny and John both who would accompany Stan to John's Hopkins. While in Knoxville, Stan had been to his own doctor for the diabetes, and also had seen the neurologist from Parkwest several times. There was no doubt Stan had diabetes. The doctor had put him on a regimen of Victoza and Metformin to control the spiking blood sugars. Since going on the medication, along with a more stringent diet, his blood sugar had receded considerably. The only issue was ensuring that Stan took the medication at the appropriate times. Edna was helping with that task, although things were not always easy.

"Mr. Stan; you do your Victoza this morning? I see pen still in holder," she would ask.

"For the love of God, Edna! Could you give me a chance to get my underwear on straight before you set the damnable medication police on me?"

"OK, Mr. Stan. I no call police. You need me come in and help straighten underwear?"

A loud sigh was heard from inside the bedroom. Stan was never one to be reminded of things left undone, particularly if in fact he actually had forgotten them.

"The Parkinson's medication," he thought. "Where the hell was that, and did I already take it? Damn, but it was getting confusing with all these medications. Edna will have to sort this out," he concluded. The Parkinson's was not a confirmed diagnosis, but the local neurologist explained that he had a number of indicators that suggested this might be the problem. In the meantime, the doctor had prescribed two medications that would help reduce the symptoms if indeed it was Parkinson's. Should that medication now be successful, it was a good indicator that he was suffering from the disease. As with the original examination for Alzheimer's, the final diagnosis was yet to be made.

*****

Jenny sat next to her father during the flight. The two of them exchanged small talk about Stan's granddaughter, Kendra, the way things were going with Edna at the house, and where they would stay when they got to Baltimore. For a majority of the flight, however, Stan worked on his puzzle book.

As they arrived at Bayview that afternoon, Jenny was thinking what a nice facility it was. They immediately proceeded to the doctor's suite where they were warmly greeted by Dr. Wu.

"Good afternoon, Mr. Beecher, how have you been? I must say, you look terrific. Now, I already know John, but is this your daughter?" Dr. Wu inquired.

"It is," Stan replied. "She wanted to come see first-hand what's been draining her inheritance."

A big concern for John was the possibility of his father calling Dr. Wu by the name Dr. Ming. Stan had gotten into such a habit of calling her by that name, John was certain a slip up might happen. Usually, these nicknames were funny and no problem, but today John warned his Dad to be watchful, and not insult the Doctor, a point to which Stan took strong exception.

"John, give me a break. Why do you always have to imply that I'm some kind of forgetful nitwit? I've been in law enforcement, and working with the public for over forty years. Do you think I don't know how to deal with people? Let's try this: how about you give me a little credit for *not* being an idiot."

Dr. Wu went around the group to ask their assessment of how things were going. Had they noticed any new concerns, or seen any signs of improvement? Neither Jenny nor John was able to say they had seen anything remarkable in either direction. The doctor moved quickly on to the subject of the diabetes, and how that was proceeding. Stan jumped in at that point.

"I think we have that one taken care of with the medication. I just went to the doctor before we came up here, and the ..." Stan had to stop; he now wasn't sure just what it was the doctor told him other than it had improved.

John stepped in to help his father. "He said the A1C was down to 6.3, and the daily blood sugars were normally under 150."

"Right, that was it. Thanks, John," his father added. "And why shouldn't they be better? Between Edna and the medicine police, along with the food detectives, it seems I can't eat *anything* anymore. Go ahead. See if you can find even as much as a damned potato chip at my place. Good luck. For snacks, me and Sandy eat Milk Bones on the sly. Pathetic, doc, freaking pathetic!"

Sensing frustration, Dr. Wu moved on. The last thing she wanted was an agitated patient during the neurological tests she planned to administer.

"Right; well, that's all good then, Mr. Beecher. Good for you. But let me move on to what your local neurologist and I have been talking about since last time. The first thing is, we both see strong indication you may have early Parkinson's. That is something we both agreed should get intervention. I know he has prescribed some medication for you to take. But I also have another more immediate concern. Your recent blood work showed elevated readings of both creatinine and potassium. This can sometimes be an indication your kidney function has been affected. Again, we will keep a very close check on this to ensure that we are providing sound care. Does everyone understand all this?"

Jenny had now moved past concerned. "Wait. So what you are saying is that Dad has damaged kidneys in addition to the diabetes, memory issues, and probable Parkinson's? How serious is all this? It sounds like an awful lot!"

Dr. Wu nodded and understood the concern this information had generated.

"Yes, well I understand; it is a lot going on at once. Let me assure you, however, we deal with multiple issues all the time. It can be done, and it can be done safely. Because we found all this now, in the early stages, we are in an excellent position to take very positive steps. We will all just need to recognize the importance of being watchful. Diligence with his medication schedule, as well as follow up visits to the doctor will all help."

Jenny nodded yes, but John stayed quiet. John's thoughts went toward just how much care was going to be required down the road. His wife, Linda, was still on his back about the amount of time he had to spend tending to his father's care and looking in on Edna. She constantly reminded him of just how that was affecting the perception of his superiors at work. If these new revelations meant even more time away from his office, it couldn't help but have a negative effect. That would not be good.

Dr. Wu wanted to turn her attention to Stan, who had become quiet during this discussion. His silence was not because he was disinterested, but rather the conversation was moving too fast for him to keep up.

"Well, everyone; it's time that Stan and I work together for a while. So, if you would just excuse us, John, I will have the desk give you a call when we're ready to get back together. It shouldn't be that long."

John and Jenny left, and went to the cafeteria for coffee. Both were concerned, but their reasons for concern were quite different. John knew that when he explained all this to Linda, she would begin harassing him again to look into an assisted living arrangement. John also knew Jenny was going to resist that idea. He would be caught in the middle of a complete firestorm.

"I don't know about you, John, but I could use a stiff drink after all that. Doesn't all this make you nervous? You seem so quiet, so...I don't know...nonchalant, I guess."

John corrected his sister; "Jenny, you couldn't be more wrong. I'm sure I'm just as concerned as you. I just want to hear what the doctor has to say after this exam. If Dad has Alzheimer's, we need to know definitively. This other stuff is just medical, and I think they know how to deal with it. Multiple health issues are Dr. Wu's specialty. Where we are with the Alzheimer's, that's what has *me* worried."

*****

Dr. Wu began gently with Stan. She knew he was already under a great deal of stress, and the revelations of the last half hour had done nothing to ease his mind.

She smiled at Stan, and asked, "So, Stan; it's just us now. Why don't you tell me how you think things have been going? Are there any changes? Are you doing anything differently?"

Stan had the answer to that question ready; "HA! A *lot* has changed since last time. First off, I now have a full time nursemaid watching my every damn move. If I put on the coffee maker, she's in there telling me she can do it. Dammit; if I wanted her to do it, I would have asked. I get treated like I'm four years old!! I put up with it to keep peace, but I don't like it one damn bit. I mean, the lady is nice and all, I don't dislike her. I just dislike being judged an incompetent asshole." Then Stan thought about what he had said. "Oh, sorry about that...I didn't mean to swear."

"It's OK, Mr. Beecher. I think I heard that one somewhere before, but go on, what else is happening?"

"I guess you know my son stole my car keys. I'm not allowed to drive anymore. Between Edna and my kids you would be amazed at all the stuff they are stealing out of my house. I have to hide things I want so no one takes them. On top of that, I had to sign some power of attorney thing so John could do my bills and all that house crap. I'm not even in charge of that anymore. I'm bloody well housebound except for walks with Sandy. Did I tell you about her? She's my dog. Great dog. Anyway, I can't do anything without some nosey Parker getting in my business. It damn well pisses me off when I think about it."

"Sometimes our family tries to act in our best interest, and instead of helpful it can seem intrusive. They are trying to be helpful, though, and I'm sure that's the case here. How about your memory, Stan? Is there anything to report there?"

"Hell, I don't know, doc. The guards on the watchtower could probably tell you more than me. I will tell you, I have started doing puzzles, and I'm trying to stay on top of this. Some of them I can do pretty well, but a lot of them...well, I don't know, the brain goes on strike or something. To be honest with you, a couple of the books somehow mysteriously flew across the room on their own, if you know what I mean."

Dr. Wu chuckled with Stan. "Yes, I know precisely what you mean. I myself have wanted to do that to several New York Times Crossword Puzzles."

"How about we just proceed, and redo some of those little tests we did last time? We won't do anything new, just the same kinds of questions. Do you remember last time? I gave you three objects to remember. Let me give you three new ones now, later we will come back, and ask you to give them back to me. Are you ready?"

Stan simply nodded. He was as ready as last time, and he remembered how that had turned out.

"OK. Here they are: *Ed Leonard......91 Belleview Avenue...... toaster.* Did you hear all those correctly, Stan?"

Again, Stan nodded. The fact was, however, he was already unsure of the name she had given. "Ed something," he recalled to himself.

Dr. Wu conducted all the same tests from their first meeting, interjected some conversation, and then came back to her list.

"OK, Stan. Can you tell me the things I asked you to remember?"

Stan just looked at her, and thought. He thought hard. Finally, he shook his head, no.

"Ed?" he said. "I think maybe the last one was oven - something to do with the kitchen, I know that."

Dr. Wu, gave him a few hints to help jog his memory. Stan added some detail that showed he had remembered some things, but specifics were lacking. Dr. Wu asked him to draw the clock face again. As was the case on his last visit, the basics were there, but not everything was positioned properly. There were also some psycho-motor issues in drawing the circle.

Dr. Wu concluded her tests, then brought everyone back into the office for their post observation meeting.

John was first to speak. "Well, Doc; what's the verdict?

Dr. Wu didn't want to keep anyone in further suspense. "I've completed all our tests, the other doctors and I have reviewed all your Dad's brain scans, plus the results of the genetics test. As I'm sure we all suspected, your father is currently suffering from late-onset Alzheimer's. It's past the early stages, but at this point is only moderate. I must add, however, he is still pretty alert and competent at times as I'm sure you've probably seen. I'm afraid that will decline in the coming months, and even more over time."

Dr. Wu went into a more complete explanation of the genetics results, and the fact that there are two basic types of Alzheimer's disease, one being "early-onset Alzheimer's" and the other, "late-onset Alzheimer's." She went on to explain both are brought on by the development of amyloid plaques and neurofibrillary tangles which is simply the loss of connections between nerve cells in the brain. The plaques, which normal brains break down, build up in Alzheimer's patients, and layer themselves to inhibit transfer of information across neurons. The neurofibrillary tangles wrap themselves around the nerves and kill them. Together, they slowly choke off the brain's ability to transmit signals and function. Late-onset Alzheimer's, which affects people over 60 and is their father's condition, has a genetic link. In their father's case, he has something called an APOE 4 allele on chromosome 19 which shows up in a significant portion of the late-onset Alzheimer's cases. Currently science doesn't know the precise mechanism by which this allele contributes to the disease, but there is strong evidence that the onset of Alzheimer's is a combination of this genetic tendency, environmental factors, and the general condition of the patient. In their father's case, the medical staff has looked at the scans, and his brain already shows signs of these deteriorations, as well as some diminishment in the hippocampus portion of his brain. She explained that the hippocampus is a small area of the brain that is important to the transfer of information from short-term to long-term memory. It also has an effect on spatial interpretation.

Dr. Wu looked at each person in the room, then said what everyone had feared: "There is no doubt. This is Alzheimer's."

Jenny listened carefully and thought how much she wished Jimmy was here to make sense of all this.

Jenny pleaded, "But there is medicine he can take to slow this down, right? There are things that will help him lead a reasonably normal life for a while longer. I've heard that...."

Dr. Wu interjected. "I hear what you're asking Jenny, and yes, there are some medications we can offer. You need to understand, however, these are not cures, nor do they really slow things down in any material way. They help relieve some of the symptoms, and you might see a difference in the overall function of his memory for a while. Just understand that everyone is different. There is no timetable, no special remedies I can offer. Stan will proceed at his own rate, and in his own way. Family, on the other hand, can be very important to help him along in daily life. I know you are already doing a great deal. I wish all my patients had the kind of family support Stan has."

Dr. Wu sat silently for a moment; then looked over at John and Jenny as she gently moved ahead with even more disheartening news. She set her pen and the charts down for the moment, and sat forward in her chair.

"But there is one more matter I need to draw to your attention before we go on with our meeting today. I mentioned earlier that Alzheimer's has a definite genetic link, and this means it can be transmitted across generations. Because it is carried on one of your father's chromosomes, there is a 50-50 chance this gene was also transmitted to any children."

Jenny took a deep breath and almost immediately blurted out, "You mean John and I could also have Alzheimer's?"

Dr. Wu tried to lessen the blow of this unexpected news as best she could.

"Well, you don't have Alzheimer's now, that's for certain. It is entirely possible you don't even carry the *APOE-4* allele. There is a test to tell if you do, but I should tell you that you are under no obligation to have that test done. Many people do not have the test done until much later. I'm just telling you the option is there should you want to rule out the possibility that you possess the *APOE-4* allele. But, I also want to add that you are both very young, and even if you should test positive, there are years ahead before you would experience any symptoms. A lot can happen over that time, and this could become a non-issue. I would suggest you just think about this for a while, then get back to me, and let me know how you would like to move forward."

This news was not something anyone had considered to this point. Jenny's hands were now visibly shaking as she tried to process what this all meant. John's mind was racing as well. Oddly, it was Stan who seemed the most calm. He just stared at Dr. Wu.

"Even my children might have this," he thought.

Stan had come to the realization that fate was now dictating the way forward, and there were no alternatives. His remaining life was mapped out; he was now on a journey with only one path and one destination. Even worse, he now had the added burden of knowing that he might well have passed this on to his children. As Stan sat there he began talking silently to himself.

"This is like a bad dream, but somehow I never expected this would happen to me. I am now in the full time business of forgetting. I'm like that big oak outside the house losing its leaves until it's bare; only in my case I'm losing my memories. I will slowly forget all those things that were always so important; they will now become unimportant. They will be gone. Will I even forget the people in my life? My family? That's what I've heard. Will I gradually just forget myself into nonexistence? Is that possible? I wonder, how long do I have? My God, I want to see my little Kendra grow up. I'm not that old! I want to do more things! How did my life get here? How did it get to this awful place? I just want to go home."

Jenny was the first to notice; it was something she had not seen a very long time. Her father's eyes were full, and tears were running down his cheeks. Those tears were the last straw; she was doing everything possible not to weep as she went over and held onto her father. John moved closer and held them both. It was perhaps as sad a day as any of them had known in a very long time.

*****

The air in John's hotel room was full of gloom. His Dad was in the bed across from him, possibly sleeping, but John could not be certain. It didn't matter. As he stood looking out his window with the rain pelting against its glass, the only thing on his mind was how totally out of control everything in his life seemed at this moment. He had a father who he knew was going to need ever increasing levels of care, a potential health crisis of his own with which he was yet to deal, and the uncertainty of a future that had once seemed so full of potential and prosperity. Everything was now enveloped in a shroud of ambiguity.

Jenny had ceased crying hours ago. She was lying on her bed in the darkened room listening to the rain. The muted sound and light from the TV was her only companion. Her hour-long call to her husband had only a marginal effect in bringing her runaway emotions under control. Somehow, Jimmy had always been able to quiet Jenny's fears when she had become lost in the past, but they had increased since the afternoon meeting at John's Hopkins. She was now certain she would lose the father she had known. The only question was when. Would she have to give up her full-time position for something part time? When would a twenty four hour home nurse in addition to Edna be required? Would that even work given what she knew of her father? How would all these other diseases play a role her father's future, and would they shorten the time he would be mentally able to interact with everyone? Beyond all of that, would she want to be tested for this Alzheimer's allele, whatever it was called, and if so, when? She had told Jimmy about the genetic test hoping he would answer that question, but all he said was that he would look into it, but not to worry because he would be there and support her decision. They would talk more when she got home.

It was 10:30 PM when John finally decided he would never get to sleep. He walked over to the night stand, quietly picked up the phone, and dialed Jenny's room number. He assumed she was probably still awake and no better off than he.

"Hi, Jenny, it's me. I can't sleep, and was wondering if you wanted to go down to the bar and talk a bit. I have to tell you, I am so torn and uncertain. I need someone to talk to."

Jenny was relieved to hear her brother's voice. At least she wasn't alone in all of this, and she knew John was facing the same questions that had been assaulting her for hours. Plus, she was eager to get out of that room.

The hotel bar was empty but for a couple sitting in a darkened booth by the wall. There was no music, no gaiety, no atmosphere of enjoyment anywhere, just an outdated TV with no sound, and pictures of the day's news flickering above the end of the bar. There was little to greet John as he arrived. He ordered a double bourbon on the rocks, and took up a table away from both the bar and the amorous couple in the far corner. As Jenny walked in, he motioned her to join him.

"What'll you have, Jenny? I've got a bourbon," John asked.

Jenny had no idea what she wanted, so simply blurted out the first drink that popped into her mind.

"I'll have a whiskey sour," she said, then thought, "Jeez, when's the last time I had one of those? Whatever...I don't care."

John called Jenny's drink order to the distant, inattentive bartender who barely acknowledged the request.

"So, Jenny, this is some mess, huh," John began. "Did you have any idea things would go in this direction when we landed here? I sure didn't."

The bartender arrived with the whiskey sour, picked up the twenty dollar bill John had waiting, and returned to the bar.

Jenny looked across at John, and saw his mind deep in thought. His eyes were not really focused on anything, arms akimbo, and a furrow in his brow wider than any she remembered having ever seen.

"Absolutely not," Jenny said answering his question. "I just thought we'd come up here, find out Dad had Alzheimer's, and go back home... you know, everything pretty much as it was, just that we would now know for sure that it was Alzheimer's. I never even considered all this other stuff."

John didn't respond. He just sat in continued thought. The bartender returned with the change, and tossed it on the table next to John.

"We close in twenty minutes; so drink up," he flatly said. With nothing further he went back to stacking his glassware, anxious to end his long day.

John finally looked back at his sister, "So what do you think? Are you going to have that test done? You talk to Jimmy yet? How's he taking all this?"

Jenny thought a moment and responded, "Yeah...I spoke to Jimmy right after we got back to our rooms. He says it's up to me, but he'll be there for me. He wasn't all that surprised by the stuff on Dad. He's been saying for a while he thought Alzheimer's was a real possibility. But what are we going to do, John? I mean Dad is going to get worse, and who knows how fast? Did you call Linda? Jeez, I forgot all about her. How do you think she's going to take all this? Oh boy, that is going to be some call. Do you want to wait until we get home, and tell her when Jimmy and I are around?"

The question of what and when to tell Linda had not escaped John's mind, not for one moment had that concern been out of his thoughts. He had pretty much decided to wait until he got home to tell her any of this. He knew his wife well enough to know that she had developed a low tolerance for more bad news concerning his father. The added burdens of his care had taken its toll over the preceding months. Today's news was not likely to be received well, and doing it over the phone was probably not the best idea.

"No...I haven't talked about this with her. I did send a text from the doctor's office that everything was done here, and we would talk about things later. I think she expects me to call tonight, but I guess I will just wait until we get home. Face to face will be better than just a phone conversation, if you know what I mean."

Jenny returned to the question of testing.

"I'm thinking of having the test done. I know there is something to living in the denial granted by ignorance, but I can't see how I won't lose sleep worrying about this anyway. I mean, living my whole life wondering, and then being paranoid every time I lose my damn keys - is that any way to live? No. I'll talk more with Jimmy, but if I had to make the call right now, I'm probably doing it," Jenny said emphatically.

"I agree with you Jenny. Knowing is better than not knowing, but I have to tell you, I'm just a bit afraid. I see how Dad is, and I've seen how people can get. I really don't want to go down that road, but if that's my fate, then I guess that's my fate. Maybe we could come back up here together after we take care of Dad, and both of us have it done all at once. Then we have to hope we both dodged the bullet. Would you want to do that? I mean, if you do, then when do you think we should come back, and have Dr. Wu make the arrangements?"

John looked at his sister, then blankly back at the TV. He hadn't planned that far ahead, but to his mind he didn't see any great urgency for the moment. He looked back at his sister with a smile although there was no hint of joy in his eyes, and said;

"I don't know, Jenny; not right away. Let's just concentrate on Dad for the moment. We need to see just what needs to be done there. Whatever those tests are going to show for us, there isn't really anything we need to do right away. Is that OK with you?"

Jenny simply nodded and looked back toward the bar and bartender who was now tallying up the register receipts. The romantic couple from the corner booth had already left, and only she and her brother remained to delay the bartender's exit.

Jenny looked back at John, who had not stopped looking at her, and said, "No, that's fine; no hurry. But we do have one other question to sort through, and again, we don't have to decide now, but we need to think about it. What about Stan Junior? Frankly, I don't see any reason to burden him with this, at least not now. He is going to have enough trouble just dealing with the declining health of his father. What do you think?"

John took another deep breath, already his mind functioning on overload, then said, "No, let's just let things be on that front. I think we've more than enough on our plates right now."

Jenny rose from her chair, took her brother's hand and looked at him. "So then, we have some ideas going forward; assuming I don't change my mind after I get home. Let's see where things go for now with Dad, and then later you and I will see about this testing; you, me, Jimmy, and Linda if she wants to come. Let's all just take things a step at a time until we get these questions answered and out of the way. God help us, John. God help us."

*****

John walked slowly up his driveway toward the door where Linda stood on the porch waiting. Linda held out her arms to give him a hug and kiss. She knew this had been a hard trip, and was reasonably certain the news was not good. John had already alerted her that Stan had Alzheimer's, but that was no surprise to her. She had been suspecting that was the case for some time. John had, however, also said there was other news he would share when he got home. It was that news Linda was anxious to hear.

"So, John; what was this other news you found out on this trip? Is it something else really wrong with your father?"

Linda had never considered the possibility that Stan's disease might directly affect John or their relationship in any way. To this point, the Alzheimer's had only been a drain on John's time, and a little bit of money. What she was about to learn went much further.

John sat down in the armchair adjacent to the couch where Linda was sitting. He looked down for a moment, then looked into his wife's eyes, and took her hand in his.

"Well, we had some very long discussions with the doctor about what Dad is suffering from, what causes it, and a lot of technical information on his current condition, which is not great, but will obviously get worse in the months ahead. Unfortunately, there's more; there's stuff we didn't know. The thing is...this disease is genetic." John paused a moment to collect his thoughts in order to word his news as well as he could. "So that means, those genes could have been passed on to Jenny and me. According to Dr. Wu, it's about 50-50 whether I have the Alzheimer's gene myself."

Linda jerked back upright in her seat while she continued to look at her husband. Her reaction could only be described as stunned amazement. She squeezed his hand, briefly looked away, then back at John. She didn't believe what she had just heard; and found it hard to accept what it meant. No, this wasn't possible. This was not going to happen. For one of the few times in her life, she was momentarily at a loss for words.

"Wait," Linda finally blurted. "You mean you could have the same condition as Stan? How will you know? Is there something that can be done if you find out early enough? I mean what will we do if that's the case?"

Linda's mind was racing with questions and fears for their future. She wondered how John could just sit there so calmly.

"This could be a disaster, and he is just sitting there," Linda frantically thought. "Does he not fully grasp what this could mean for us? He can't just be sitting there. We have to do something."

John finally answered at least one of her questions when he added, "I know the possibilities. They're all I have been thinking about for the last two days. However, before we all jump to conclusions, we need to just understand nothing is certain at this point. I probably don't even have the dumb gene. On the other hand, at some point I will need to make sure. Jenny and I have talked it over, and decided that the best thing is for us to make an appointment to go get the tests done once we see where things are going with Dad. We can all go up to Hopkins. If you want to go too, we'll figure this out together. Once we do the tests, we'll either be in the clear, or we will just have to deal with what comes. But before I do anything or make a final decision, I want to hear what you think."

Linda sat and looked at her husband, her mind still racing. Get the test done? She didn't know. And when? Her concern was the total change of direction their life would take if that test came back positive. As John sat waiting for her answer, she withdrew her hand from his, rose from the couch, breathed heavily.

"Whatever you think, John," she said with a distant but resigned voice. "I guess if you and Jenny think it's best to get this dealt with, then that's what we'll do." But in her mind, Linda was thinking, "Good God, just when everything was going so well for us, now we have this... can we ever catch a break in this family?"

*****

Upon his return home, Stan continued to live as he had prior to the trip. Edna had become his daily helper; no, she was more. Edna had become a companion. But more bad news was just around the corner.

Edna arrived at her usual eight o'clock, John just slightly later. As Stan emerged from his bedroom, he was surprised to see them both standing in the living room.

"Uh oh. What the hell did I do now?" Stan asked in a cheery voice. "Edna? Did you squeal that I've been leaving the toilet seat up again," he said in a humorous tone.

"No, Mr. Stan. I no tell bad stories. I love you now."

Stan was caught off guard by Edna's confession. It struck him to his heart. As he thought about it, he realized he had come to love Edna as well. She was like part of his family.

"But I not happy today, Mr. Stan. My husband, he transferred by company. We have to move to far away," Edna said sadly.

"You're leaving, Edna?" Stan said, almost in shock. "When? Not today, I hope."

"No, but end of week is last day I stay. I sorry. I want to stay longer."

Stan was crushed...again. He didn't know what to say. Moreover, he didn't know what he was going to do. He actually had come to depend on Edna, although he sure as hell was not about to admit it any time soon. He walked into the kitchen and sat at his table. Silence was the only response he had.

John came in and began to say something, but Stan raised a hand and stopped him.

"Not now, John. I beg you, not now. We can talk later, maybe whenever it is you come to do the bills. Just let me be in peace right now. In fact, I think I'll go back in my room and lie down a little more." Stan said nothing further, got up, walked into his bedroom, and left John standing outside the door.

John looked at Edna. Her tears were streaming down her face.

"Well. We are going to miss you. Stan is going to miss you the most. If you need anything - letter of reference, some expense money, anything. You let me know. I'll stop in again tomorrow to see you."

John went down the drive to his car. For a few moments he just sat, trying to gather his thoughts. What else could happen? What other calamities could be added to this ongoing nightmare? Seeing his father's reaction hurt him so deeply he felt physically ill. He sighed, then picked up the phone to dial Jenny's number. This was a conversation he did not want to have.

*****

Jenny, on one of her weekly days off, picked up her cell phone when she saw John's caller ID. She hoped it wasn't bad news, but of course it was.

"Hey, Jenny," John said trying to speak with a level voice. "Are you home now?"

"Yes, yes. I was just getting Kendra ready for the day. We are supposed to go out in a little bit."

"Oh, well let me swing by so I can tell you about an unexpected development we need to work through."

Jenny felt her chest tighten. "Dad's OK, right? Nothing happened over there?"

John tried to set his sister's mind at ease, "No, nothing like that. But we have an issue that needs attention. I don't want to go over this on the phone. I'll be at your house in about ten minutes. We can talk then." With that, he rang off. He didn't want to give Jenny the opportunity to continue questioning. Actually, he had a couple of things to tell her, and he knew at least one of them was going to cause real problems.

As John came into Jenny's house, Kendra was just finishing her breakfast. Jenny was at the sink doing a few dishes as John sat down in her living room. The room was cluttered with toys that Jenny had begun picking up as she was walking through.

"OK, John…so what happened at Dad's?"

John came directly to his first point. "Edna has to quit. She is leaving at the end of the week. Her husband was transferred, and she won't be able to stay in Knoxville."

"Oh my God," said Jenny, falling into a nearby chair. "It was almost impossible to get Dad to accept this one. I can't imagine what another homecare person will be like. How did Dad take this news? Was he really upset? Did he yell or anything?"

"Yeah," said John. "He was really hurt. He didn't say much, but you could see it in his face. Even though they have a bit of a love-hate relationship, he really likes her. When I left, he had gone back in his room."

Jenny offered a solution almost immediately. "Between the two of us, or maybe another home care lady, we can all get over there, and help out enough that he won't have to have a full time professional care situation. Maybe you and I will just have to play a larger role. It can be done - you will just have to be willing to help out a little and do it with me."

John took a deep breath before offering the next, even more explosive revelation; one he knew was likely to create friction.

"Well. That's the other thing I've been meaning to talk with you about."

"I don't like it already," Jenny said immediately. "So let's hear it."

John cautiously continued. "Well…" and he paused for a few seconds, "the fact is that I might not be here to help, at least not that much longer. I've been offered a promotion to manage the branch of Wright, Johnson, and Willoughby in Nashville. It's a one-time thing. If I turn it down, I'll never get offered a promotion like it again. It's a huge advancement, pay raise, and if I ever want to be made partner, I have to accept this post now."

Jenny's anger was felt right to her core, and she exploded at John, "You have got to be absolutely kidding me! We have a father in crisis who needs our help, and you're biggest concern is your career? Really, John? You've become that selfish, that self-centered?"

John countered, "Really, Jenny? I don't think you understand this at all. It's a one-time thing, and refusing it will stall my career forever. And besides....

Jenny cut him off mid-sentence, "Oh I understand! I understand completely. You have a cushy position you want, and Dad is somehow now in the way. So let's enlist Jenny's help, and get him off to a nursing home so everything can turn out sweet for me!!! Oh I get it. So let me tell you how it is and how I see it. You have become one selfish bastard!! How's that play?"

It did not play well at all. In fact, it hurt him deeply. He wanted to strike back, but John knew if he did that, he might alienate his sister for the foreseeable future; he needed her on his side. John needed Jenny to be part of a solution, not an angry enemy. He wanted to choose his words carefully, but some of his anger crept into his response.

"See Jenny, this is why I've hesitated bringing this opportunity to your attention. I knew how you'd react. It's how you always react. For you, everyone lives in this Rebecca of Sunnybrook Farm existence where the realities of life can somehow always work out the way you want them, and when they don't, then someone must be to blame!"

Seeing Jenny's body language and facial anger at that statement, John tried to move to a less confrontational stance.

"Really, Jenny; I'm sorry. I didn't mean that. I mean, given the circumstances for us, I know that's not true. This is just really hard. Do you honestly think I *like the timing of this?* Do you think I don't wish this could be pushed back? But it can't. Henry just called me into his office and made the offer. I didn't go in and ask him. So, it is what it is, and I have to be the one making a hard choice. My firm is not an understanding place about these things. Please don't make me into the villain."

Jenny, however, was not to be appeased that easily. She was hurt, she was angry, and she was frightened about what her father's future would become. In fact she was worried about everyone's future. She had a daughter who was not out of danger, and this had been weighing so heavily on her mind she could hardly take a free waking breath. Now, the idea of her brother being absent for all this was almost too much to bear.

"Villain? Villain? I'm making you into a villain? No, John, that's what you're making yourself. Our father, *your* father, is fighting for his life here. This family is fighting for *its* life. We're fighting for our lives, our children's lives, but for you this is just black and white? I've got this deal; and it's too good to turn down. So everyone else has to pick up the slack! Villain? You're not a villain," Jenny said in a lower but disgusted tone. "You're just a man like you've always been, a man who lives in a world that is all about him. Sad. Really sad."

John again tried to reduce the intensity of the argument.

"Look. Let's just stop arguing for just one minute, OK? Let's look at this rationally."

Instead of reducing Jenny's hostility, her brother's request only raised it.

"Oh yeah, 'rationally'... that's your strong suit isn't it! Fine: Let's do that. I want to hear what this *rational mind* of yours is going to come up with this time to justify your behavior. We don't have enough on our plates already? And you know we still have to go for those tests, right? Or did you forget that in your glee about this position? Suppose I have this stupid gene? I'm going to be here by myself to handle this? Let's see how the *rational mind* handles all this...can't wait to hear!"

John allowed that remark to pass. He simply moved on with what he felt might show Jenny that this situation was not simply driven by personal greed.

"OK...I'm letting all that go. Just listen. We both know, and you have seen, Dad is no longer able to live alone. He thinks he can, but in reality, he no longer takes care of himself, nor does he always behave in fully rational ways. We have tried the daily home care person, and that has come to an end with very little hope of going forward with a new caretaker. He would chew them up like candy. Whether we like it or not, Dad's temper has also become a problem. So what are we left with? Option A: Professional Care in a very nice setting where he will want for nothing. Option B: He comes lives with one of us. Can he live with you Jenny? Could that work? That would be impossible, there's no room, and you are not in a position to quit your job to stay with him. Of those choices, there's only one!"

"Or he stays with you," Jenny shouted in anger. "Then we get someone in to help while we're at work!! I can come over on my days off and help as well. How about that?"

"For reasons I just explained, that is not an option Linda and I will be able to make work. I am going to have to make this move. We are all going to have to sit together, and try to develop a way forward. You and Jimmy, Linda, me, Dad, Stan Junior, all of us. We need to work together."

John decided, there was little likelihood that he and his sister would find a solution today. He would need to save the rest of the discussion for another time. He knew the move to Nashville was something about which his wife was adamant. In that regard, he had no line of retreat. The future was uncertain, and sure to result in family pain.

7

Decisions

L inda had just returned from her weekly luncheon with the ladies at the Cherokee Country Club, and was waiting for John to return from Jenny's. She knew if John had told her about the Nashville move, it had to have resulted in a major argument. It wasn't so much that she disliked Jenny, but she always felt Jenny had very little appreciation for her brother's career or situation in life. Even though John had done more for his sister than she thought required, Linda felt Jenny had taken much of it for granted, and that annoyed her.

When John had told her of Mr. Wright's offer to head up the entire Nashville operation, she was thrilled. John had been working for this break all his life, now it had finally come. They would move to Franklin, a small, upscale community just outside Nashville. With the near doubling in salary and bonus schedule, they could enjoy everything the area and life had to offer. The only cloud on the horizon was that the genetic test would be positive, but that was off in the future somewhere. Just thinking of all the possibilities made Linda happier than she had ever been. However, between her and that life stood Jenny, and her father-in-law's health.

When she saw John's face as he ascended the walk, she knew things had not gone well. She was just hoping John hadn't caved in, and agreed to something that would jeopardize their future. A tension was mounting in her.

"My God, John, you look terrible. What happened? How did it go? I guess you told her," Linda said in a comforting voice.

"Ohhhhhhh yeah; I told her. Let's just say, she isn't at all pleased with me, *or* with our projected move to Nashville. The words, 'selfish bastard' come immediately to mind, along with a few other uncomplimentary allegations about my lack of concern for my father," John offered.

Linda blew up. "Are you kidding me? *We're* the selfish ones? Who was it who took Stan to Baltimore at his own expense - twice? Who is it goes over to his father's house, cleans it up, and picks up the dog crap three or four times a week? Who was it that took Stan Junior into their house like a son? Who is it that takes care of all the monthly paper work, writes his checks, and does every other financial thing under the sun for Stan? Who is it that has everyone over for dinner a couple of times a month along with almost any other damned family occasion at their expense? And to top everything off just beautifully, at some point we have to go up and have this test done. And what if that comes out positive? We can't have a little sunshine in this life? It all has to be about her, and the drama around this family? You want me to go on? I hope you didn't let that little bit…you know what…get away with that statement. 'Selfish!' I could just throw something!"

John was now dead center in the crossfire.

"No, Linda…good grief, calm down a little. I mean we both expected she was going to be upset, so it should come as no surprise that she feels everything is going to fall on her. And anyway, this isn't about what we've done in the past. Frankly, I've been the one having to carry this, and it hasn't really affected the two of us all that much.

We just need to find a way to move things forward for the future, something that will work for all of us," John offered.

"Wait. You don't think this has affected me at all? You think this is all you? My God, you are really too much. I can't believe you would say that."

"Come on Linda! You know I didn't mean it that way. I'm just saying Jenny sees this as basically a failure on my part to keep helping Dad. And to a degree, I see her point. She feels alone. Surely you can see why she would be upset, right?"

Linda was not put off. She added in a disgusted tone of voice, "Oh, good grief, John, isn't that just like you. Now you take her side against me, and try to make it somehow sound like she's the victim and I'm the bitch. Well, it isn't OK. It isn't OK that she attacks you like you're the one who caused all this. I'm sick and tired of her twisting everything so you are the one...like we won't carry *our share* of the burden. That's crap!!! You know it, and I know it. The only one who *doesn't* know it is Jenny!"

"Regardless of who's right or who's wrong, I need to think about how we can make this work out," John soberly countered as he retreated toward the living room window trying to get a little more distance between himself and Linda's fury.

That did nothing to lessen Linda's sense of frustration as she followed on his heels not yielding an inch. She then added: "Well, my little darling, I want to see just how you are going to pull that one off. In the meantime, here are a few simple facts of life your little sister better just get used to. First: this opportunity in Nashville is a once in a lifetime offer that you *are not* taking a pass on. Second: whenever Henry Wright says we have to be there, we are there. Whatever needs to be done here, that's fine. We will do what we can, but people better get used to the idea that future help may damned well be coming from Nashville, or Franklin, or wherever it is we decide to live. And finally, *our* family is just as important as hers! So, if she needs me to remind her of that little item, I will be only too happy to do so. We are *not* letting her be the only one calling the shots on this, no sir, not this time," Linda fumed.

John buried his head in his hands, and tried his best to calm the situation. "I understand, Linda, and I agree with you. Really I do, honey. I have to take the new position. I know that, and we will have to do what we have to do. That's vital for all of us. We just need a way to convince Jenny...and my father as well...that a professional care situation is best, and that day might be sooner rather than later."

John didn't want Linda to lose sight of the fact that not only would Jenny need to become comfortable with an assisted living arrangement, his father would need to accept that decision as well. That might actually be the more difficult task.

John took a deep breath as he looked out the window and said, "Just let me think a little. Something will come to me. I'm sure we will have some opportunities to make this work. We just need to press forward." John needed a plan, but the simple fact was he had no idea how he could make all these moving parts come together. In the all too near future, however, there would be events to move this discussion to a new level.

*****

Jenny pulled into the driveway at 12:30 to have lunch with her father. She and John had been doing this for some weeks in order to straighten the house, see to it that Stan was eating at least one good meal, and check on Sandy. When she walked into the kitchen, she saw that along with the usual housekeeping issues, Sandy had not had much attention either. The mud room smelled awful; and both the water dish and food bowl were empty. She could hear Sandy in the back yard crying.

When Jenny opened the back door, she saw Sandy wound around her house with only a few feet of lead rope remaining. She went out, unhooked her, and the dog immediately ran about the yard ready to play. It always amazed Jenny how a dog could bounce back from such circumstances, and still be so happy. Jenny went back toward the house, as Sandy ran past her up the stairs heading straight for her water bowl.

"Poor thing," Jenny thought. "She must be dying of thirst."

She wondered where her father was. He was nowhere in the front of the house. She knocked on the bedroom door, and could hear her father talking inside.

"Now, now. I know...that's...don't come then."

He seemed to be having a conversation with himself, but it was all non sequiturs, just fragments of statements. "He must think he is talking to someone," she thought. She knocked again.

"Edna, is that you?"

"No, Dad; it's me, Jenny, your daughter."

There was a little silence, then Stan answered. "Oh. OK...I'll be right out. I'm just getting a few things I need together."

Jenny had no idea what he thought he needed, but it was pretty clear he had forgotten their lunch date.

Jenny had brought some sandwiches and fresh fruit. As they sat and ate, Jenny made a decision. She sat trying to formulate what she was going to say in her mind.

"You know, Dad; I think it's time Sandy had a bath. I will take her with me when I go, then I can get her all fixed up. Besides, she is way overdue for that vet appointment we decided on last week." No vet appointment had ever been discussed, but Jenny was relying on the fact that her father might not recall.

"Really," said Stan. "Who needs a bath? Whatever; go ahead if you want," her father said as he looked out the window. Stan was not always paying attention in recent weeks. When he talked, there were sometimes gaps in his responses. At other times, he was lucid, and seemingly in command of the conversation. This was particularly true when he lost his temper.

"Also, Dad, are you keeping up with your medications? I know you take them when John and I are here, but I'm wondering what you do when we're not here." She and John tried to be sure one of them was there every day to oversee his medication routine, but it wasn't always easy to do.

"Medications," Stan said, acting surprised by the question. Stan usually remembered he needed take the medicine lined up in the bathroom, but exactly which medication, how much, and at what time had become muddled. Of course he had his little weekly medication organizer that Jenny or John would put together. He just had to decide which day it was, and take whatever was in the compartment. He really didn't know what they were in most cases. He sometimes looked at the bottle labels, but he was no longer always certain what they said. The fact was when Jenny or John was not there, he sometimes just guessed at whether he was on schedule.

"Oh...that ...." He paused to organize a few words, "those pills and things. Right. Well, I try."

Jenny knew that "I try" was code for "not really."

As to the question of the effectiveness of the various medications, except for the diabetes, Jenny had not seen any great improvements. His balance seemed a bit better, and the tremor his Knoxville doctor had identified seemed less pronounced. At least he wasn't falling into walls or tables any longer. Jenny had been watching for signs that the tremor had worsened, but to date hadn't seen it. Perhaps that medication was working. As Dr. Wu had warned, her father was progressing in his own way and in his own time.

Jenny and John had attempted to replace Edna with some full time help to make sure their father was looked after, but it hadn't worked out. Stan fired the first person after one day, alleging she was stealing things from his room. He didn't want to see her again, "or he'd call the police." The second woman lasted a little over a week before the agency called and said she refused to return. She gave as her reason that Stan was abusive, prone to fits of violence, and constantly accused her of stealing. Now, there was the unfortunate fact that a continued search for a new homecare person was appearing less likely to be successful.

After lunch, Jenny collected Sandy, and took her to the car. She really did need a good bath. As she backed out, her father stood in his usual place at the window, and waved to her as she drove away. Jenny had no intention of ever placing Sandy back in the house full time. She would bring her over whenever she could, but she had decided she and Jimmy would take full time care of Sandy.

*****

Stan Senior woke with a start. He knew it was dark, and probably quite late. But where was Sandy? He thought out loud, "I haven't seen her since dinner time."

Actually, Sandy had been living with Jenny and Jimmy for over two weeks. The last time he had seen her was closer to three days ago. Such time lapses were not totally uncommon; he had had them several times in recent months.

Stan got up, and began frantically looking through the house. He called Sandy's name, yelled for her out the door, he even went into the back yard to see if she had somehow gotten out. Of course, she was nowhere to be found.

"My God," he thought. "She's gotten loose and run away. Maybe she's lost." He had to find her. He threw on the first pair of pants he found, grabbed his orange hat, and set out to search the neighborhood. "She can't be far," he thought. "She wouldn't run far, not Sandy."

He walked for what seemed quite some time without success. He had reached a main street, although at this time of night, cars were few. Suddenly he looked around, and was totally unsure where he was. Stan started to walk toward the corner. He looked up at the sign, but the street names made no sense. He turned and looked in every direction to get his bearings. "Oh no," he thought. "I can't be lost again!" He wasn't sure which emotion was taking over his thinking: anger or fear.

Stan walked out toward the middle of the street, and saw a building he thought he recognized. It was a church he thought. If nothing else, perhaps someone in there could help him get his bearings. He was certain he knew the neighborhood. He just needed a little help. He walked up to the large red doors and knocked. There was no answer. He knocked again, only a little harder this time, but with the same results.

A black car that had cruised by him several times, slowly rolled up alongside the curb. Suddenly there were flashing blue lights and a spotlight shining on him. The man inside the car called as Stan squinted to see who it was. He recognized the blue uniform, it was a police officer.

The officer called out again from the car, "Excuse me. Excuse me. What are you doing, sir? Are you OK?"

The officer was certainly justified to ask. Stan was dressed in bedroom slippers, pajama top, slacks with no belt, and his tattered, orange Tennessee hat. At first Stan did not realize the officer was talking to him, so he came down the steps and continued to walk. After a quick report to the dispatcher, the officer exited his vehicle to speak with this strange man.

"Sir, is there something we can help you with? It's a little late to be out walking. What are you doing at this door? Everything is closed this time of night."

"Yes, yes…my dog. I think she ran away. Have you seen her? She's a yellow retriever. Nice dog, she'll come right up to you. She won't bite. I just saw her. Name is Sandy. I don't…" and his voice trailed off as he tried to think where he was taking this conversation.

"I'll call around and ask. Can you tell me your name, sir; where you live?"

For some reason, perhaps reaching back to his days on the KPD, he answered, "Of course, I can tell you my name…I'm Detective Beecher. I work with you, I thought you would have known that…and I live right back over there," he pointed in no particular direction.

"Oh yes, Detective Beecher. Sure," said the officer. "You don't happen to have any identification with you, do you?"

Stan said nothing. He looked at the officer, but had no words that fit the conversation. He had nothing. Although the police officer had been with the force less than a year, he thought he knew the name "Beecher." But, was this man actually Detective Beecher? If so, why he was out here wandering around at almost 2 am in the morning? It was fairly certain the man was disoriented, plus it wasn't entirely safe for him to be out at this time wandering by himself. Since the man had no identification or address information, he decided the best thing would be to take him to Police Headquarters where everything could be better handled.

The officer called back to headquarters, "Could you let the desk sergeant know I am bringing in a gentleman, about sixty five years old who claims to be a Detective Beecher."

The radio crackled its response, "Unit six two…you said, Detective Beecher? If that's who it is, I think Detective Newsome knows him. Just bring him in."

The officer stepped away, and coaxed Stan into the car.

"Detective Beecher… why don't you get in the passenger seat …we'll go look for your dog. We can cover more ground that way."

"Right. Good idea," Stan answered, happy to be back "on the job." Besides, he didn't know where he would go if this person left.

As they rode in the car, Stan told the officer nonstop fragments of stories about cases in which he had been involved. He had over forty years on the force, worked homicides, on and on. As they pulled into the station garage, Stan got out of the car, and walked right into the building as if he knew exactly where to go. Once inside, Stan was brought upstairs to the detective unit where he sat with the cup of coffee they had given him. It was only a short time before Ted Newsome arrived. Ted nodded his head to the attending officer that this was indeed Stan Beecher. He would take care of things from here. Ted began by trying to make light of Stan having been picked up off Broadway.

"Hey Stan, I hear you've been working a missing canine case without inviting your old pal in on the investigation."

Stan was elated to see his friend. "Absolutely," he said. "You remember, Sandy, my dog, right? Well, somehow," Stan paused to try and remember exactly what it was he was trying to say. Finally, he added, "She's gotten loose...Nope...Can't find her anywhere. So, if you want in on the case, just let me know," Stan laughed at his little joke.

"OK, Stan. Let me make a few calls. I bet we get this one solved in a hurry."

The first call Ted made was to John who he looked up on Stan's emergency call card still on file in the office.

No one likes a call in the middle of the night, but there was no one else to contact.

*****

As the house phone rang, John opened his eyes and looked at the clock on the nightstand; it read 2:25. "Oh this can't be good," he thought as he picked up the receiver.

"Hello...who's this?"

"John...Ted Newsome, your father's friend in the detective unit. Look, I'm sorry to call and disturb you in the middle of the night like this, but we have your father here at the station. Nothing wrong, he isn't hurt or in any trouble, but one of our officers found him out on Broadway at about 1:30 am. Apparently, he was looking for Sandy, his dog. He thinks she might have run away. Can you shed any light on this?"

Linda was up and asking, "Who is that? Is it about your father? What did he do this time? Is he OK?"

John put up his hand to silence the questions, and simply nodded that he was OK, but Linda kept talking as she got out of bed to put on her robe.

"I knew something like this was going to happen. This is really going to be the death of me at some point. Why is it *we're* the only ones who think this is a problem? This entire situation is *totally* out of hand, and we do nothing. Can you believe it? Nothing," she said to no one in particular as she paced the room.

John sighed resignedly.

Linda went on as she raised her hand and turned away, "Fine... OK...you handle it. It's *your* father, not mine," she intoned in her most sarcastic voice.

John answered, "Oh, right Ted, no, no. Jenny has Sandy at her house, she didn't run away. Jenny decided to keep the dog with her for now. Dad must have woken up and just forgot."

Linda made a wry face, and added under her breath, but not so silently John didn't hear, "Oh, I just bet he did, he's become an expert at forgetting these days." Another icy stare with the hidden message of "please" was all John could muster in response.

John continued with Ted, "No, I understand. I'll be right down to pick him up. Just tell him I'm on my way...Oh...and tell him Jenny has Sandy, and not to worry. Gee, I'm really sorry to have caused this trouble. Dad hasn't been himself lately."

As soon as the receiver was back in the cradle, Linda was outlining to John what he had to do now.

Linda wryly said, mimicking John's voice, "OK, see? Everything is going to be fine." Then she sarcastically added, "You and Jenny could just do spot visits, your father would be taken care of. And that great plan has taken us where? Phone calls in the middle of the night about your father wandering who knows where! No...that's not dangerous, not dangerous at all. Well, you go down and pick him up, and while you're on your way, you call up that sister of yours, and let her know of tonight's little adventure. Why should she get a nice cozy sleep while the rest of us are *up dealing with this in middle of the night!*"

Ted was well aware of Stan's memory problem. It had obviously grown considerably worse; he felt sad for his friend. As the two waited for John to arrive, Ted informed Stan that Sandy was fine and at Jenny's house.

"Really," Stan said with an air of complete surprise. "What do you know about that? She somehow escapes from the house, and goes over there. Funny, she's never done that before."

John called Jenny as soon as he was in the car. When she answered, John explained what had happened as briefly as possible. He wisely omitted the entire list of discussion points Linda had insisted he explain. Jenny wanted to come with him to the police station, but John asked, "And why? What would that accomplish? That would just mean two more people out in the middle of the night." He promised to call back, and let her know when he finally got Stan home. That didn't really meet Jenny's idea of what her role should be.

"OK, look, I'll go over to the house while you go get Dad. I'll just make sure everything is OK there, and you can bring him back."

"Right, I'll meet you back at the house when I get Dad."

By the time John arrived at the police station, it was almost 3 am. Ted had Stan waiting near the door. Ted and John exchanged a few pleasantries, as John again apologized. Ted simply smiled and said it was no problem.

During the ride home, Stan was remarkably quiet about the evening's events. He offered no explanation of why he would go out in the middle of the night, or not call him or Jenny. John doubted his father even had an explanation to offer. He had just imagined Sandy missing, panicked, and out the door he went.

"What were you thinking, Dad? Why didn't you call someone if you thought the dog was gone? You know you shouldn't be out by yourself that time of night," John said in an angry voice.

"Oh really! Now I need your permission to go look for my dog? I don't need anyone's permission to do anything. You do nothing but try to make me look like a fool, like I can't be trusted with as much as a, a, a piece of chewing gum! You know how that makes me feel? Do you?" Stan was shouting at this point. John wisely let the discussion drop.

"Fine, Dad…the important thing is you're here, and we'll get you home."

Once they arrived home, Stan had worked himself up into an angry, confrontational mood. As he walked in the door, Jenny was there to meet him. Unfortunately she had no idea of what had happened in the car or her father's frame of mind.

"Dad, my goodness, I was so worried…" which was as far as she got before Stan launched an angry tirade.

"You two make me laugh. Worried? You're not worried. You just have to meddle in my business, and upset your mother! Well, we're sick of it! Both of us!"

Jenny looked at her brother who looked back at her, and she shook her head. Her father had so lost track of things in his anger, he was now bringing Marilyn back to life. Jenny tried to correct his thinking.

"Dad…Dad…look at me. Mom is gone, she died in an accident and….

Stan flew into a rage, and shoved Jenny out of his way, knocking her off her feet and back into a table, as he lunged toward the bedroom.

"Don't you EVER SAY THAT ABOUT YOUR MOTHER AGAIN!! YOU HEAR ME!!"

With that Stan went into his bedroom and began to undress. Opening and closing drawers, he couldn't find any nightwear and called out.

"Jenny. Do you know where my pajamas are? I can't find them."

Both Jenny and John were in a state of shock. John had gone over to pick up his sister who had been more shaken than physically hurt. On the other hand, Stan had moved on, and was now just concerned about getting ready for bed. He had already dismissed the incident.

"Jenny, are you all right? You hit that table pretty hard."

Near tears, Jenny looked at John with that "what are we going to do" sense of bewilderment. This had never happened before. Yes, her father had had lots of temper problems, but except for throwing inanimate objects, he had never physically assaulted anyone.

John and Jenny did not want to leave the house with their father so out of sorts. John was now afraid to leave his sister alone with their father in his current state of mind. Cautiously, Jenny went to the door of the bedroom to check on what her father was doing. Looking in, she saw Stan on top of the bed covers, still dressed, and sound asleep.

Jenny decided to call Jimmy and have him come over so John could go home. Linda would begin to get worried, and she didn't want to have to deal with her right now.

Once Jimmy arrived with Kendra, John went home. Jenny and Jimmy did not sleep. She told him what had happened, and the rest of the night was spent by Jimmy holding his wife and comforting her. Her heart was broken. She went from intermittent sobbing to just holding her husband, and asking what else she could do.

On the drive home, John made a decision. It was time for another family meeting. It was a meeting he truly wished could be avoided, but things had come to a point at which a serious discussion about Stan's future was needed.

*****

John had been fretting about this upcoming family meeting for days. He decided to do it in conjunction with the Sunday family dinner. That way might seem a bit less ominous. The only difference was he had asked Jenny if a baby sitter could be arranged for Kendra to avoid the distraction. Reluctantly, she agreed. She knew this was a night for a long overdue talk.

He and Jenny had already agreed that after dinner they would have a family discussion about their father's little "walkabout," and the growing fear that he was becoming more physically abusive. John also wanted to give everyone the opportunity to assess the situation, and try to reach a consensus as to what steps were next. Jenny was well aware of the magnitude of the occasion, and had enlisted Jimmy's support in advance.

"Sweetheart; I need you tonight. I know John is going to push hard for the assisted care option, and I suspect that Linda is behind it. I have no idea how Dad will receive that suggestion, but I have the sinking feeling that it could get ugly. Just remember, we're on Dad's side if it comes to that."

Jimmy was uneasy for his wife. He knew the arguments for John's case on an assisted living arrangement were rapidly mounting. He didn't know if Jenny was correct about Linda's role as the key decision-maker, but he had seen Linda's sharp side any number of times at family gatherings. Linda liked Stan, but it was in her own way. It was certainly not "unconditional love." Jimmy tried to stay out of things as best he could, but tonight he saw no way to sit things out. No, tonight was going to be a night he dreaded.

At John's house, Linda had given John her full support. He planned to take charge, present the best case for assisted living, and not allow his sister to minimize the importance of his job offer in Nashville. John never told Linda about Stan's shoving Jenny against the table, or the episode when his father thought Marilyn was still alive. He had enough trouble as it was. He had taken the additional step of asking Jenny not to mention it either.

Linda said: "Don't let her make us feel like we're selfish so and so's for wanting to make this move. You have a family just like her, so it isn't a matter of *convenience*; it's literally a matter of what kind of life we will have *forever*. John, you have worked countless hours, weekends, nights, any time they needed you, all just to get this kind of break. Well, now it's here, but you and I both know if you hesitate there are at least two or three others down there who will slit your throat in a heartbeat, and take this position. Don't let your sister badger you out of it. I will have your back, so don't let her do it, John, don't let her do it."

Stan Senior knew something big was afoot. When he heard his granddaughter was staying home, every red flag he knew went up. Unfortunately, he also realized he was starting to get worse. Tricks to mask his problem were no longer working. He was making mistakes more often, and he needed notes to himself for almost everything. He just hoped people could be civil to one another. The last thing he wanted was an all out battle. He knew Linda was growing short on patience with him. He could see she was unhappy with both him and the family pressure this disease was causing.

As far as he could tell, Linda had always felt a bit like an outsider in the family. What he could not tell was whether this was something she wanted, or did she just not know how to fit in. Stan also knew that his caustic sense of humor, occasional sarcasm, and temper issues were adding to the problem. "Well," he thought, "I can't go back and change history, so I will just have to sit there and see what happens."

Stan Junior, as was too often the case, was almost completely ignored in this equation. His opinion had rarely been sought, his feelings rarely considered. As it had been for so much of his life, he had unknowingly become invisible. He had heard lots of arguments, or at least loud conversation, between John and Linda. He was afraid Linda didn't really love his Dad, not really, and this frightened him. Linda would tell John to confront his sister, *make* her understand things, and *"not* let her get away with it." Stan Junior never quite knew what the "it" was, but he did know John and Jenny were likely to have an argument. He hated arguments. Tonight was going to be bad. Linda had been talking to John all week, and tonight was when he was supposed to "get things in the open." Stan Junior desperately wished there was something he could say, something he could do, something to eliminate all this anger. Nothing came to mind. He would have to let things take their course. He was helpless.

When everyone was seated at the dining room table, Jenny said a short grace, and dinner proceeded. Despite the small talk, there was an unmistakable air of nervousness hanging over the room. Stan Senior did not even make any of his usual funny statements about Linda's dishes. "Not surprising," she thought. Once dinner was over, Linda and

Jenny cleared the table, and set the dishes in the kitchen. They would do them later, but for now, there were bigger issues to tackle.

The group assembled in Linda and John's large living room. John took a very deep breath, and began:

"Well. Thanks everybody. We all know there have been a few difficult days, and we need to talk about what we think might be some good options for Dad as we move ahead." John paused to collect his thoughts, then proceeded. "Right now, I think we will want to take a moment to consider at just what point we need to look at some additional professional care for Dad." John thought about what he had just said and panicked, "Jesus, but that came out stupid."

"Oh my God," thought Linda. "He's already waffling and getting cold feet." She wasn't about to let things get away from her by sitting idly by as their entire future went down the drain. This was no time to be timid. What had to said, had to be said.

"Yes," Linda added. "As everyone now knows, John has been offered a senior position in the Willoughby firm, but it's in Nashville. That will mean we will not be able to be as involved as we have been in the past. We will need to put that into our plan going forward."

"Oh indeed," Jenny jumped in. "Well, that may be just great for you guys, but sucks for everyone else, doesn't it. Oh by the way, just in case no one noticed, we also have a father who will need our maximum support in these next months. Can we at least discuss all options to ensure he gets that support here in Knoxville?"

John tried to regain command of the discussion, but the first shots had been fired. He was cut off before he could utter a sound.

Linda continued with added sharpness, "Jenny. I know...and John knows...you would prefer we stay. Under other circumstances we would, but where we are right now is unique. You cannot expect John to pass up the opportunity of a lifetime so we can try to add a few months of independence for your father. That just isn't fair."

The gloves were off. "Not fair! You talk about fair? All that is being asked is that you help out here. No one is asking that John turn himself inside out, or pledge to a life of full time servitude. I'm pretty sure if John explained his situation the firm would understand, and perhaps afford him a little time before the move would have to be made. Why isn't that an option on the table? The least we can expect is that we all just do our share here."

Linda jumped out of her seat. John started to talk, but Linda motioned him to sit back down. "Oh you do have some nerve with that statement, Jenny. How dare you suggest we haven't 'done *our share!*' We've been doing a *lot more* than *our share* in this family for quite some time, and you know exactly what I mean. So, don't even go there with that sanctimonious argument about us holding up our end. It's *been* done, and *continues* to be done...and don't you dare try to tell me otherwise!"

Jenny knew exactly what Linda meant. She was referring to taking Stan Junior in their home after he graduated from high school. It was an arrangement Linda was all for at the time, but always felt a bit underappreciated for the effort.

Jimmy tried to jump in before things got worse.

"OK. OK. I get it; and Linda, absolutely. You and John have always been there for us, and we all appreciate it. Where we are tonight, however, is a little bit unique in that we are talking about trying to buy some time for the future. I don't think I'm talking out of turn when I say you guys, all of us, want Stan Senior to have as much quality of life as possible. We're just trying to find a way to do that. So please, let's just all of us try to keep our cool and work together. Yelling at one another is just going to make things harder and piss everyone off; it won't get us anywhere."

John was uncomfortable with the exchange between Jenny and Linda. He knew there were no great connections between the two, but until tonight there had been at least some degree of respect and civility. John also knew things that Linda didn't, so he couldn't just leave his sister on her own in the discussion.

"I know this is a tough time for all of us. And Jenny, you have been the best through all of it. But the things that have happened recently, and Jenny, you know what I mean, kind of put us in a new place. I know Linda didn't mean to be so sharp, but we are all just trying to look for something that will meet everyone's needs."

Before John could go further, Stan Senior, quiet until now, unexpectedly spoke. He had been sitting there listening to people talk as if he were not even in the room. He had been having trouble keeping up with the discussion, but he certainly knew what this argument was about...it was about *him*. It was about the eight hundred pound gorilla in the room called Alzheimer's. That was the thing about this disease. There was no doubt about its direction or consequences, and no doubt about the end game. What Stan Senior was witnessing, however, was his entire family at one another's throats over *him*. He was watching the disintegration of his family, the destruction of the very people he loved most, and who had given his life purpose. It was no secret, eventually the effects the disease would force him into a full care situation. He was convinced that in the end there would be no other option. He was certain. Since that was the case, he was not about to let his family fall apart over this damnable disease! It would not happen to *his* family.

"Excuse me for asking, but will I ever get a chance to speak, or do I have to wait until the bell rings after the tenth round?" Stan began.

Everyone fell silent. Until that time, no one had even considered asking the most important person in the room what he thought. Stan continued.

"So John...and Linda...am I right? You guys have a great job offer that's going to mean you have to move? First I'm hearing of it," Stan said in a subdued voice. He went on, a little bit louder, "But just so you know, I'm happy for you. I think it's great, and you'd be a pair of dumbasses to pass it up." Stan paused, not entirely sure where he was taking this conversation; took a breath and restarted. "So let's not confuse my situation with yours. Ahhhh ... I think I want you to do what's best for you and your future. I know my son has worked damn hard to get where he is, so I guess my advice is don't blow it now. Anyway, that's what I think about that."

Out of the corner of his eye Stan saw his daughter's pained expression. He turned and looked Jenny in the eye. "Jenny, honey, you are too sweet. Really, you are. But...I hear all this yelling, and I don't want you guys...any of you...getting all upset simply on my account. At some point..." Stan lost his train of thought. "We all know I can't ...by myself...stay in that house forever." Stan took a breath as he looked down at the floor, "I guess it's only a matter of time until a change has to be made. Anyway, if that time is now, that time is now. I'm OK with it."

There was a long pause; then Stan got up from his chair. He wobbled a bit, and went over to lean on the fireplace, then continued.

"So...there...maybe it would be good." He wanted to get this right in his mind before he spoke, but suddenly there were too many ideas, so he simply offered, "Why don't we all just go look at a few of these places ... maybe we ... let's look. I'll be good with that. OK? Looking."

Jenny sat stunned for the moment. This was not something she expected. Finally, she questioned, "You're sure about this, Daddy? This is not something I ever heard you say."

Stan could not resist the opportunity. "Mmmmmmm...what? No. You've been too busy arguing with your brother," he said with a laugh to ensure everyone knew he was kidding. "But yes. This is fine. You can help me look."

John said, "I wasn't expecting you would want to go in this direction...at least not yet. But it's a great idea. We go look. I'm all in for it."

The yelling had stopped. Stan Junior was now breathing again. He wished he could think of something to make people laugh. But everyone was just staring at one another. Stan Junior felt alone in the room.

"OK," said Stan softly. "John, you and Jenny will let me know when we're going, and Stan Junior, you will accompany me as my right hand man. Now...didn't I hear something earlier about ice cream? I don't get to eat it often, so Jenny...you get the plates."

For the moment, things seemed somewhat resolved. Their father seemed comfortable with the idea that an assisted living arrangement would be satisfactory. As with everything else, however, things would not proceed so smoothly.

As the meeting broke up, John stood on the porch saying goodbye to everyone, especially his sister. He knew she had been hurt, and he knew she was still angry with him about the move. He didn't know exactly how to put things like this into words, so instead just hugged his sister.

"I'll call you tomorrow, OK? We'll talk. Everything will work out," John added, not knowing how anything at all could work out. Jenny just nodded and motioned toward the car with her head. She could see Linda waiting, looking straightforward in the passenger seat.

*****

The family had been visiting assisted living facilities for over a week. For Stan, everything had been one big blur. All of the facilities, routines, and information ran together in his mind. He really could not say which place was the best. He knew he had to come up with an answer, but the only place he remembered was the last place he visited, so he decided to go with that.

"Well, I will tell you what, Jenny. They all seem about the same to me. That last one, what was its name?"

"Willow Grove," Jenny answered.

"Right. Willow Grove," Stan said flatly. "That one had the most stuff, and I guess the apartment on the first floor was OK. I liked that you could walk out to your own little patio. And that director--what was her name? I'm calling her Warden Legree, but I know that is not her name."

Stan was trying to use his wit, "and that business guy – God, he asked so many questions. He was like that Spanish Inquisition priest, Bernardo Gui."

John chuckled at the reference, because he had the same impression of the business agent.

Stan didn't especially like any of the places they had visited, but "none of the above" was not an option. As he thought about it, Willow Grove was as good as any, and knew looking at more places would not make any difference.

"Anyway," Stan finally said, "Willow Grove is an OK place, but I want the first floor apartment. What do you think, Stan Junior? Is it a good choice?"

Stan Junior was caught by surprise by the question, but recovered and found an answer. "Definitely, Dad. That was a real nice place. Maybe we can have lunch in that nice dining room some time."

Stan liked that idea, "Absolutely, Stan Junior. And we won't let that Bernardo Gui guy know. We don't want him charging extra, and running up the bill on poor John here."

"That does it then. Since Stan Junior agrees, John, you do whatever you do. I'm sure Bernardo Gui will have lots of papers to sign. Most of all, he'll want money handed over."

Jenny could not believe this was going so fast. She was certain that her father was not as in favor of all this as he was letting on. But what could she say? Short of starting another argument, there just didn't seem any way to stop this train wreck.

When Stan got home, and after everyone had left, he sat in his living room in the dark. He could not believe the hand fate had dealt him. Sometimes he thought this all must be a bad dream. But no; it was real. In a decision he had thought necessary to save his family, he was signing away his independence. He guessed this day was inevitable, but now that there was an actual timetable, he was no longer certain he had made the right decision. His emotions shifted between sadness and anger. "Why me?" he thought. "Why do I have to have this disease? Why do I have to lose everything?" Once again, he felt totally abandoned. No one could help him; no one could understand his level of pain. He didn't know what would become of his life as it moved painfully in a direction he dreaded. He just knew it wouldn't be the same. "At the end of the day," he thought, "I will have lost everything. I will be just waiting to die."

All that was left now was to wait for John to give him the date.

*****

John and Jenny had already been at the Johns Hopkins Center for two days where they were asked to complete the "Informed Consent" documents for the genetic test. They had been counseled by the staff geneticist, and had provided the samples of their cheek cells for testing. This was a limited test that analyzed one specific genetic marker; thus the process was not expected to take a long time. Jimmy and Linda had accompanied them, and as best they could, the four were taking in a few sights trying to make a mini-vacation of the time. This was not easy. Some of the scars left from the family meeting at which Linda and Jenny had clashed had not fully healed. Today, however, was not a vacation, nor was it a time when old conflicts were to be re-addressed. Today, the results of the test were back, and the doctor's meeting with John and Jenny had been scheduled for that afternoon.

Against some opposition, at John's request, it had been decided that John and Jenny would meet first with Dr. Wu alone. Everyone would gather later if there were questions. As Dr. Wu entered, she was smiling, and that gave both Jenny and John a feeling of hope.

"Jenny, John, we have everything back. I've looked at all the results, and met with the laboratory director and our geneticist to evaluate what we see. So let's start with you Jenny."

It is difficult to describe the apprehension Jenny was feeling at that precise moment. Terrified is an insufficient word. Jenny was not only frightened for herself, and what might happen in her own life if the test was positive, but she was petrified for her daughter. Her hands were soaked with perspiration. She was well aware that if she had the APOE-4 allele, there was a 50-50 possibility it had already been passed to Kendra. If that was the case, Jenny knew she could never forgive herself. The fact that it wasn't her fault would be no consolation whatsoever. She literally held her breath and squeezed both her eyes shut as Dr. Wu delivered the results.

"Jenny, we have looked at your results very carefully, and none of us see any evidence of the APOE-4 allele in your genotype. Everything we saw in the genetic analysis was perfectly normal. I know you and James were worried, but I think you can put those fears aside now. I'm very happy for you."

Jenny could no longer contain her emotions, and just began to silently weep in her chair. She had just had the weight of the world lifted from her shoulders, and she wanted to run around the desk and kiss Dr. Wu. Instead, she sat in her chair, and hugged her brother as she looked up at him and smiled through her tears.

As Dr. Wu closed Jenny's file and moved the second folder in front of her, John sat holding his breath. This was a moment in time he dreaded. His heart was pounding so hard in his chest he could actually feel it beat. Jenny had moved her chair closer to her brother's, and was now pressing against him, gripping his hand and arm tightly.

Dr. Wu looked up at John with a smile, and pushed some papers from the folder into her direct view. She adjusted her glasses, looked back down and continued.

"John; well, we have also looked closely at your results downstairs. In fact we did the test twice. Unfortunately, we do find the APOE-4 in your chromosomal makeup. However, before you read too much into that, I do want to give you some better news. Right now this gene is doing nothing, and it is likely to be at least thirty more years before it might become a factor in your life. In genetics research that is a lot of time. My hope is that we have made significant progress by then as to what we can do to mitigate this result. In the meantime, we will be here for you in any capacity you wish. We have counseling services, health services, and would be more than ready to work with you and Linda in whatever way we can."

Jenny put her head on John's shoulder, and squeezed his arm even tighter. As happy as she had been just seconds before, her gladness had now been replaced by grief for her brother. She looked at his face for some sign as to how this news had been received, but for the moment John just sat there. He wasn't shocked or frightened; he was just resigned. For some reason, he had been expecting the worst for some time. He had been preparing for this moment for over a month. Now that it was here, John simply took a deep breath, sat back in his chair, and looked up at Dr. Wu with a request.

"I'm not surprised," John said. "I don't know why, but I just thought this was probably going to be the case. I'm just relieved that it isn't both of us." He smiled ruefully at his sister, and added, "I'm really, really glad for you, sis; really glad." He then leaned over to her and kissed her on the forehead.

"But," John continued as he redirected his attention back to Dr. Wu, "I do have a request. I'd like my results to be just between us. I'd appreciate it if you would keep these results private, and just let Jenny and me decide how we want to deal with them as far as our families go. I think that's best."

Dr. Wu looked back at John and said, "Absolutely, John. These results are private, and we are bound by patient confidentiality to keep them that way. That said; if there is anything you would want me to do in this regard, you only have to ask."

"Do you think Jenny and I could have a few moments alone right now? And if you would, could you not go out into the waiting area where our families are sitting just yet? We just need a minute to process," John said, mustering the best smile he could.

As Dr. Wu exited through the back door of her office, John looked over at Jenny. Her eyes were totally blood shot, and her hairline had actually become wet from all the perspiration. He patted her hand, got up, and walked toward the window before he began to speak.

As he gazed through the window overlooking the grounds, he said, "Jenny. I'm going to ask a big favor. I know we haven't discussed what would happen if one or both of us had this gene, but I've thought about it a great deal. Please don't tell Linda. In fact, I think we should tell Linda and Dad both that we are each in the clear."

He turned to look at his sister and raised his hand before she could respond. "I know. It's a lie, and at some point will probably be found out, but for now why should we ruin the lives of others? I mean, hasn't this damn disease done enough damage to our father and this family already? Why make Dad feel worse than he already does? What's to be gained? If he thinks we're both free, then perhaps it will give him just a little more peace. And as for Linda, well, why ruin her life? I'm going to be fine for a long time, and like Dr. Wu says, by the time I need to say anything, maybe they will have found a cure or medication or something. In fact, let's just let everyone go on living with the idea everything is fine. I'd rather we just did something along those lines. Are you OK with that?"

Jenny, for the first time in many months, looked at her brother through different eyes. This was not the man she had accused of being self-centered. At this moment she felt very small, and very guilty for some of the comments she had made to her brother. She really didn't know how to react to this request. Of course, she planned to honor every word, but a new bridge between them had just been built. All she could do was to walk over to him, hug him, and give him her answer.

"Yes. Absolutely. We will keep this to ourselves. Let's give Dad some peace, and Linda can move with you to Nashville next month as you had planned. She'll be happy."

As Jenny and John went to the waiting area, Jimmy and Linda rose in fearful anticipation. The two of them had been sitting there for almost an hour in near total silence. Both had felt somewhat excluded after coming all that way, but neither had wanted to debate John's decision.

Jenny walked back in the waiting room, smiled and said, "It's all good!" John simply looked at Linda and gave a thumbs-up. Words were not exchanged. A loud cheer erupted from everyone as the entire reception room looked up to see what had happened to cause the commotion. Hugs were exchanged, and the four exited the building to find the nearest steak house with a good bar. Happy voices, loving hugs, and spirited exchanges of laughter accompanied their ride to the restaurant as they each admitted how worried they had been, and how happy they were now. For that brief moment in time, all seemed well, and everyone could concentrate on Stan. Even though this news would make Stan Senior happy to hear, his transition to Willow Grove was still on the horizon.

8

Willow Grove

As Stan and his three children were walking to the front entrance of Willow Grove for Stan's first day, the front door opened, and they were greeted by the director, Nettie Lanier. She motioned everyone to come into the lobby. Inside was a small group who served as part of a "welcoming team" to greet new residents. Ms. Lanier introduced everyone, and told Stan they were here to help him feel welcome. Stan was somewhat surprised, although still quietly angry about being there at all. He had not yet fully recovered from leaving his lifelong home and the argument with his son.

"Mr. Beecher," Ms. Lanier said. "It's so nice to see you again, and I see your family has all come to help you get settled. I know you were here earlier speaking with our Administrative Assistant, Mr. Barnard. Did he answer all your questions and make you feel welcome?"

Stan remembered meeting the man, whatever his name was, and the fact that he had asked a lot of questions.

"Well, Warden, I'm not sure about his 'answering *our* questions' but he certainly examined us enough to get answers to all *his* questions," Stan said, accenting the word "his."

Ms. Lanier smiled and said, "Well, Mr. Beecher, what we would like to do now is show you to your apartment. Art and Sal have it all set up for you. Why don't we go down there now."

"Yes," said John, "let's go see if we can get you settled in."

"Right, yes. By all means…let's go check these accommodations," said Stan, but could not resist the opportunity to add a little of his own brand of humor. "You realize, however Warden, I never stay in any places other than five stars. I hope your establishment maintains that high standard. Butler service, twenty four hour room service, you know, the usual."

Ms. Lanier ignored Stan's comment, and wasn't certain she liked being referred to as "warden" either. As far as a butler and room services were concerned, she was confident Stan was merely exercising his sense of humor. Perhaps, she faintly hoped, he might come around later.

"Everything is ready, Dad. You're going to love it. Here's a TV, there are cold drinks in your little refrigerator over here, and all your clothes and things are ready to be put away. Over here, Dad, is a neat bathroom. And it's got all these bars and things so you won't fall," Stan Junior enthusiastically explained.

Stan looked at his son and smiled. He rumpled his hair and said, "You've done a 4-0 job here Stan Junior. It's a good thing the Warden over there has someone like you to help her out. I was just about to lower the rating on this place to three stars, but you've raised it back to five."

Sandy was already lying down next to the bed, her eyes moving back and forth between people speaking in the room.

"Don't get too comfortable over there, Sandy, you can't stay," warned Stan. "Nope, girl… Bernardo Gui said your too fat and overweight."

Ms. Lanier, wishing to move things in a different direction, added, "Well, I think she looks beautiful, and she is welcome to visit you here for as long as she wants, any time she wants. We love pets here at Willow Grove."

Stan Junior joined in to help, "And I'll bring her with me every time I come, Dad. I promise."

"Wellllllll, I guess it's OK then. How about you, Sandy? That OK with you?" Sandy got up, and slightly wagging her tail, sat closer to Stan.

Stan Junior was proving a valuable ally in helping reduce Stan's hostility over the new living arrangements.

John and Jenny walked with their father back to the front doors, preparing for their departure, as they wanted their father to have some time on his own. Stan Junior was outside helping Sandy explore the grounds. Everyone said their goodbyes, and Jenny promised to be back the next day.

"Dad, Jimmy and I are coming by tomorrow, and we'll all go to lunch. It will be fun. So you just settle in and relax. OK?"

Stan had any number of responses to the perfunctory, "OK" question, but for once that day, he just said, "Yeah...sure. I'm fine. You guys go ahead. I think Gui said we have dinner at 5:30, so I'll just wait for that highlight of the evening. Should be interesting...."

Jenny knew her father wasn't happy, not one bit. She felt absolutely saddened about it, but it was too late now. In her heart she knew it was way too early to be making this move. Her father could easily have stayed in his house longer if only everyone were ready to pitch in and help. But no, a few bad incidents plus John's career path had altered everything. Add to that, Linda's insistence on the move to Nashville, and it seemed everything had conspired to uproot her father to Willow Grove, and make him unhappy. She was so annoyed at herself for not stepping up more forcefully with an alternate solution. If she didn't know what she did about her brother's condition, she would likely have still been angry with him; and with Linda as well for her lack of consideration of any solution other than her own. She really could have cried, but instead just hugged her father and gave him a kiss.

"See you tomorrow, Dad…can't wait."

As Stan watched the car pull away, his heart sunk. Why the hell he had done this to himself was still a mystery even to him. It was like a big ball that had started rolling, and he had no way to stop it.

Stan went to his apartment, closed the door, and sat by the doors leading out to his little patio. He thought to himself, his life would now revolve around what was left of old memories and days that would never return. He would not be making any new memories, at least not ones he thought would be worth keeping. Worse than that, he sighed, Alzheimer's would eventually claim every one of those old memories as well. What would be left then, survival? Sad as it seemed, that was where he saw his future going.

*****

The weeks came and went. Stan slowly began adjusting to his new surroundings. He had made a new friend in his primary caretaker, Kevin Willis. Kevin was a very large African American, about 42 or 43 years old. He had a jovial personality, and loved Stan's somewhat acerbic sense of humor. He especially enjoyed some of the nicknames Stan had given people on the staff. He would walk Stan to the dining room, or help him with getting ready for the day. If Stan needed anything, Kevin was the man to whom he turned.

One afternoon, Kevin looked at Stan and said: "You know, Stan, we have a "happy hour" later this afternoon. I'd love to have a beer with you then if you want."

"Good plan, Kevin," Stan said, perking up. "That's the best offer I've had today."

That happy hour was one of the pleasant surprises Stan had found at Willow Grove. They actually did have a happy hour during which you could get wine or beer…as long as the doctors said it was OK. He was thinking it was a good thing Dr. Ming wasn't around; he'd be lucky to get a bottle of water and crust of bread. That woman was still calling and talking to his doctors about what he could or couldn't do, what medications he should have, and who knows what! All Stan knew was that every time he thought he'd like to do something, someone said they had to check with Dr. Ming! "Meddling pain in my ass," Stan had concluded.

Stan went to his apartment, turned on the TV, and sat in his chair. He had come to enjoy watching some of the older TV shows like *Law and Order*. I doubt anyone could properly explain the attraction between senior people and a show like *Law and Order*, but there was definitely a clear link unexplained by modern science. In any event, Kevin had found a great channel that aired all the old TV shows, and for that, Stan was eternally grateful. "That Kevin," thought Stan, "what a good man to have around."

As he sat there, he slowly drifted off to sleep, missed Happy Hour, and didn't wake up until someone came to remind him of dinner. This was becoming his life.

*****

Stan was sitting in the dining room after dinner, well after everyone had left. He was just staring off into space when Kevin arrived. The lights had been dimmed, all the table cloths removed, and a silence filled the air but for the hum of the refrigeration units. The remnants of a faint aroma left over from the evening's pork stew still hung in the glum atmosphere of solitude in which Stan sat.

"You want to walk back to your room with me, Stan, or do you want to go upstairs and hang out with the folks?" Kevin asked.

"Oh, hi...uhhhh, Kevin... No, I'm just going back to my room I think. I was just sitting here thinking," Stan said, blankly looking forward. "You know, when I first came here, I was really pissed at my two kids, blamed them for everything. Then I blamed myself; I realized

I was the one who just let things happen. At some point, I guess I must have said it was OK. But in reality, Kevin - in reality, they weren't to blame, and neither was I. It was none of us. What landed me here was this damned disease … damned disease," Stan repeated. "Alzheimer's is a terrible thing, Kevin, a terrible thing. Every day you forget something else; or maybe a lot of something elses … you don't even know how many. I don't at least."

Stan sighed and took a deep breath. He paused a moment, looked around trying to put together what he wanted to say. "Every time I forget something, I lose another part of myself, you know? I'm like a big, old, abandoned building that is falling apart. A brick falls off over here, a window comes out over there, then another brick..." Stan stopped and put his head down, then, not looking at anyone, he said in a soft voice, "Pretty soon there is nothing left but a big empty space where a nice building used to stand, Kevin -- a real nice building," Stan said, now barely audible. Then he perked up again, looking Kevin in the eye. "And you know the hell of it, Kevin? People who knew that building, perhaps even admired it…now they just walk by, and forget there ever even *was* a building there. Just totally forget. You're gone."

Kevin felt sorry for old Stan. He knew he was losing pieces of himself, and was helpless to do a damn thing about it. It had to be the worst feeling in the world. The only bright light in Stan's comments was it was the most clearly spoken he had been in weeks. At this point in time, Stan was having his good days, and his not so good days. Today was obviously a good one.

"Come on, Stan. Let me walk you back to your room. I'll find us something good on that TV you got down there."

Stan lifted up out of his chair, and slowly walked, with Kevin's help, toward his room, his home.

*****

Saturdays had become one of Stan's favorite days. That was usually when Jenny or John had come to visit. If he was lucky, they would bring Kendra. He loved seeing her. The usual plan was to visit for a while, go out for lunch, and perhaps take a drive. Stan had genuinely looked forward to these occasions, and made sure Kevin kept him informed what day it was so he wouldn't miss them.

It was a nice spring day as Stan sat on one of the benches outside waiting. One of the nurses from his unit came to see if he needed anything. Today, it was Rosa Aviles, a very attractive woman with a Spanish accent.

"Mr. Beecher. You OK out here? You want something to drink?" she asked.

"Right as rain there, right as rain. No nothing, thanks."

A bit later, Jenny arrived with Jimmy and their daughter, Kendra. Kendra ran from the parking lot toward Stan yelling, "Grandpa!" She jumped at him and put her arms around his neck, hugging him so hard it almost hurt.

"So then, who is this big girl?" Stan asked.

"We're all going to lunch today, Daddy said. Are you coming too, Grandpa?"

Stan just smiled and said, "Well I am hungry but who are you and why are we going together?"

Jenny, devastated, exclaimed: "Oh Dad, stop joking with Kendra! You know we always come on Saturdays to go to lunch."

Suddenly it all flooded back, and Stan realized that this little girl was his dear granddaughter, and gave her a big hug.

At lunch, Jenny wanted to know how things had been going, if he was finding any new things to do, had he made any new friends; the kinds of questions that would tell her if he was finding any pleasure in life at all.

"Oh yeah…you know, they have that whole activity schedule here and all…most of it is crap I don't care about, but they said Dr. Ming now insists I be in one of those exercise programs in the morning. I go just to maintain peace." There were quarterly medical reviews of every resident, and the staff, along with Dr. Wu, had been keeping up with Stan's various health issues. The new exercise program was the latest recommendation.

"Oh hey...while I remember, I have to tell you something really funny that happened," Stan said. Just then, the waitress arrived with their meals. They started to eat, and Jimmy asked about the story, saying: "We could all use a good laugh, so what was that story?" Stan looked at him blankly, and continued eating. No story was to come. Jenny and Jimmy exchanged a worried glance, but did not mention the incident again.

At the end of their visit, Jenny thought she would throw in something funny to close their time together. Her father had always hated baseball...too slow he thought. As he would explain it, "I'm a football junkie, don't give a flip about baseball. I wouldn't walk across the street for a pair of free tickets." Her husband, Jimmy, on the other hand, was the opposite. Having been a semi-pro baseball player in his younger days, he loved baseball, and as often as possible would take Jenny to the games. Jenny had always playfully annoyed her father by inviting him along although she knew her invitations would be turned down. Still, it was fun to keep asking, and having him decline. It was a game they had played with one another since her first year of marriage.

Jenny started her little amusement, "So next Saturday, Dad, Tennessee is playing Florida in baseball over at the stadium. Big game...you wanna go with us?"

Without hesitation, Stan said, "Sure. What time will you pick me up?"

Jenny was stunned. "What? You mean that? You will go with us?"

"Yeah, certainly, what time? I need to tell Kevin so I don't forget."

"But you hate baseball," Jenny reminded him.

"Oh? I do?" Stan puzzled. "Well, Marilyn, I love you."

*****

Kevin was making his last sweep through the unit when he heard Stan's frantic voice sounding from behind his closed door.

"Fuck, fuck fuck!! I'm totally fucked," he was shouting.

Kevin knocked on the door.

"Are you OK in there, Stan?"

"Does it sound like I'm OK? No! I'm screwed. I'm done."

Kevin opened the door, and what he saw shocked him. The sight was totally unexpected. The room looked as if an earthquake had taken place; it was completely ransacked. Drawers had been flung open and thrown on the floor, clothes were scattered throughout the room, nothing was left on hangers in the closet; even the bathroom drawers had been emptied onto the floor.

Stan looked even worse than the room. He was disheveled, his hair was a mess, and he was only half dressed.

Seeing Kevin, Stan came over and grabbed his arm.

"You've got to help me here, Kevin. Start looking," Stan pleaded.

"What are you looking for Stan," Kevin asked.

"Oh, how screwed am I if these are lost. How screwed am I," he near hysterically repeated. "My badge and service revolver! Both of them are gone. Oh shit, maybe they were out somewhere and someone stole them. Holy hell, do you have any idea what kind of shit storm will happen if I show up at the department and I've lost them? Do you!! I could get fucking suspended for losing those. Look for me Kevin. Find them, please."

Stan was in a state of total panic. Kevin had to diffuse the situation quickly; he needed help to get Stan back under control. He signaled for assistance.

"OK, Stan. OK. I understand. Sure, I'll help you right now. But come on over here and sit down a minute while I look for you. I'm sure we'll sort this out. Let's just sit a bit and collect our thoughts. OK?"

Stan felt a little better since Kevin was going to help, but he was still beside himself with fear. He didn't know what he was going to do. This had never happened to him before. He let Kevin lead him toward the bed, and the two of them sat down. In the meantime, two other nurses arrived, one of them with the medications cart.

"Oh SHIT!" Stan yelled. "It's the damned medication police!" Stan got up and moved away from them, further toward the back patio door.

"It's OK, Stan. It's OK. They are just here to help. I told them we needed help to look for your things," Kevin said.

"Listen, anyone not here helping, get the hell out!" Stan said in a somewhat lower tone. Slowly, he was calming down. Kevin sat next to him rubbing his back, continuing to try and soothe him.

"Don't you worry, Stan. We are going to get this all sorted out. You won't be in any trouble." After a few moments, one of the nurses gave Kevin a pill to give to Stan. They wanted to lower his blood pressure and reduce the panic, perhaps make him sleep.

Once Stan laid back and fell asleep, Kevin began the task of putting things back into some order so he could move about the room. He would have the office call Stan's home, and have someone come over tomorrow to restore things the way Stan would want.

As Kevin left, he told the nurses to keep checking on him. "Call me if you need me. Don't worry about the time."

Kevin had seen this kind of behavior many times. People suffering from Alzheimer's often suffered bouts of paranoia or panic. Poor Stan had just had a bad one. It would not be his last.

*****

Stan's daily routines had been slowly changing over time. In the early months, he would get up, have his breakfast, then bring a cup of coffee to Ned Barnard; the man he referred to as *Bernardo Gui*. At first, Ned was somewhat annoyed by this nickname, but over time realized this was just part of Stan's character. It was meant as humor, not disparagement. Stan didn't come every day, and never stayed long; he would just pop his head in the office, leave the coffee, and occasionally add a barb or two to entertain himself.

Over time, Stan's morning coffee visits had dramatically declined. He had even stopped referring to Ned as Bernardo Gui, nor was he continuing to refer to the director as Warden Legree. In fact, he barely paid attention to either of them. Kevin was about the only staff person with whom Stan would directly interact.

At almost any time of the day, it was not unusual to see Stan slowly walking with his cane in the outdoor area of the quadrangle between the Willow Grove wings. This was a large, self contained, rectangular area with oversized concrete walkways crisscrossing between mounded gardens of small colorful plantings and shrubs. There were white tables with chairs, and small two-seater white benches strategically placed for people to sit. Stan enjoyed his time in the outdoor area where he would walk a bit, then sit on one of the benches to rest. He would spend several hours in this activity. Sometimes Kevin even needed to retrieve him for dinner or medications.

When Stan was inside, he would be either sitting in his room watching Cartoon Network, or be up in the TV area where the ladies watched soap operas, or perhaps *The Price is Right* game show. Stan rarely paid attention to the women, but that didn't deter the women from paying attention to him.

"Good morning, Stan...you doing OK today?" one would ask.

"Hmph," Stan would answer in response. "What's this crap you're watching? Makes my hair hurt."

"Really, Stan? Oh, we watch it nearly every day. We try to guess the prices. It's amazing how close we can get."

Stan would just blankly stare at them, saying nothing. He had no real idea of what was happening on those shows. For him, it was just noise and figures moving on a screen. His daily life was becoming a slow withdrawal into himself. He no longer recognized a lot of the speech taking place around him, and conversation was pretty much becoming a lost art. The world was beginning to dim and close in around him.

*****

Two incidents took place that turned Stan's life in a different direction. In the first, Kevin was helping Stan get ready for bed. It was late and he wanted to go home, but Stan was being obstinate. He wanted to go out for a walk, and was refusing to go to bed. He wasn't going, and that was final! Kevin just continued getting him in his pajamas, ignoring the continued requests to go outside, as well as the rise in Stan's voice. Finally, Stan decided he was just going to go, and tried to shove his way past Kevin. Kevin, however, being a very large man, just put out his shoulder and arm. As Stan came in contact, he fell back, lost his balance, and tumbled onto the bed. With that, he lost his temper.

"LEAVE ME ALONE, YOU FAT BASTARD! GET THE HELL OUT OF HERE!!"

Kevin just looked at Stan. He knew enough to step out and return when Stan was calmer. He went out in the hall, and began laughing to himself. A nurse was outside the room across the hall, and wondered what had happened.

Kevin looked at her and laughed. "Did you hear that? Stan just called me a 'fat bastard.'" Kevin thought that was hilarious. He knew it was just the disease talking, exacerbated by Stan's increasing anger management issues.

Kevin knocked on the door.

"Excuse me, Stan...it's me Kevin, can I come in?"

From inside, Stan yelled back, "Yeah, come in here a minute. I want to tell you something."

When Kevin went in, Stan was sitting back upright on the edge of the bed.

"Hey, Kevin. I'm glad you're here. I want you to do something for me. Look around outside. There was just a big, black guy in here pushing me around. See if you can find him and throw him the hell out. He's really mean," Stan explained.

"Really, Stan? Sure, I'll go look right now. In the meantime, should I turn on the TV for you so you can rest?"

Stan nodded agreement, and Kevin put on the TV as he turned out the overhead light. The voices from the TV were soothing to Stan, often helping him relax and sleep.

As Kevin went out to the hall where the other nurse was still standing, he said,

"I think he'll be fine now. I'll come back before I leave to look in on him."

In the back of his mind, however, he was hoping this was not the beginning of new phase in which Stan would become more physical or violent. Patients who represented a threat to themselves or others would have to be transferred once it passed a certain point.

The second incident came when Kevin had the night shift. As he was walking through the main reception area, he looked through the window to see Stan sitting outside on one of the white benches. As it was nearly 2 AM, Kevin thought it best to bring him in and put him to bed. Walks at odd hours had become more common for Stan. He even would walk the halls, hands behind his back, patrolling as he perhaps had when he was a police officer on the beat. It seemed he always wanted to walk. Even after just returning from outside, he would often suggest another walk five minutes later.

As Kevin approached, he saw Stan shoeless, dressed in blue dress pants, a brown sport jacket, and a night shirt.

Stan looked up and said, "Hi; you looking..." and he paused searching for the word to describe what he had in his mind..."for the bus?"

"Maybe. What bus is it that you're waiting for, Stan?"

"Oh, it's the one... downtown...you know...work. I don't...don't be late."

"That bus, oh yes. Well, it's not going to be here for a bit, why don't we go inside and wait for it?" Kevin said, coaxing Stan back toward his room.

"Mmmmmmm," answered Stan, not really certain why this man wanted the same bus.

Kevin went over, took Stan by the elbow, gathered up his cane, and gently helped him to his feet. Slowly, Kevin walked him back in the direction of his room.

Once Stan was settled, Kevin thought to himself, it might be time to suggest moving Stan up to the Pavilion unit. The Pavilion had Willow Grove's highest level of care, a memory care unit where most of their advanced Alzheimer's patients were taken when it became less safe for them to live in the assisted care area.

*****

The meeting among the doctors, director, Kevin, and the family was fairly brief. The staff provided a total review of Stan's overall health, something which had noticeably declined. They then moved to a discussion of his general behavior and detachment, along with their recommendation that Stan would be better served at a higher level of care.

John sat silently, looking at each of the staff. As the discussion unfolded, Jenny kept her head down. At the conclusion, John looked at Jenny.

"What do you think, Jenny? Have you seen anything that makes you feel differently," John asked.

Jenny looked up at him, and simply shook her head, no. For some time, she had been finding it almost impossible to communicate with her father during visits. Even when she brought Sandy, her father did not seem to perk up the way he had in the past, although he did like petting her. It was so sad. Day by day they were losing pieces of their father. He no longer really recognized any of them. On one occasion, her father thought little Kendra was Jenny. If he was reminded who they were, he would simply smile, and sometimes say, "hello" or "thanks for coming." For the most part, he just sat next to them staring into space. Jenny told him stories of the old days, reminded him of happy events that had taken place, and tried to jog his memory of something pleasant. She desperately tried to do something to make their time together more enjoyable. Every now and then, when she told him something and asked if he remembered, he smiled and said, "Yes. Yes. I remember that." For Jenny, those had become red-letter days.

The staff physician painted a rather bleak outlook of Stan's overall health. The Parkinson's was near a point where even the cane or walker no longer ensured safety. Kevin and the nursing staff had begun putting Stan in a wheel chair to take him places. There was a noticeable tremor that often prevented Stan from successfully holding things in his hands. Feeding him was becoming a chore as well. Sometimes Stan would try to eat, at other times refused to eat. He no longer knew exactly which utensil to use. He even needed to be reminded of what foods he liked. Swallowing was becoming a major effort as well. Food and meals were not enjoyable.

Stan's kidney function had also been declining. The doctors were monitoring this on a daily basis, but they were concerned about the likelihood of this becoming a larger issue down the road.

Overall, it was clear to everyone. The Pavilion would be Stan's next stop.

*****

The Willow Grove Pavilion was a self contained area where the residents with Alzheimer's could receive maximum care. John and Jenny were both pleased with the round the clock medical staff, and the progressive program to assist dementia patients. On his arrival, Stan was immediately provided added sensory stimulation programs, reminiscence materials, and more coordinated medical support.

One of the more unique features of the Pavilion was an aviary, something certain to catch the interest of Stan Junior. The aviary contained a wide variety of birds in a natural habitat that patients could watch. Although birds had never been of particular interest to Stan Senior, it provided a common ground where he and Stan Junior were able to make their visits more enjoyable.

On days when Stan Junior came, he sat next to his father near the aviary, and spent hours telling him about the birds they were watching. Stan didn't really know what Stan Junior was telling him, but he did like looking at the birds, and his companion was nice to him.

"Stan, this is your son, Stan Junior. You remember him? He's going to sit with you for a while so you can watch the birds. Would you like that?" the nurse would ask.

Stan would smile, sometimes wave his hand, and then go back to watching the aviary.

When Jenny or John was there, they would wheel Stan's chair outside, and walk about the garden area with him. Stan always enjoyed feeling the sun on his face. Even when the weather was cooler, Stan wanted to go outside. As the winter set in, however, that became less an option. On warmer days, Jenny would sometimes put a blanket around Stan, and they could go out for just a few minutes, but the staff didn't want him out too long. Colds were especially dangerous. It was best to be safe.

Both Jenny and John could see it. Their father's days were becoming limited. Stan was clearly entering his last days.

9

The Last Days

As the weeks rolled by, Jenny tried to get to Willow Grove as often as she could. John, Linda, and Stan Junior had moved, and had lived in Franklin for some time now. As a result, their visits until recently had been limited to a couple of times a month. Stan's general health had continued to decline, and he had been moved to the more intensive hospital unit of Willow Grove. He had become totally incontinent, and was now in adult diapers. His ability to communicate was nearly gone. He was making different sounds, single words, or looks to communicate, but he was often difficult to understand. Jenny was becoming depressed over everything, while Jimmy was finding it full time work to keep his wife from despair. Sometimes all he could do was hold her as she told him stories of Stan and their past family life. Perhaps these were last ditch attempts to keep her father's good memories alive.

John called Jenny two or three times a week, and they talked about what was happening with their father. It was never good news. Jenny had stopped being angry with her brother long ago. After returning home from Baltimore, she and John had grown far closer even though he now lived three hours away. It was the disease claiming her Dad's life, and nothing that John or she could do was going to change that. Even if John was there every day, nothing was going to improve. Hospice had already been notified, and was on the scene arranging things with the family and Willow Grove for whatever they needed.

Stan Junior spent a lot of time in his room with Bonkers. He felt sad, out of touch, continuously wanting to visit his father.

"John, do you think we could go up this week to see Dad? I hope he's feeling better. I'd like to show him some of those birds again. I've looked up all the ones they have in that pen. Some of them are really interesting. Maybe we could even bring Sandy. He really loves her. It seems to make him happy when she puts her head in his lap."

John answered his brother, "Let me look at things and see what we can do. It would be good to go see Dad, wouldn't it. Let's make it happen."

Over the last month, he and Stan Junior had been coming every weekend. John had come to realize there would not be too many more Saturdays when they could visit. Time was growing short. He and Stan Junior came on both Saturday and Sunday, and if things looked tenuous, he planned to call work and stay on. Jenny, it seemed, was almost always there now. She had taken a short leave of absence from the hospital. Her supervisor was most understanding, and told her to take as much time as she needed.

Stan had retreated into his own world. He was moving back and forth between consciousness and some other place. He was coming nearer the end. He often found himself traveling outside the boundaries of his small room.

Stan's eyes remained closed, his physical body still in the bed. He was alone in his room, yet he was not alone. He felt a breeze, almost like a powerful wind coming into him. He gradually felt himself lift above the bed. He could actually look down and see himself. As he drifted higher, he began to see a beautiful white, almost blinding, whiteness, a light perhaps? No, it was more. On the way up toward that light there were puffy clouds of pastel shades and colors. He looked at these for some time, floating among them, but moving higher, then above them.

Far above the clouds he saw scores of forms trailing streaks of light in their paths. They didn't have a human form, yet he recognized them as having human qualities. They didn't speak, but there were loud sounds, almost like music, coming from somewhere within them. It wasn't melodies, but just a joyous, nondescript sound of...perhaps more like love? It wasn't a romantic love, or friend-like love; not any singular type love. It was a combination of all love. The best description was that it was perhaps a total love. The only way Stan's mind could wrap around this feeling was that it was some kind of love he had never before felt that was filling his soul. It was the most calming thing he had ever experienced.

From almost the very beginning of this experience, he had sensed a being traveling next to him. No, not traveling really, more like guiding. It was a woman, a woman with beautiful, strong but tender facial features. Features he was certain he recognized, but yet couldn't exactly place. He knew her; he knew her well. Was it his mother? Or no, was it Marilyn? He knew her somehow! She was not dressed like a person, nor did she actually even look exactly like a person. There were long, flowing feather light garments trailing with her. Although she was not saying anything in words, she was communicating with him, a kind of mental telepathy or direct transfer of thoughts. She was guiding him upward toward the brighter light. He tried to ask her about those streaking beings, but all she communicated to him was, "*They are all here for you.*"

There was also a great darkness far above. Inside that was a beautiful glowing orb of intense brightness. It was almost too bright to directly look at. The spirit guide smiled, taking him gently in the direction of the orb, and pointing it out to him, but then told him, "*Not yet, but soon.*" He thought this must be the hands of God or His light, but before he could go there, his spirit guide had other messages to communicate first.

The message had three parts that Stan felt, rather than heard. The first was:

"You are loved, and cherished here above all else,"

She smiled and seemed to hold Stan closer.

Stan thought back.

"Who are you? Who am I? Am I now dead? Where are we going?"

But, the spirit did not answer his questions; she simply sent him a second, even more powerful message:

"There is nothing for you to fear here. You are totally safe with all of us by you."

Stan thought, "Who is 'all of us?' How do I know you? Are you me?"

The spirit's third and last message was perhaps the one of most comfort to Stan. She gazed at him, and seemed almost to envelop him in her love.

"There is nothing you can do wrong here."

Stan continued his journey with the spirit. He saw butterfly-like creatures floating up toward the light. The spirit told him they were prayers, thoughts of love from the world below. He was amazed at their numbers. She then said again,

"It is not yet time. Soon."

Stan gradually started coming back toward his room and his body. He didn't want to go back. He didn't want to leave her. He didn't want to have to be afraid again, to be limited. As he came back into his human form, his eyes opened. There were people in the room. They all seemed to get up and come over to him once he became more conscious of their presence. They seemed happy. A man joined them.

*****

Jenny had asked Father Joseph to come to the nursing home, to be with the family as they realized their father had limited time. He sat with her, John, and Stan Junior as the four of them prayed silently together.

Father Joseph was holding Jenny's hand when the doctors came in to explain that Stan's kidneys were beginning to shut down, and at any time there could be a major health crisis such as a heart attack, or just a general organ failure. The doctor told them they were going to examine him again, and perhaps keep him comfortable with a morphine drip. He assured Jenny they would see to it her father would be in no discomfort whatsoever. At this point it seemed all the discomfort in that room was embodied in the Beecher children.

"Father, what happens when we die?" Jenny asked. "Does God or Jesus come and take us?"

Joseph answered, "That is one of the mysteries about which we have so little information. We don't really know. What we believe, however, is that when our spirit finally departs us, it goes directly into the presence of God. That is what will happen to your father. In fact, I believe God's spirit has already descended into this room, and is with your father right now, comforting him."

Stan Junior asked, "Does my Dad know He's here? Does he actually see Him?"

"Well," said Joseph, "I believe in our hours of need, we do see Him. I think Stan sees him better now than he ever has in his life. He will feel safe in God's arms; you can trust me on that."

"Yes," said Stan Junior. "I trust you."

The doctor came back again and began to examine Stan. Stan was looking straight at them, but making no sounds. As the doctor turned to Jenny and John, he smiled and said,

"Well, your father seems to have come through another crisis. His heart is relatively stable, and his vital signs are not really too bad. His blood pressure is a little low and his heart rate is a bit elevated. Other than that, he is resting comfortably. I'll come back again in a little bit to check on him.

As night fell, Father Joseph left, promising Jenny he would come back the next day, but if she needed him, he gave her a number to call. She thanked him, and promised she would be in touch.

Before Joseph left, Jenny added with tear filled eyes, "If we lose him, Father, I would like to have his funeral at Saint John's. Do you think that would be possible? I mean, most of his life he was over at Saint James, but he hasn't been there in a long time. I would feel so much better if we could do it at our church."

"Oh, Jenny; of course we can do that. We will take care of him, and your family as well. You needn't concern yourself about these matters at all. But for now, your Dad's not at that place. We will just add our prayers together for him. Remember; call me if you need me."

None of the Beecher children would leave their father alone in the room that night. Off and on they slept. Their father lay beside them also drifting in and out of sleep.

Stan was in constant contact with his spirit guide. He would often leave his body and move above the room toward that ever present light. He was no longer afraid or worried about what was to come. His spirit guide was constantly beside him, showing him things he had never seen, providing him comfort beyond anything he had ever felt.

*****

The following morning, Kevin saw Stan Junior, obviously upset, standing outside his father's room. As he neared, Stan Junior looked up to him trying to find the words of a question weighing heavily on his mind.

"Kevin, I don't think Dad knows me, or hears anything I'm saying to him. When I try to talk to him he just lies there, I guess asleep."

Kevin offered what few words of help he could manage, "Well, actually your Dad *is* in a kind of sleep. But I've heard that in that kind of sleep, when loved ones speak, they actually do hear them."

"Really?" Stan Junior asked with a quizzical look. "I don't know. He certainly doesn't seem to hear, at least not like some of the other times when we were here. Will I ever be able to talk to him like that again, Kevin?" Stan Junior asked in a pleading tone.

"I don't really know for sure," answered Kevin. "But you know what? I've also heard that if you write something down for them on a piece of paper, then when they are a little more awake, they will see that, and know you were there talking to them. Do you think you would want to try that?"

Kevin didn't really believe what he was telling Stan Junior; but in that moment, it was all he could think of to offer as some consolation.

"That's a good idea, Kevin. I think that's what I'm going to do. Where should I put it?"

"Oh, that's the easy part, my friend. You just place it in his hand so it's there for him later. If you give it to me, I can do it for you if you like," offered Kevin.

Stan Junior went out toward the office where he got a small piece of paper and pencil, then began to write. He soon returned with the note which he handed to Kevin.

"This is all, Kevin. Will you give it to Dad, then?"

"Absolutely, Stan, absolutely; I'll do it for you right away," Kevin assured him.

The Beecher children all sat at the bedside of their dying father. Each was quiet in his or her own thoughts, thoughts of their childhood home, their father's devotion to their mother, their family in general. They had come a long way over these last years. They had all fought what was to be a losing battle against Alzheimer's and the ravages of age. It was a battle with no winners, only survivors. The battle had left many wounds and scars, wounds that would take a long time to heal, if they ever healed at all.

Prayers were being said, but in their hearts, the children knew there would be no last minute reprieve. Jenny asked God to forgive her for failing to help her father spend more time at home, and for not being a more resourceful person in finding a better answer than having him enter Willow Grove too soon. Jenny then simply prayed that her father would find peace in the hands of his God. It was a God for whom, in his last years, ravaged by mounting ailments, her father had shown little regard. She was certain God would forgive him; she asked Him now for that forgiveness. Quietly she wept for this man she so dearly loved.

John prayed for forgiveness. No one in the room felt worse about how things had gotten so out of hand over the last years. He prayed his sister would forgive him for being so single minded, so inattentive to her and Stan Junior's pain. He prayed his father would forgive him for placing his own needs first. Of course, obtaining God's forgiveness would be the easy part. Would he ever forgive himself was the question. These were burdens John would bear forever. In light of what fate had in store for him later, he asked for redemption, and he pledged he would be a better brother, a better man in future. In his heart, he wondered if he actually would.

Stan Junior sat silently and wondered. What would life be like without his Dad? Who would be that person he came to with every problem, every small discovery, every story of his day? For Stan Junior, life was now full of uncertainty. He wondered if there was something he could have done to make his father's last months happier. Could he have been a better brother to Jenny and John? He often wanted to do or say something to make them stop arguing, but nothing ever came to mind fast enough. Now, with his Dad near the end of his time, Stan Junior felt helpless, a feeling with which he had become well acquainted over his years.

For Stanton Beecher, he simply continued to lie in bed with Stan Junior's note loosely held in his hand. He was slowly drifting toward that quiet place of restful peace that at some future time will claim us all. There was no further struggling with words, no fear of forgetfulness.

He was nearing a place where he felt totally safe and completely loved. As he slowly traveled with his spirit guide beside him, he felt absolute calm. His hand opened. Stan Junior's note slipped silently to the floor, where it landed face up for the three Beecher children to read. It seemed fitting that Stan Junior's note was the last thing his father would ever possess. It captured the essence of all that was good in that room. It simply read:

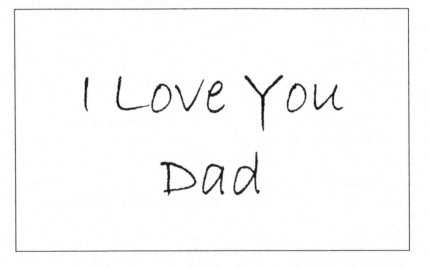

For Stan, his battle was over, and as the spirit guide had told him, "There was nothing he could do wrong here." He was home.......

For Stanton W. Beecher, it was his last day.

Epilogue

S tanton William Beecher was buried out of Saint John's Cathedral on March 21, 2014. He was survived by his sons, John and Stan, daughter Jenny, son-in-law, James Carter, daughter-in-law, Linda Ethridge Beecher, and granddaughter Kendra; as well as his trusted companion, Sandy. The pall bearers included his two sons, Detective Ted Newsome of the Knoxville Police Department, Kevin Willis of Willow Grove Assisted Care, and son-in-law, Jimmy Ray Carter. His funeral was attended by over 150 uniformed police and fire officers from over 11 Tennessee counties. An honor guard of six Knoxville Police officers fired a three salvo salute at his graveside.

Jenny and Jimmy Ray still work at Parkwest Hospital. They now have two children; James and Kendra Ann, who is a stand out member of her school and church. One of the things of which the family is most proud is the repurchase of the family house on Gill Avenue. It seems, however, the family member happiest to return to Gill was Sandy. She knew every nook and every cranny of the house, backyard, and street. It was an adjustment for Sandy in one respect; her lifetime companion and master, Stanton, had left his scent all over the house. She went from room to room looking for him, and wagging her tail or crying. When she was unable to find him, she sometimes came and barked at Jenny, probably trying to enlist her help in the search. Ultimately, Sandy became content to just lie in the room where Stan had slept for over forty years. At dinners with Stan Junior, one of the stories they loved to retell was how Jenny had defended Stan Junior against Kyle the Bully at Knox Central. Stan Junior always liked it when the family was laughing.

John is now a senior manager for the Nashville offices of Wright, Johnson, and Willoughby. He has been elected three times to the Franklin town council, and is currently the treasurer for the University of Tennessee Alumni Association. The big change in John's life occurred when Linda called him during one of her frequent visits home to tell him she wouldn't be coming back to Franklin. She thought a trial separation was needed for them to "re-examine their relationship." The toll taken by the family arguments, and her sense that John had not always supported her as strongly as he should have created a rift that hadn't healed. Beyond that, John's reluctance to start a family had only added to Linda's sense of disappointment in their overall relationship. John and Linda's marriage had become just one more casualty in a family tragedy brought on by Alzheimer's. John was saddened by Linda's decision, but her absence removed a great deal of stress that had been growing over the years. He had little hope they would ever get back together.

Stan Junior continued to live with John for a few months after Linda's move back to Knoxville, but arrangements for times when John was at work were troublesome. Ultimately, it was decided that Stan Junior would move back to the house on Gill to live with Jenny and Jimmy. It was an adjustment, but in reality, the only viable option. Once Stan Junior was back on Gill Avenue, Jimmy helped him find a part time job with Petco in the stocking department. He also volunteered at the Golden Retriever Rescue Center, where he helped to maintain the kennels and feed the dogs. Life was full for Stan Junior, but he missed his father and their times together.

Each year, the Beecher family comes together on March 17th to celebrate two things. First, it is Saint Patrick's Day when it had always been a family tradition to have a corned beef and cabbage dinner with Irish soda bread, boiled potatoes, and some good Irish beer. It was well known to the family that Stan Senior was "a corned beef junkie." The second reason was that March 17th was the day Stan Senior had passed away. Tradition holds that everyone raises his or her glass, and repeats the family toast; "To the greatest father a family ever had: Stanton Beecher!"

Had Stanton actually been alive for such a toast, he most assuredly would have added that his dying on March 17th was God's ultimate practical joke.

"To think of it! Me! A born and bred Englishman going all the way back to bloody Sir Edmund Stanton of York; and God makes me die on March 17th……. a sodded Irish holiday!"

Here's to Stanton Beecher.

Made in the USA
Coppell, TX
11 February 2022

73422173R00125